THE HANGING PSALM

THE HANGING PSALM

A Simon Westow mystery

Chris Nickson

This first world edition published 2018
in Great Britain and 2019 in the USA by
SEVERN HOUSE PUBLISHERS LTD of
Eardley House, 4 Uxbridge Street, London W8 7SY.
Trade paperback edition first published
in Great Britain and the USA 2019 by
SEVERN HOUSE PUBLISHERS LTD.

British Library Cataloguing in Publication Data
A CIP catalogue record for this title is available from the British Library.

ISBN-13: 978-0-7278-8831-0 (cased)
ISBN-13: 978-1-84751-957-3 (trade paper)
ISBN-13: 978-1-4483-0166-9 (e-book)

Typeset by Palimpsest Book Production Ltd.,
Falkirk, Stirlingshire, Scotland.

Leeds, 1820

They were grave men. Sober men, neat in their black coats, white stocks snowy and clean, tied tight at the neck. Important people, businessmen and landowners. Men who believed that wealth and position gave them a heaven-sent command of life. Three of them together at the carefully polished table, papers arranged in piles before them. The one in the middle spoke.

'Your name is Simon Westow. Is that correct?'

He waited for a moment before he answered. Let them look at me, he thought. Let them *see* me.

'That's right.'

'How old are you?'

'Thirty in July. If I was told the truth.' He wasn't about to call them sir. If they wanted his respect, let them bloody earn it.

'You were in the workhouse, I believe?' The man kept his voice even, glancing at the sheet he held.

'I went there when I was four, after my parents died. There was no one else to take me in.' He could hear the scratch of a pen as the clerk in the corner took down his answers.

'How did they treat you? When did they put you out to work?'

'Are you really sure you want to know that?'

That made them stop. Just for a second. But he had their attention. The man behind the desk gave a condescending smile.

'Of course we do. That's the purpose of this commission and these questions. Our intention is to find out about child labour.' A slight pause. 'But you must know that. I understand it was made perfectly clear to you.'

Oh yes, he thought. Perfectly.

'They set us on at the mill when we were six, and let the manufactories do their worst.'

'Their worst?' He laid a soft emphasis on the word. 'And what might that be? Were you beaten often?'

'We were,' Simon told him. 'Boys and girls alike.'

The man looked down and shuffled a few of his papers.

'More than once the overseer made us take off our shirts, climb into one of the bins on the floor, and he'd hit us with his stick until we were bloody.' He let his words remain steady as the memories raged through his mind. The facts could speak loudly enough.

'I see. What else?'

'They'd tie a two-stone weight to our backs and make us work. Two of them for the bigger lads. They said it would make us strong so we'd be able to work harder.'

They looked a little uncomfortable now, all of them shifting on their seats. Good.

'There was one boy who could never do his job fast enough,' Simon said. 'He tried, but he couldn't manage it. Every week the overseer hung him from a beam by his wrists and used a strap on his back to try and teach him a lesson.'

'Did he improve?'

'He died. He was seven years old.'

The men were staring now. The clerk had stopped his writing. The only sound in the room was the soft tick of the longclock. But he hadn't finished yet.

'Once they took a pair of vises, and screwed one to each of my ears. Then they had me work half the day with them in place.'

The man grimaced. 'Why would they do that? How could it improve you?'

'It was for their own amusement. I still have the scars.'

But they wouldn't want to see, he knew that. He'd leave this room and they'd try to forget everything he told them. Maybe it would return in their dreams tonight. Every night to come. Exactly the way it had for him for years after it was over.

'Don't you want to know where it happened?' Simon asked. 'Don't you want the name of the mills and their owners?'

The man shook his head. 'That's not part of this inquiry. We're here to discover facts, not blame people for things that happened in the past.' His voice changed, becoming oilier, trying to appease. 'How long did you work there?'

'Until I was thirteen. Seven years.'

'Thank you, Mr Westow.'

He stood, back straight, and walked to the door. A final question made him turn.

'What is your occupation now?'

He stared at them. 'I'm a thief-taker.'

ONE

As he left the Moot Hall, Simon curled his hands into fists and pushed them into the pockets of his trousers. Briggate was thick with carts and people, and he moved between them without noticing. His head was filled with the faces from the past. The children who fainted after working for twelve hours without any break for food or water, because the overseer wanted the most from them. The boy who lost three fingers in a machine and just stood and stared at the stumps, not able to say a word.

And finally, the day he carried a girl back to the workhouse, the bloody patch steadily growing on her skirt after two men had their pleasure with her during their dinner break. Catherine was her name. She'd just turned eleven the week before; that was all he ever knew about her. She moaned in his arms, in too much pain to cry.

He was thirteen then, grown big and strong and defiant. He pushed the door of the matron's office wide, and gently laid Catherine on her desk. The woman protested, shouted, but he didn't want to hear anything she had to say. He'd heard enough, day after day: piety, duty, gratitude. Instead, Simon turned on his heel. He was never going back.

There was an early April chill in the air as he stood and gazed down on the river. The water moved slowly, putrid and dirty. Swirls of red and ochre and blue eddied on the surface, waste from the dyeworks. A dead dog bobbed lazily up and down in the current.

Simon took off his hat and ran a hand through his hair. He needed to let his thoughts ebb away. He needed to forget. To let the fire burn down to embers again.

From the corner of his eye he noticed a movement, a shadow.

'It's only me.' The girl kept a wary distance, eyes on him. She was fourteen, older perhaps, maybe even younger. Sometimes she seemed old, ageless, silent and looking. And as invisible as any of the children who roamed the streets in Leeds. An old, patched dress that was too small for her. Stockings that were more holes than wool, battered clogs on her feet. A pale face and hands and a threadbare shawl over her blonde hair. 'Rosie sent me after you. I saw you leave the Moot Hall and followed you here. You're all dressed up today.'

Simon had worn his good suit, the short, double-breasted jacket in fine worsted with long swallowtails and tight, narrow trousers. A ruffle at the front of his shirt and a tall-crowned hat with a curled brim on his head. He'd wanted to make an impression, to show them that a boy from the workhouse could be a success. But by now he probably no longer even existed for them.

'What does she want?' He took a breath, tasting the soot that spewed from the factory chimneys. Slowly, he felt the anger recede.

'Someone's waiting to see you. I caught a glimpse before she sent me out. Looks like a servant.' She waited a moment. 'Are you coming?'

'Tell her I'll be there soon.'

He watched her move away, melting into the press of people. Who noticed a child? Who noticed a girl? That was what made Jane so useful. She could follow without being seen, she could overhear a conversation without anyone realizing she was close.

Simon gazed around. Grim faces everywhere. People who looked as if they were just clinging on to life. He began to walk. The anger started to fade. But it would never vanish.

The house stood on Swinegate, right on the curve of the street. He could hear his wife in the kitchen, talking to the twins as she worked. She raised her head as he entered, pushing a lock of hair away from her cheek. An apron covered her muslin dress. She brought the knife down sharply on a piece of meat.

'Jane found you, then?' Rosie asked.

He nodded. 'Where is he?'

'I gave him a cup of ale and left him in the front room. He arrived about half an hour ago.' She raised an eyebrow. 'He seems to have a high opinion of himself. Didn't want to talk to a mere woman.'

Simon nodded. Too many men like that.

'How was it?' she asked.

'What you'd expect. Give them three lifetimes and they'd never understand. All it did was drag up the past.'

She offered him a tender smile. 'It'll go again. It always does, Simon.'

'I suppose it will.' She was right; it always had before. His sons peered at him around the corner of the table, two small, identical heads. He stuck out his tongue and they began to laugh. They were the best medicine he knew.

His smile vanished as he opened the door and walked into the front room. The man in the chair jerked his head up at the sound as if he'd been sleeping.

'I'm Simon Westow. You wanted to see me?'

'My master does.'

Jane was right. He was a servant. But a trusted one, if someone was sending him here. Older, with sparse grey hair and a stiff, formal manner to match his dark clothes. Haughty; Rosie had pegged him well.

People didn't normally seek Simon out. They placed a notice in the *Mercury* or *Intelligencer* for their stolen property. He found it, returned it, and gave them the name of the thief. In exchange, he received the reward. If they chose to prosecute, they could take their chances in court.

That was how a thief-taker worked. Only a few came here to buy his services. When they did, it meant the job needed discretion.

'Who's your master?'

'He'd rather not say just yet.' The man gave a forbidding smile. 'But he'd like to meet you today.'

'Why?'

'It's a delicate matter. He'd prefer to tell you himself.' The man reached into his waistcoat pocket with two long fingers and drew out a sovereign. 'He believed this might convince you.'

The gold felt heavy in Simon's palm. Solid. Real.

'Where and when?'

'Three o'clock. Do you know Drony Laith?'

'Yes.' Out beyond Gott's big mill at Bean Ing. Just woods and fields, where the town ended and the countryside began.

The man stood and gave a small bow.

'What would you have done if I'd refused?' Simon asked.

'My master gave me a second sovereign. He'll see you at three.'

*   *   *

He tossed the coin and watched it skitter across the kitchen table. Rosie's hand moved swiftly and it vanished into the pocket of her skirt.

'Handsome money,' she said and grinned. 'Who does he want you to kill?'

'I'll find out this afternoon.' He poured a mug of ale and drained half of it in a gulp.

She kneaded the bread dough, fingers spread as she pushed it down. She'd given the boys a small scrap; they sat, stretching it between them until it snapped, then starting over again.

This was where he felt complete. This was home.

Rosie began to shape the loaves, concentrating on her work. She'd blossomed, he thought, so different from the girl he'd seen sitting at the side of the road all those years before, staring helplessly at a mile marker.

'I hope you can read, mister,' she'd said. 'Which way is it to London? The words are all a jumble to me.'

He'd told her, but she didn't pick up her bundle and start walking. Instead, he sat next to her. They talked. An hour later they were heading back into Leeds. He had four shillings in his pocket, all his money in the world. Enough to rent them a room and buy food. He'd earn more tomorrow. He had a reason now.

After the workhouse, he'd starved for twelve months, taking any work he could find, stealing food when there was nothing. He slept in old buildings until he had the money to share a bed in a doss house. An old soldier taught him the alphabet, and to read a few words. From there, he learned on his own. A newspaper someone had thrown away lasted a week, struggling through it in the night by the light from candle stubs until he could read properly. Then he noticed the advertisements for missing property and the rewards for their return. Simon had met plenty of criminals. He listened well, he was large and strong.

And he discovered he had a talent for the work. He'd been doing it for two years when he met Rosie.

Fourteen years later, she was still here. He'd taught her her letters and her numbers, and she learned quickly. She balanced his anger with her humour.

'Who sent him, do you know?' Deftly, she slid the loaves into the oven.

'Not yet. Has Jane come back?'

'I heard her go upstairs.'

He knocked quietly, waiting for her reply. The attic was almost bare, just a bed, a basin and jug on a small table, and a haze of ragged curtain covering the window.

She'd been here for two years, yet there was nothing of her in the room. No trace; as soon as she walked out, she might never have been there. But he understood. Own nothing you couldn't carry. A portable life, always ready to move, to run. Until he met Rosie, he'd felt the same way.

'I saw him leave.'

'I need you to go out to Drony Laith,' Simon said. 'I'm meeting his master there at three.'

He didn't have to tell her to keep out of sight. It was habit; she'd learned it on the streets. Don't let anyone see you steal. Keep clear of authority. Get caught and you'd end up in chains, waiting for Botany Bay. Maybe the noose if you drew a hanging judge.

'I saw his face this time. I know him. He works for John Milner.'

That was interesting, he thought. Milner owned property all over Leeds. He had investments in two of the new manufactories that had sprung up since Napoleon's defeat. They'd never spoken, but Simon had seen him in town, a sour prig of a man with a miserly face.

But what property had he lost that needed to remain such a secret?

'Let me know if anyone comes along with him or if anyone's following.'

The girl nodded.

'Dinner will be ready soon.'

The tenter poles stood on Drony Laith, but no cloth was stretching on the hooks today. It was nothing more than a barren field that ran down to the water, past the rubble of the demolished dye works, a copse of oak and ash rising on the far side. Simon stood and waited. Behind him, the brute, ugly mass of Bean Ing Mill rose like a monster from a tale, swallowing people in the morning and spewing them back out at night. Above the building, the sky was blurred with smoke rising from the chimneys.

He wasn't old enough to remember Leeds before the factories. Even when he was young a few had already been there. Now more and more were rising every single year. They drew the hopeful and the poor from all over Yorkshire. Simon saw them arrive, looking around in wonder as they imagined good work and steady wages ahead. Then he'd spot them again a few months later, broken and ragged and wondering why they'd exchanged the field for the factory.

Jane would be somewhere close, concealed from sight, watching and ready. Simon idled, letting the minutes pass. He'd changed into his working clothes, an old jacket, heavy trousers that clung to his legs, a felt hat, and boots with thick, sturdy soles. Milner would see exactly the kind of man he expected to find.

The man was late; the echo of the bell tolling the hour at the parish church had long since faded when he came strolling along. He had an easy gait, shoulders back, a walking cane giving rhythm to his step. Even from a distance, his clothes were well cut, expensive, a thick coat with a waist-length cape, stock tied into a soft bow, his hair a bristly grey burr over his skull.

But it was his face that told the real tale. It was tight, his lips pressed together as if he was desperately trying to hold something inside. Pale eyes, the skin around them dark and smudged. A man having sleepless nights, he thought.

'You're Westow?'

'I am.' He nodded. 'Simon Westow.'

For a moment Milner said nothing, examining him. He could look till the cows come home, but he'd find nothing beyond a blank stare.

'You're the thief-taker.'

'Yes.'

'What do you charge?'

Only the venal ones asked that question first. Weighing whether it was worth the fee.

'It depends what's been stolen.'

Another silence, longer than the first. It seemed to grow until it overwhelmed the space between them.

'My daughter,' Milner said finally.

Westow had retrieved silver plate, cloth, bonds, too many things to count. But never a woman. Yet a woman was property; that was the law. She belonged to her father, then to her husband. She was his possession. A daughter had value for the marriage she might make. Or the worth she could so easily lose.

'When did it happen?' he asked.

'Yesterday. In the afternoon.' Milner's jaw tightened. 'The stupid girl wanted another gown. She and two of her friends went to the dressmaker to select the fabric. And when she finished there, she had to go to the milliner for a new hat and God knows where else.' He raised his head. 'She didn't come home.'

'You didn't send a servant with her?'

'No. Why would I? She had the other girls to chaperone her. This is Leeds. There's never been a problem.' Milner's face was strained. He reached into his pocket and brought out a folded sheet of paper. 'This was delivered this morning.' His hand shook a little as he passed it over.

> *I have your daughter with me. She has undergone no harm. She is unsullied and perfectly content for the present.*
>
> *But this situation cannot last, as I'm certain you will appreciate. After all, sir, it costs money to keep a girl.*
>
> *With that in mind, I propose a bargain between gentlemen. In return for a fair payment I will ensure that she's returned to you entirely unharmed. Given who she is and who she might become, I believe £1000 is a reasonable figure.*
>
> *Should you not comply, of course, her fate will be a little different. I will take pains to let it be known what has happened to her. After that, you will understand, no decent man will be willing to take her for a wife.*
>
> *The choice lies with you. I shall send another letter with more instructions.*

A thousand pounds. It was an outrageous sum. More than half a dozen working men might hope to see in their working lives. A ransom for one girl. Simon took a deep breath.

'That's a fortune.'

'I know exactly how much it is, Westow. To the penny.'

'Do you have that much?'

'That's my business.' Milner glared at him. 'But yes, I do. And whoever sent this seems to know what I'm worth.'

Simon tried to clear his head. Talking about money wasn't going to find her. 'Who brought this?'

'A boy. He handed it to one of the servants and ran off.'

'Do you have any idea who sent it?'

'No.' A curt, angry reply. 'If I did, I'd kill him myself.'

'Are you negotiating a marriage for your daughter?'

'Not yet. But there are some prospects.'

'What's her name?' She was a person, not an item.

'Hannah.'

'What does she look like?'

Milner considered for a moment. He seemed to have difficulty conjuring her into his mind.

'Fair hair. A pretty enough face, I suppose. Small; she doesn't stand to my shoulder.'

About five feet tall, Simon judged.

'What was she wearing?'

The man shook his head. 'I don't know. I was at work.'

'It would be helpful to find out. Nobody's courting her?'

'I told you, no. She attends the dances at the Assembly Rooms. But her mother always accompanies her when she goes. That's as much as I'll allow.'

The man believed he was as hard as iron. Yet someone had quickly found the point where he'd break. He'd been forced to see that he had weaknesses. A man like Milner wouldn't enjoy that.

He wanted his daughter back. For the girl herself, but even more for what she could bring to his family's future. How a good marriage could burnish him.

'I'll need the names of the friends she was with.'

Milner banged the tip of his cane against the ground. 'You don't talk to them. Not a word of this gets out.'

Any rumour could ruin Hannah Milner's marriage chances. Even suspicion would be enough to tarnish her reputation. She'd be soiled goods, unsaleable to any respectable bidder.

'That's fine.' He kept his voice even. The job would be harder, but he'd have to manage. 'It would help if I could speak to your wife.' Mothers knew more about their daughters than any father might suspect.

'No.' It was an answer that brooked no argument. 'She's taken to her bed. You don't come anywhere near my house. The next

I want to hear from you is that you've found her, untouched. And not even a hint about what's happened. Not now, not ever. You understand? Milner's mouth curled a little and he licked his lips. 'They tell me you're good at what you do. Bring her back before the money's due and I'll pay you two hundred guineas.'

That was far more than Simon had made in his very best year. But if he could afford to pay out a thousand pounds, the man could afford it.

'All right,' he agreed.

'And I want it done fast. Before people get it in their minds to talk.' The man started to turn away, then stopped. 'And before I have to pay this damned ransom. I expect success. Ask anyone – I don't take to people who fail me.'

Simon stood and watched until the man was no more than a smudged figure in the distance.

TWO

He was halfway home by the time Jane caught him.

'He had a man keeping watch,' she said. 'Over in the trees.'

'Did he see you?'

She didn't bother to reply. He should have known better than to ask. No one spotted her unless she wanted it. But she took in everything, noticed every detail. That was how they'd met. She'd appeared at his side one day when he was following a man who'd stolen two pounds' worth of parts from a watchmaker. Simon had lost him in one of the courts down near the river, not sure which way to turn.

'He went to the right.' A girl was suddenly whispering. 'I've been watching you trail behind him all morning.'

He hadn't seen her. He hadn't even sensed her there. Simon gave her a shilling from the reward. She stared at the coin in her palm and eyed him with a curious innocence.

'Does this mean I work for you now?'

They'd never said more about it. Jane was simply there every day, entwined in his work. Then in his life, once she moved into the room up in the rafters. She was there. To anyone outside, she might have been part of the family. But that was just surface. Underneath, Jane kept her distance. Her world was inside her head. They'd worked together for a few years, but he still knew little about her. Most of the time he had no idea where she went or what she did. But he accepted that. She was good at this work. The best he'd ever seen. The rest was her choice. Long before they ever met, she'd built a wall between herself and the world. Even now, she remained wary, untrusting of everything. As if this could all crumble to nothing one day and she'd be left on her own again.

'Someone's snatched his daughter. Her name's Hannah. Wants a thousand for her.'

'A thousand?' she asked as if the figure couldn't exist. 'Is that what the rich are worth these days? I've seen her going in and out of the shops.' Her mouth hardened. 'She giggles a lot.'

That was her judgement. A frivolous girl without a serious thought in her mind. Someone with everything laid out before her. Perhaps it was true, but it didn't matter. Their job was to bring her home safe.

'He doesn't want anyone to know.'

'That's going to make things difficult for us,' Jane said.

'We've no choice on this job. Start asking around.'

'I will.' And she was gone.

In the house, the boys ran to him and Simon knelt and hugged them close. Three years old, growing each day. They were twins, but he could always tell them apart. Richard was impulsive and daring, with a shy, beguiling twist to his grin, while Amos looked at everything with Rosie's forthright, evaluating stare. Before the baptism he'd plucked their names from the graveyard outside the parish church, hunting for anything at all to call them. What did it matter, anyway?

He'd been named for his father; he had the faint memory of his mother telling him that once. Sometimes he believed he could even recall the sweet tone of her words as she said it; it seemed like a dream of the time before his parents died, when he still had his innocence. But in the end, the name was all his father was able to pass on to him. And any weight it possessed ended when they put him in the ground.

He stood, a son wriggling in each arm as he gripped them tight. He was dwelling too much on the past. It was the session that morning. He'd thought it might help. Instead, it just painted the old pictures again, bringing them back in vivid colours.

Rosie came through from the kitchen, wiping her hands on an old piece of linen.

'Did he want something important for his sovereign?'

He told her, taking out the letter and waiting as she read.

'A thousand pounds?' She stared at him in disbelief. It was beyond counting. 'Do you think she might have eloped? Maybe they're using this to get some money.'

'Milner claims no one's courting her.'

Rosie snorted. 'He's the father. What would he know? Most men can't see in front of their faces.'

'He's convinced she's been taken.'

'And he wants his property back,' she said. 'The poor lass must be terrified, Simon. Did he bother to think about that? Or just what she's worth?'

He didn't need to answer. Hannah Milner was a commodity. To her father, to the man who'd taken her. Even to him. A commodity worth her weight in gold.

'Maybe he'll see things differently when she's home and safe.'

'Come on. You know he won't. Men like that only see the world in pounds, shillings and pence.'

She was right. But he'd never change the Milners of this world. It wasn't his job. He'd leave that to the Radicals and the agitators, for all the good it would do them.

'Do you think of me as your property?' Rosie asked as he took a small box from its hiding place under the stairs, selected a few coins and slipped them into his purse.

He looked at her. 'I wouldn't dare, and you know it. I'll be back later,' he said as he kissed her. No point in promising a time.

'Bring her home quickly,' she said. 'And safely.'

'That's what I intend to do.'

'And make sure Milner doesn't start giving you those ideas.' Her smile was warm. 'Not if you value your existence, Simon Westow. A thousand? I hope you're stinging him well for this.'

'Two hundred,' Simon told her, watching Rosie's eyes widen in astonishment and greed. He grinned. 'Guineas.'

Jane wandered and listened. Nobody noticed her; down here she was one more ghost among so many. All these folk cared about was surviving until the next morning. Some food, a bed indoors, keeping their babies alive, the formless wish of work for the men tomorrow.

No scrubbing would ever remove the grime ingrained in their skin. Few talked. Words were nothing more than wasted breath. Some had given up caring, slumped and staring at the wall.

None of them was likely to know about Hannah Milner. But Jane came here anyway. This was where she always began. It focused her mind, reminded her who she'd once been. She'd spent years among these people. She knew who they were, how they felt. Sometimes their despair even rested comfortably on her shoulders. And very occasionally she'd catch a spark that sent her in the right direction.

Not this afternoon. The only thing around here was the fracture of hope.

She left, gathering her old shawl over her head as she moved up and down Briggate, stopping to gaze in the shop windows. Another ragged girl looking at things she could never afford. Jane smiled to herself. They didn't know she had nigh on a hundred pounds hidden away where no one else would ever find it. Not even Simon.

In the glass she saw the reflection of two young women, prattling as they passed by. She'd seen them before, arm-in-arm with the missing girl. Quietly, she followed. Close enough to hear them, but far enough away not to be noticed. They had no thought for anyone but themselves, anyway.

Along Boar Lane, listening as they commented on this and that – a woman's dress, how handsome a passing young man might be – then up West Street by the side of the Mixed Cloth Hall, Jane remained behind them like a pale shadow.

Finally, as they approached St Paul's Church on the edge of Park Square, one said: 'Did you hear about Hannah?'

Suddenly Jane was alert, aware of every word.

'No,' the other replied. 'Where is she? I thought she was coming out with us today.'

'I called for her earlier. The servant told me she'd had to go to York. Her grandmama's been taken ill.'

'Poor thing. I hate having to go and see relatives when they're unwell, don't you? Especially the old ones. It's not as if I can do anything to help them and the sick rooms always smell so awful. About the only reason I'd go is if I was in the will.'

'I don't know. It might have its good points. I've heard the dragoons are there at the moment. Maybe Hannah will meet an officer. A good-looking captain. Even a colonel.'

The other girl snorted. 'They won't bother with a little stick like her. When is she coming back, anyway?'

'The servant didn't say. She'll probably find herself a rich husband and never return.'

The pair of them giggled and walked on into the square, arms still linked together, the hems of their skirts just above the dusty pavement.

Jane didn't follow. She'd be too visible, her appearance too out of place there; someone would see. Still, she had something to pass to Simon. The family had made an excuse for her absence. More importantly, her friends believed it. That would buy them a little time.

She walked slowly back into Leeds from the west end of town, always aware of the people around her, their faces, the way they moved. There were times she imagined she saw her mother in the distance and her heart would start pounding in her chest as she darted through the crowd. But the resemblance always vanished when she drew close.

Eight years old, waking in the morning with her father's weight on top of her. His coaxing words, the smell of his breath, his sweat against her skin. Then the sharp, awful pain between her legs that made her scream. When she turned her head her mother was standing in the doorway, mouth open, the basket of shopping tumbling out of her hands on to the floor. Jane cried out for her. She shouted and begged.

But her mother was already calculating. It was in her eyes. A husband meant security. He brought in wages. A growing girl was nothing more than temptation. Before her tears could even dry, Jane's mother had forced her out of the door. She heard the key turn in the lock.

It was all illusion. That woman would never come searching for her daughter.

He passed a pair of drunks snarling at each other on Briggate. One yelled and lurched forward. In a moment they were rolling on the cobbles, throwing feeble punches that hit nothing but air. A man offered odds on a winner.

Simon strode along, weaving between people, jumping out of the path of a coach as it careened out of the Talbot Inn. The man he wanted to see had his office on the far side of the Head Row, close to old St John's Church.

George Mudie ran the *Leeds Gazette*. Once he'd been the editor of the *Intelligencer*, a power in the town, but when it was sold the new owners wanted fresh blood. Now he ran a small paper that always tottered on the verge of bankruptcy.

The printing press stood at the back of the small office, filling most of the space. Mudie was a fastidious man, always well-barbered and shaved, a suit of good wool, his linen crisp and white. Everything but his fingertips; they were permanently black after a lifetime of setting type. He was sitting behind his desk. Except for a bottle of rum and a glass, the surface was bare.

'That's it,' he said with grim satisfaction. 'The final edition's on the street. No more *Gazette*. We're out of business. Want a drink to celebrate?'

When Simon shook his head, Mudie poured a tot and raised it.

'To new ventures,' he toasted, and swallowed the rum in a single gulp. He jerked his head towards the machinery behind him. 'Do you know anyone who needs a press?'

'Half the Radicals in town would probably love it. They'd be able to print up their pamphlets.'

'That's not a bad idea.' Mudie sighed. 'What can I do for you, Simon? The only thing that's been stolen here is my livelihood, and you can't get that back for me. I couldn't afford your fee, anyway.'

'Information.'

'My stock-in-trade.' He gave a wry smile and poured another glass. 'If I still had a trade, of course.'

'I want to know about John Milner.'

'Do you have a reason?' Mudie asked, and it was Simon's turn to grin.

'Nothing you can print.'

'Touché.' He drained the last of the bottle into the glass and stared at it. 'He and his brothers inherited from their father. There are four of them, I think. Milner sold his share of the estate to the others and put his capital to work in town. Bought a few houses, good ones, and rented them out. He invested in Park Square; that's probably paid off well. I know he has interests in two manufactories and those might as well print money these days.' He lifted the rum to his lips and sipped. 'What else do you want?'

'Family?'

Mudie grimaced and drank a little more.

'Married, of course, although the rumour is that it was never happy. His wife seems to have faded into the woodwork. About the only time you see her these days is at the balls and assemblies. I know for a fact he's had a mistress for years; installed her in a place he owns just up the street from his house and visits twice a week like clockwork. Had five—' He paused for a moment and corrected himself. 'No, six children, but only one survived. A daughter.' Mudie cocked his head. 'Why the interest? It must be something important.'

'I'm curious.'

'The only time you're curious is when money's involved.'

'Money's involved in everything these days, George. You ought to have learned that by now. What about his enemies?' Simon asked. 'Who hates him?'

Mudie had a question of his own: 'Have you ever met him?'

'Yes.' No need for details.

'Then you can probably guess the answer to that.'

'Anyone in particular?'

'Easy enough. Arthur Standish. Last year he was keen on a match between his oldest son and Milner's daughter. Milner told the boy to come back when he was worth more. Standish cursed him up and down. Swore he'd ruin him.'

Simon never paid attention to feuds between the wealthy. Words didn't pay his bills. But he'd done a little work for Standish, retrieved some plate a servant had stolen. The man had chosen to prosecute; the thief had been transported to Australia for fourteen years.

'Standish is cheap.' He'd tried to haggle on the reward.

'They all are, Simon. It's why they stay rich and the rest of us
are poor.' Mudie stood. 'I'm going to buy another bottle and go
home.'

'I wish you good luck.'

He sighed. 'So would I, if I knew what it was.'

THREE

S tandish? It sounded very plausible, especially if the man had
his heart set on revenge.

Still, it was good news of a sort. When he was pursuing
the thief, he'd spent time cultivating the housekeeper. The shank
end of the afternoon would be a quiet time for her. Just right for
a visit.

The house lay out along Long Balk Lane, half a mile beyond
town. Coaches and carriages passed, a straggle of people on foot,
every one of them heading to Leeds, bent under the possessions
loaded on their backs. Coming to search for their fortunes.

He breathed in the clearer air, saw plants starting to grow in
the fields, young leaves fluttering on the branches and the early
flowers of spring waving their colours. Not like town, where hardly
a tree still stood. Nature there was stone and brick and slate.

The house was impressive, graceful and pleasing to the eye.
But Simon knew better than to present himself at the big double
doors in front. It was the tradesman's entrance at the back for him,
standing inside a cobbled courtyard. He pushed the door wide and
walked into the kitchen.

'Well, well, well. Look what the cat dragged in.'

Martha was sitting in her rocking chair by the fire, a pipe
clenched between her teeth, knitting on her lap. She was larger
than ever, a mob cap over her hair and an apron wrapped around
her bulging waist. A jug of ale sat on the floor beside her.

'I wouldn't say no to a drop of that,' Simon said.

'I daresay you wouldn't.' But she didn't move. 'Is that your
idea of a greeting? I don't see you for a year or more, then you

stroll in like you own the place, demanding a drink. Forgotten your manners, have you, *Mister* Westow?'

That was him told. He needed her sweet and talkative.

'It's a pleasure to see you, Mrs Dawson.'

She eyed him suspiciously.

'You're a lying beggar, Simon Westow. You've not walked out here to pass the time of day with me.'

'No,' he admitted. 'I'm hoping to learn a few things.'

Her eyes glittered. 'Is that right? And might these things be worth a little?'

'They might.' He opened his hand and a silver coin shimmered in the light. 'Like this?'

He flicked it with his thumb. It turned over and over in the air and landed in her lap.

'Aye, that'd be the ticket. Get yourself a mug and wet your whistle.'

He knew he needed to phrase his questions carefully, not to give anything away. Martha Dawson was sharp; she'd pounce on any crumb.

'Has the master lost any more things lately?'

She laughed. 'Touting for business now, are you? Things must be bad.'

'Never hurts to ask. I've been hearing a few things about his son, the eldest one—'

'William?' She looked at him sharply. 'What about him?'

'That he's been getting loud around town.' He knew nothing about the lad, but it would make her talk.

Martha snorted. 'Someone's been having you on. He wouldn't say boo to a goose, that one. Anyway, he's not even in Leeds. He's in London. His father sent him down there months ago to stop him mooning over that lass as turned him down.'

'The Milner girl?'

'That's the one. A right baggage, she is, too. Came here for dinner with her parents once, and spent the evening staring at everything as if she was weighing its worth.' She shook her head in disgust at the memory. 'If you ask me, young Will's better off without her. Him so studious and her with nowt but feathers in her head. But the master was furious when old Milner said no to the marriage, mind. You'd think the sky had fallen in.' She moved in her chair, slowly easing her bulk around until she gave a small sigh of comfort. 'Why do you want to know about William, anyway?'

'Something I overheard,' Simon replied with a shrug. 'Like you said, they must have been wrong.'

'Aye,' she said doubtfully. 'They must.'

She was suspicious now. He could see it in the set of her mouth. But he hadn't given her a sniff of anything worthwhile. She could worry at it all night and never discover the truth. He set his mug on the table.

'I'd better be on my way.'

'Value for money, was it?'

'No,' he told her bluntly. 'But that's how it goes sometimes. You can't always find a winner.'

He knew better than to ask Martha about Standish. The son was one thing, the father quite another. She was fiercely loyal to her employer; questions would just cause her hackles to rise. He left certain of one thing, though: Hannah Milner wasn't there.

Outside, the light had shifted. Evening was close. Somewhere nearby, birds were singing, their trills and warbles filling the air. He gathered his coat around himself and set off back to Leeds.

Tonight he'd be in the taverns and dram shops, asking more questions, listening for anything out of the ordinary. That was where he did most of his work. First, though, an hour or so at home.

'And her friends believed the story about York?' Simon asked.

'Yes,' Jane told him. They leaned against the battered kitchen table and talked while Rosie cut bread and cheese and sliced the cold remains of the beef as the twins played a game of some kind around their feet. 'I've been thinking.'

'Go on.' He'd learned to listen to her ideas.

'I don't believe it's anyone wealthy who's taken her.'

He was surprised. 'Why?'

'Servants,' she replied, and it was explanation enough. They saw everything in a house. If one didn't talk, another would; by now it would be common knowledge.

Simon nodded. 'Then who is it?' he asked.

'I don't know. But he must have enough space to keep her quiet,' Jane said. 'Someone who lives alone.'

'Maybe he has an accomplice,' Rosie suggested. 'Or perhaps he owns somewhere lonely.' She put the food on plates and handed them around. 'You two,' she told the boys. 'Sit and eat. Now.'

They knew her tone well enough to obey.

'And it can't be too far from Leeds.' Simon let his thoughts roam. 'Still, there are enough who live alone. He'd need a reason for taking her, though.'

'I'd say a thousand pounds is a very good reason, wouldn't you?' Rosie said. 'It's a lifetime's wealth. If we had money like that—'

'You wouldn't know what to do with yourself.'

She looked at him and arched an eyebrow. 'Living like a lord and lady? I'm sure I'd find a few amusements.'

Simon pursed his lips. 'This feels personal to me. The kidnapper picked her out for something more than money.'

Most thieves were stupid, greedy. They saw a chance, grabbed anything of value and ran. They had no plan. That was why it rarely took him more than a few hours to retrieve stolen property. A question or two dropped in the right ears, the clink of coins changing hands, and he was knocking on the door.

But this was different. A person wasn't an object that anyone could snatch. This took care and thought.

'What is it?' Rosie asked him.

'I'm not sure.' He believed he was groping his way towards something. Some understanding. He just didn't know what it was yet.

'Eat,' she told him. 'Maybe that will help.'

The night was quieter than the day. Shops were shuttered. Lamps flickered in the houses. People safe behind locked doors.

But another Leeds arose in the darkness. A different population that came to life with the shadows. Simon had known them for years, people like Colonel Warburton, the former soldier who always wore the tattered French officer's coat he claimed to have stripped from a corpse on the battlefield at Waterloo. He held court in a back room of the Boot and Shoe, a bottle of good brandy on the table, quietly buying and selling stolen bonds.

Or Hetty Marcombe. She looked like a harmless, vacant old woman wandering forlornly around the yards of the coaching inns. But she had quiet cunning behind the empty eyes, ready to make off with any case that passengers didn't keep close. Josh Hartley, Silver Dexter, all the flash men and burglars, and the whores who strutted up and down Briggate. Once the daylight faded, Leeds belonged to them.

Simon was at ease in their company. He talked a little and listened as they spoke. With a word or a nod, one person often led him to another. He learned who'd stolen what, if it had been sold and for how much. Information he'd be able to use in the coming weeks. But tonight his eyes were open for a particular man.

At the Cross Keys, just across the river in Holbeck, he stood inside the door and watched the crowd. Almost every face was young, drinking with the grim determination that dashed headlong towards oblivion. A few more years and most of them would be gone. Violence, disease, the gallows, a ship to the other side of the world. Something would carry them away. And deep inside, they knew it. So they forced out their pleasures like duty.

Strange, Simon thought, Harry Smith didn't seem to be anywhere tonight. People called him the Vulture. He'd earned the name; he relished it like an honour. Smith fed himself on the weak, the gang of young boys who worked for him, picking pockets and robbing shops.

But Harry heard things that didn't reach other ears. He was sly, he understood that knowledge brought a good price. And he always knew who'd be willing to pay.

Simon moved on. By the time the clock struck ten he'd gone all round the town. No word of anyone anticipating a fortune soon. Finally, close to midnight, he turned his key in the lock and climbed up to bed.

'You're a pretty thing. How much do you charge?'

Jane turned away and the man laughed.

'Don't play coy, luv. Tuppence and you'll get the bargain. You might even like it for once.'

She began to walk down Kirkgate, but he staggered along behind, drunk, cursing her. She'd survived the nights out here for too long.

She knew the men who populated them. This one was harmless, all drink and bluster and noise. Still, she reached into the pocket of her dress and curled her fingers around the handle of her knife.

The voice faded and she forgot he'd ever been there. No one behind her now. With the shawl over her head, she slipped in and out of the shadows. People passed without a glance. The only light came from gaps in the shutters, but she knew her way around in the darkness.

Lizzie Henry lived out on Black Flags Lane, the far side of Quarry Hill. The building stood alone, looking as if it had once been a large farmhouse. Now, as she entered, she saw a series of rooms off a long hallway. The lamps had been lit and trimmed, the floorboards swept, paintings on the walls; everything was clean and tidy. The faint sound of talk leaked from behind closed doors. But she had no sense of joy from the place.

Jane had heard tales. This was a house that catered to the worst things men desired, anything at all if the fee was right. From somewhere upstairs there was a stifled scream, then silence. She paused for a second, feeling the beat of her heart and the breath in her lungs, then walked on to the open door ahead. Beyond it, a neat, ordered parlour and Lizzie herself sitting in an armchair, close to the blazing fire.

Jane had always pictured the woman as a hag. Instead, she was slim, darkly attractive, dressed in an elegant, fashionable gown whose material shimmered and sparkled in the light. She had power and wealth, and wore them easily, a woman who held her secrets close – the names of the men who came here, what they did, those who went too far.

She'd never have difficulty finding girls to serve in the house. Too many were desperate. All it took was the promise of a meal and a bed. And then enough gin and laudanum to dull the pain of living and the agony men inflicted. If a few died, there was ample land for the burials. Girls without names, without pasts; no one would ever ask questions.

Lizzie Henry looked up and her mouth curled into a frown.

'Who are you? How did you get in?' Her voice had a harsh rasp. But there was no trace of worry or fear on her face. Beside her, a decanter, a glass and a bell sat on a small wooden table.

'It wasn't locked.' Jane could feel the heat from the grate.

'You're lying.'

Jane shrugged. The handle had turned under her touch. No one had come to stop her.

'What do you want? I don't need more girls at the moment.' She cocked her head a little. Jane knew exactly what the woman would see: a ragged, scrawny thing. A pauper who looked as if she was clinging to the edge of life. 'Still, I suppose one or two might prefer your type. What's your name?'

'It doesn't matter who I am.' She kept her grip tight on the knife. 'I've come looking for something.'

Lizzie raised an eyebrow and moved on the seat. She filled the glass, the liquid the deep colour of rubies, and took a small sip.

'And what's this something you're after?' The words mocked quietly.

'Truth.'

'Truth, is it?' She stretched in the chair. 'What sort of truth would a girl like you want?'

'The names of the men who come here.'

Lizzie began to laugh.

'For God's sake, child, don't be so stupid. Do you honestly believe you can breeze in here like Lady Muck and demand something like that? Get out. Run off and play before something bad happens to you. Be grateful I'm feeling generous tonight.' She gave a cold smile. And edged her hand closer to the bell. 'It would be so easy. And nobody would ever know.'

For a second they stared at each other. Then Jane turned, feeling the chill wrap around her as she stepped into hall, and listened, expecting the tinkle of the bell.

Outside, she took a breath, trying not to shiver. For a moment, she'd felt death at her shoulder. It could happen so easily, the woman had said. Not a threat; a purr of anticipation.

'You went to see Lizzie Henry?' Simon asked in disbelief. 'On your own?'

'You know the type of men that go there.'

'Of course we do. Everybody knows. Pious and proper until their trousers are down,' Rosie said. The boys had been fed; now they were playing in the small yard behind the house. She placed her fingertips on the back of Jane's hand. 'Simon's right. You shouldn't have gone by yourself.'

'I thought she might talk to a girl.' She sat, and tore a piece of bread into crumbs, eyes stinging as she stared down at the kitchen table.

'What did you want to know?' He was struggling to contain his temper. Christ Almighty, how could she do something so idiotic? She ought to know better. The girls who walked through that door rarely came out again, and none of them dared enter with demands.

'The names of the men who go there.'

Simon glanced at his wife for a moment, then he pushed his plate away, stood, and stalked out of the room.

'I thought it might help,' Jane said. She looked at his empty chair.

'He worries about you,' Rosie told her. 'We both do. We don't want anything to happen to you, that's all. You're family. And you're too valuable to him.'

Jane said nothing. Her fingers swirled through the breadcrumbs.

'Lizzie Henry's very dangerous,' Rosie said.

Slowly, Jane stood. Her chair groaned on the floorboards. In the doorway she turned.

'She told me to get out. She called me a child.'

'Then you were lucky. She's murdered people before. And that's not just a tale.'

'She said nobody would ever know if she did.'

'No,' Rosie answered, 'she's wrong there. Simon would have found out, and he'd have had to kill her.'

'Should I say sorry to him?'

'There's no need. He knows.'

Halfway up Swinegate he stopped, slapping his palm against the wall and slowly exhaling. Anything to rid himself of the anger. In some ways Jane was still very young. She was so good at what she did that he often forgot that. She showed a blank face to the world, she kept everything at bay. But somewhere down in her core, there was some little piece of innocence that life hadn't torn away yet.

Going to Lizzie Henry, wanting information like that . . . and

in her own home, for the love of God. It was asking to be murdered.
Jane had been luckier than she'd ever know. At least four girls
had died out there. Probably more. But Lizzie would never see
the inside of a courtroom. She knew too much about the people
who ran Leeds. As long as she lived, she was free and clear.

Damn it, he should have thought of going to her himself. She'd
talk to him.

Nine years before, Lizzie had sent him a note. A locket she
owned had gone missing, vanished with one of the servants. The
jewellery wasn't valuable, but she wanted it back. It was important
to her. Less than a day later he appeared at Black Flags Lane.

He'd found the piece. And the man who claimed he'd
bought it from another fellow who'd mysteriously vanished. The
servant who'd stolen the locket was dead, raped before she'd been
murdered, her body tossed on a piece of waste ground.

Lizzie had prosecuted the man for theft.

The shutters were closed as Simon banged on the door. A dull,
grey morning with a hint of rain in the air. He slammed his fist
on the wood again until finally a man drew back the bolts, his
face angry, still puffy with sleep.

'What?'

'Tell your mistress that Simon Westow is here.'

A contemptuous look, and the door closed again, the key turning
in the lock. Two minutes by his pocket watch until it opened once
more.

'Come in.'

Nothing had changed in the years since he'd been here. Still
the only room that seemed alive belonged to Lizzie. She was
dressed, perfumed and coiffed, smiling as he entered.

'Mr Westow.' A tiny curtsey. 'It's been too long since I've
enjoyed the pleasure of your company.'

He smiled. 'There's been no need, has there?'

'That's true,' she agreed. 'But you're always a welcome visitor.'

He'd never taken the reward for returning the locket. Lizzie
Henry was someone he preferred to have in his debt. Information
she could give was worth far more than money.

'I'm pleased to hear that.'

She gestured at a chair and they sat. The formalities were over.

'So you've come for payment at last. What is it?'

'I want a list of the men who come here.'

She remained silent so long that he wondered if she'd ever reply.

'A girl was here last night, looking for the same thing,' Lizzie said thoughtfully. 'I wonder why everyone suddenly wants to know.'

'The girl's name is Jane. She works for me.'

Lizzie gave a small nod. 'She should have told me.'

'I had no idea that she was coming.'

'I see.' She hesitated. 'Is it important to know the names?'

'It is,' Simon said.

'It would go no further than you?'

'My word on it,' he told her. 'I'll destroy it afterwards.'

Yet still it took time.

'All right. I'll send it to your house,' she agreed. 'Before noon. We keep different hours here. I haven't even breakfasted yet.' He saw a faint blush cross her face.

'Thank you.' He stood, extending a hand for her to shake. 'One more thing: nothing happens to Jane. Nothing at all.'

'Agreed. You expect a high price for your services, Mr Westow.'

He'd never doubted she would give him the names. Before he returned the locket, Simon had examined it. It was made of cheap plate, not real gold, and well-worn; third-rate work. He'd found the catch and opened it. A lock of dark hair, and a miniature of a young man dressed in the colours of the Thirty-Third. At the bottom, a date: 1795.

No value, perhaps, but worth the world to her. Now the debt was paid.

FOUR

Simon stood on Black Flags Lane and looked down towards Leeds. A thin haze of smoke hung over the town. Hannah Milner was there. Somewhere. Alive, he was certain of that. But terrified. Alone.

He was aware of every minute that passed. The man who'd taken her would send another letter today. He'd want to arrange quick delivery of his money. A threat in the note to keep the girl's father alert and compliant. That was what someone with intelligence would do. And whoever took her had a brain.

Jane tried not to think. As she left the house, she blinked back tears. She should never have told Simon. It would have been better to keep it inside, her quiet, private humiliation. She'd seen the fury in his look, the way he glared at her as if she was an ignorant little girl.

She didn't need to go back there. She could walk away from it all. The money she had saved was enough to keep her for a long time. Start walking and keep going until she was in a new town. Somewhere far away, where no one knew a thing about her. An invisible girl.

Standing on the bridge, not even noticing the water moving under her feet, Jane knew they were empty ideas. She'd never go anywhere. However hard she tried to push them away, Simon and Rosie and the twins cared about her. Working with him, for the first time in her life she believed she had a use. Until last night.

Maybe she really was as stupid as that woman said. Maybe she'd never learn.

Jane scraped her knuckles against the stone parapet until the skin was raw and burning. Then more, harder, enough to make her wince with the pain. The blood came, dripping on to the dark grit. She wanted to punish herself. She needed to hurt. She deserved it.

Eventually it was enough. She took out her handkerchief and wrapped it around her hand, satisfied as the red stain grew on the linen.

The town was alive, so many people jostling and bumping along Commercial Street. She stood in a shop doorway, eyes watching the pickpockets as they worked. At least three sets that she could see, quick fingers that slid out a wallet or a purse and passed it to an accomplice before darting away.

She'd never done that, her hands were always too clumsy; she didn't possess the light touch the trade needed. But she'd stolen: pieces of fruit when a shopkeeper's back was turned, anything she could sell to keep herself alive. No need of that any longer. There was food on the table every day. A room of her own with a bed. If Simon still wanted her after this.

She stopped suddenly in the middle of the pavement. She'd find the Vulture. He heard things, and she knew exactly where he'd be at this hour. As she began to move, Jane felt the faint trail of small fingers edging towards her pocket. She grabbed the wrist and turned. A girl stood, scared, bewildered, the way Jane must have always looked during that first year on the street.

'Go,' she said. 'Get out of here. Now.'

Market morning and Leeds was loud. People cried their wares, one voice drowning out another like waves. Stalls lined both sides of Briggate, the road so cramped that coaches could barely pass.

People shoved and pushed by each other as they tried to see the displays – terrified chickens crammed into wooden cages, sacks of onions and potatoes, thick blocks of pale butter. At the entrance to a court an old woman sat slumped with her back against the wall. In her lap she held a box with the broken remnants of her life. A penny each, she croaked. Just a penny, sir, nice for your wife or sweetheart. No one even heard her.

It took Simon five minutes to squeeze his way through. Finally he was beyond the crush, exhaling the stink of bodies. The noise dulled as he slid between carts and barrows and turned on to Kirkgate.

Charles Press was standing behind the bar in the Wellington, a piece of rag tossed over his heavy leather apron. His curly hair was beginning to recede, showing a ruddy forehead and a broad, smiling face.

He'd fought with the Duke's army across Portugal and Spain, survived three wounds, and been with the troops as they took Paris. He'd been clever with the loot he gathered, keeping enough back to buy this tavern and name it for his commander.

Press kept his sharpshooter's rifle in easy reach, a bayonet and club on his belt. The Wellington was an orderly place.

'Early to see you, Simon.' He picked up a mug, ready to pour from the barrel.

'Not this morning, Charley. I'm looking for Harry Smith. Has he been in yet today?'

Press shook his head. 'No.' He chewed his bottom lip. 'Didn't see him yesterday, now I think about it.'

Not in the Cross Keys last night or the Wellington today. That was strange; Harry Smith was a man of habit.

'Is he dying?' the boy asked. His eyes moved around, trying to look at anything but the man lying on his bed of rags.

'I don't know,' Jane lied. 'Is there any water down in the court?'

He shook his head. 'We use the pump on Kirkgate.'

She found a cracked jug in the corner.

'Go and fill this.'

Alone, she looked down at the Vulture. His skin burned when she touched it, a sheen of sweat glistening on his forehead. But he was shivering with cold. Jane laid a torn coat on top of him. It wouldn't help, but it was one thing she could do.

The boy returned, moving awkwardly as he tried to balance the jug. He looked nine, perhaps ten, his body hewn away to flesh and bone, no shoes or stockings, dressed in tattered breeches and a shirt made for a man.

'Where are the others?' Jane asked.

'They left,' he replied. 'They all went when he took like this yesterday morning.' The Vulture's crew had abandoned him to die; there was nothing here to keep them. Jane picked a piece of cloth from the floor, wetted it and washed the man's face. His lips twitched into a brief smile.

'Why did you stay?' She turned her head to watch the boy, surprised by his loyalty.

'I don't have anywhere else to go.'

'You'd better find somewhere. He probably won't be alive much longer.'

It wouldn't be the first death the boy had seen; she knew it wouldn't be the last. Probably gentler than some. He gave a small, weary nod, then darted to two different corners of the room, digging around for something, before walking out without a backward glance.

Jane stayed. It wouldn't be long now. It didn't matter what kind of man the Vulture been in life, he deserved someone with him when he died. She talked to him, asking questions, but he was beyond speech.

She kept bathing his face until it was clean enough to meet his maker. The Vulture's breathing became ragged, as if he was fighting for each gasp, then it stopped altogether. Quietly, Jane closed the door as she left.

'He's dead?' Simon asked. 'No one said anything. I was looking for him. Nobody's seen him since the day before yesterday.' Word of Harry Smith's passing should have rolled around Leeds like thunder.

'It only happened an hour or so ago.'

'Who told you?'

'I was there,' Jane said. 'It was quiet, in his bed. Fever.'

He'd never been able to learn where Smith lived. The man had always held that very close, even in his drunkest nights. But she knew.

'I don't suppose he said anything?'

'No. I don't think he even knew I was there.'

Twice she'd surprised him today. First with her naiveté, now with her cunning. How could someone possess both of those? But the Vulture's death meant no information. Whatever Harry knew had gone with him to the devil. He sighed.

Simon had come home to an empty house. A sealed letter, his name written on it in an elegant hand, waited on the kitchen table. Lizzie Henry had been as good as her word. Name after name, each with his particular taste. No John Milner, he noticed as he went through the list; a mistress must be enough for his needs. But many of the great and the good in Leeds. And one or two who might be willing to kidnap a girl to revive their flagging fortunes.

He put the paper in the hidden place under the stairs. Only he and Rosie knew it existed. After they moved here, they'd agreed not to employ servants. It meant more work for her, on top of the boys and the cooking and the accounts, but it was safer – no one would be tempted to pry and sell their knowledge. Everything neat, secure, and in the family.

'What do we do now?' Jane interrupted his thoughts.

'There are some we can try. Do you know Daniel Saville?' His name had been among Lizzie Henry's clients.

'No.' She cut a piece of cheese and tore off a hunk of fresh bread. 'Who is he?'

'One of a pair. He has a brother called Taylor. They live out on

the far side of Woodhouse Moor. Their father left them well-off,
but I know for a fact that they've spent their way through it all. Last
year they sold off all the land they owned, so there's no more
income.'

He was about to say more when the door crashed open and the
boys roared through into the kitchen, shouting in their high voices,
faces flushed with excitement. He could make out the tracks of
tears through the dust caking Richard's cheeks. Rosie followed,
her arms weighed down with shopping from the market.

'I swear, these two are going to be the death of me.' With a
grunt, she put everything on the table and rubbed her hands. She
glared at the twins. 'Richard decided to try and run out in front
of a cart. If a man hadn't grabbed him, he'd be dead now.'

But he was alive, Simon thought gratefully. And unhurt. If they
lasted until they were five, they'd grow to be men, that was what
folk said. Survive past twenty and they might see old age.

'I hope your mother taught you a lesson.'

'Oh, I did,' she said. 'He won't forget that in a hurry.'

The lad nodded and hung his head. Simon turned to Amos.

'And you'd better have learned it, too.'

'Yes, Da.' A quiet, composed reply. But that was his way. Never
impulsive, always thinking everything through.

'Go and wash,' Rosie ordered. 'You've both got enough dirt on
you to make a field.'

He waited until the boys had cleaned their hands and faces and
run off up the stairs.

'The Savilles aren't much older than Hannah Milner,' Simon
continued. 'They probably know her from the assemblies and
balls.'

'How many work for them?' Jane asked.

'I've no idea.'

'Doesn't matter. Someone will talk.'

'That was clever, finding Harry,' Simon told her as she left.

She shrugged. 'I just followed him home once. I suppose there'll
be another Vulture soon enough.'

'And another and another,' he agreed.

FIVE

A mail coach rushed down the Woodhouse Turnpike, the driver cracking his whip above the horses. The sun peered through the clouds for a moment, long enough for Jane to see the sweat shining on the animals' skin.

A few cows and sheep grazed, barely raising their heads as she walked over the moor. All this space, the openness, left her feeling exposed. She was used to town, secure where she could blend into a crowd and be invisible. Out here there was nowhere to hide. Anyone could see her.

A hundred yards further along, a few cottages clustered by the side of the road. A woman feeding her hens pointed out the Saville house. She eyed Jane and said, 'I wouldn't go up there if I were you, luv.'

'Why not?'

'Because they're devils, them brothers. Reckon they can do as they please.' She snorted. 'Not even got two pennies to rub together any more but that dun't stop them.'

'I've walked out here, I might as well see. Do you think they need a kitchen maid?'

She snorted in disgust.

'They need everything but they pay for nowt. Still owe me for eggs.' The woman twisted her mouth. 'It's on your own head. But I wouldn't let any lass of mine near that place.'

A few years ago it had been grand, Jane decided. But that had been when there was money to care for it. Now it looked worn at the edges, ignored. Barely spring but already plenty of weeds thriving by the drive. The house was forgotten, unloved. A few slates had gone from the roof, a window broken, rags stuffed where the glass had been.

Yet she could still smell the memory of wealth here.

A rutted track led to the back and a walled yard by a plain door. She knocked and entered a large kitchen with a flagstone floor, the open fire throwing out warmth. The fatty sizzle of roasting meat made her belly rumble.

'What do you want?' A thick-set woman bustled into the room, arms around a large bowl. Her face was pink with the heat.

A woman, Jane thought. Women knew the secrets. She gave a hopeful smile.

'I'm looking for work, missus. Someone said you needed staff here.'

'Is that right? Aye, well, they're not wrong.' She hefted the bowl on to a long wooden table and straightened up, a scowl of pain passing over her face. Her fingertips pressed against the small of her back. 'Are you experienced? Done all this before, have you?'

'No.' Jane stared down at the ground then raised her head again, eyes wide. 'But I learn fast and I work hard. Honest, I do.'

The cook snorted and eased herself on to a stool. 'You look more like one of them mill lasses to me. You're scraggy enough for one.'

'I've worked in a mill.' That was true enough, at least; two years as a doffing girl before the morning her life changed.

She smiled, pleased to be right. 'Thought so. I can always spot them a mile off. Always look like they've never seen daylight or a good scrubbing.' Her gaze was sharp. 'Why do you want to come here?'

'It's like I said, missus. I need work.'

The woman coughed. 'That'll be two of us soon enough.'

Suddenly Jane was very interested. Something was happening in this house.

'Why missus?' she asked. 'Are you leaving?'

'I am. This used to be a good place when old Mr Saville was alive. Everyone treated right and fair. These days I wouldn't wish it on my worst enemy. I'm putting in me notice at the end of the month.'

'Why?'

'His sons inherited. Two brothers. They were a right handful while the master was alive. Since then the pair of them have run riot.'

No loyalty to them. Even better; she should be able to learn a few things.

'What are they like?'

The cook pursed her lips into a frown. 'Mr Daniel and Mr Taylor, that's what they're called. They expect the world, then give you nowt to do it with.' Her expression softened for a moment. 'Honestly, lass, you don't want to work here, not if you have an ounce of sense.'

Jane remained attentive, standing with hands clasped in front of her body. 'Was there money? What have they done with it?'

'Spent it all.' The woman shook her head. 'Every penny they were left, and it were a fair lot. Most of the time they're not even here. Off in Leeds or somewhere. But once they're home they want this, want that, and want t'other, and don't give me a farthing to buy it with.' She pointed at the hearth. 'You see that meat over there? I had to beg it from the butcher. They haven't paid him in half a year. There are only three of us still working here now, and we'll all be gone before they know it.' She sighed. 'Take my advice, lass; for your own sake, look somewhere else.'

'Are they here now?' They must be, if she was cooking.

'Mr Daniel's out riding.' The cook frowned again. 'And God only knows where Mr Taylor's got hissen to.' She hefted herself upright and sighed again. 'Onions. Always forget something.' She began to waddle away. 'I daresay you're a decent girl. Best thing to do is walk away. Find yourself a position somewhere else. If you wait till I'm back, I'll give you a crust.'

'Thank you, missus.' Jane gave a nervous smile, shifting from foot to foot until the woman had gone. As soon as she was alone, she took her chance, slipping along a corridor, keeping each step quiet, listening for the slightest noise, any voice. The cook would think she'd simply left.

The house was like a tomb. Upstairs, two of the rooms had clothes tossed over the chairs and the sheets all tangled. All she found elsewhere was neglect – beds stripped and shutters closed. Jane darted out through a door to the stables. A horse whinnied in its stall as she entered. Nothing in the hayloft as she climbed the ladder.

The byre and the barn were both empty. Hardly any wood left to feed the fires. In the distance she spotted a rider crossing the fields, keeping his horse at a hard gallop before reining it in hard as he came to the cobbles by the stable. For a moment her chest tightened. Good timing. Much longer and she'd have been trapped there. Five more minutes and she was hurrying back towards town.

No sign that Hannah Milner had ever been near the place.

The knock came just as Simon was ready to leave. He pulled the door open, seeing Milner's tall servant.

'My master said I should bring you this.'

The smallest of bows and he was gone.

'Who is it?' Rosie called.

'Another note,' he said. Exactly as he'd thought. She came through, wiping her hands on her apron.

'What does it say?'

> *Sir,*
>
> *I understand full well that even a gentleman like yourself might need a little time to draw together one thousand pounds in notes. After all, you put your capital to work, rather than in a strongbox somewhere. But a day has passed, and I'm certain that you've made this your most important task. After all, you and your wife want to be reunited with your daughter. But in the event of difficulties, I shall grant you an extra twenty-four hours to ensure you have the <u>full</u> sum in your possession.*
>
> *On the day after tomorrow at noon by the parish church clock, be standing in the middle of the bridge, on the Eastern side. Have the money in a bag. A man will approach you and ask for your prediction on the weather. Give him the bag, wait two minutes, then go home. Your daughter will be returned unharmed and unsullied during the afternoon. She's being well-cared-for. You have my word on that.*
>
> *I'm sure I have no need to say it, but I would advise you not to try and cheat me. Someone will be watching. If there are any problems, the consequences would be disastrous for your daughter and your family.*

'It's very precise,' she said.

'Clever, too,' Simon pointed out. 'He could go either way from the bridge.'

'Then we need to be prepared.'

'No, what we need is to find her before this happens. That's when we make our money.'

Rosie was frowning as she read the letter once more.

'Look at it again,' she said slowly. 'The tone. There's something wrong with it.'

'What do you mean?' Simon was already thinking ahead, trying to make a plan for the bridge and hoping he'd never need to use it.

'It's a mixture of . . . I don't know. Grovelling and warning. And the handwriting . . . see? It's too careful, like someone who doesn't use a pen often. Do you have the first one?'

He brought it from his coat.

'It's the same person,' he told her. 'There, you can see the way he makes some of the letters. Why, do you have an idea?'

Rosie bit her lip. 'I need to think about it.'

So did he. And there was a man he needed to visit.

Afternoon now, and off towards the hills the clouds looked dark and heavy. An hour, maybe less, and the rain would begin. Already the air felt cloying and thick. He could taste the soot from all the chimneys on his tongue as he followed the streets. At least a good downpour would cleanse the town.

Someone will be watching . . . was that real or bluff? Two men behind this would make sense. If they *were* both men. Possibly a woman; she could have lured Hannah, and be there to ease her terror now. He could see that. But none of it helped worth a damn.

Park Square was ordered, precise. Hushed, as if it somehow managed to hold the clamour of Leeds at bay. The houses in the terraces had subtle differences, enough to please the eye. But there was also an easy, flowing unity to the design. Nothing overpowering, but with the quiet taste of wealth.

Lawrence Jordan had his law practice on the far side of the square, the office on the ground floor and his quarters above. The man had sent him work in the past, clients who'd been robbed, swindled, an intimate letter plucked from their pocket. He'd found their items and taken his fee.

'Simon.' Jordan rose, hand extended. He was still in his court robes, the wig tossed carelessly on his desk. He blinked through a pair of spectacles. 'Did we have an appointment? I'm sorry, I don't recall . . .'

'No. Nothing like that. But I need to talk to you. In private.'

The lawyer cocked his head. He was a tall man, his back stooped, the fringe of hair around his bald head mostly silver now. He walked to the corner and closed the door that led to the clerks' office.

'Are you in trouble?' He settled in his chair, tucking the black gown around himself.

'No. I want some information.'

'Ah.' He steepled his fingers under his chin. 'Information. Sometimes I think I know far too many things, Simon. Far more than I want. They weigh me down. It's a curse of the profession. But I can never tell what's passed to me in confidence. You should understand that.'

'You might have to.'

'I can't do that.'

'Lizzie Henry gave me a list of people who use her house. I was surprised to see your name there.'

'Mine and many others, I'm sure.' His voice was colder.

Simon acknowledged it with a nod. 'But very few of them have your particular preferences. I'm not after all your secrets, Lawrence. I wouldn't even be here unless it was vital.'

'And may I ask why?'

'No.'

'I see. Not exactly fair and equitable, is it?' But Lawrence Jordan had been an attorney longer than Simon had been alive. He knew when to fight and when to surrender.

'That's the way it has to be. I'm not here to bleed you to death. A few questions and that's all. My word on it.'

Simon had little respect for lawyers. Most could vanish overnight and the world would be a better place. Jordan had been one of the few exceptions until he saw Lizzie's list. Now he had an advantage, and he was going to press it home to get what he wanted.

'You'd better tell me what you need, then.'

'Who do you know who has money troubles?'

Jordan's laugh came out like a bark. 'Good God, that's half the people who come to me. Probably more, from the time it takes for them to pay my bills.'

He wasn't going to let the man distract him.

'And how many of them also want to climb in society?' Simon considered for a moment. 'Let's say someone unmarried or widowed.'

'That's a smaller number,' Jordan replied.

'He might also be a dangerous man.'

'I'm not sure I'd call any of my clients dangerous. Not in the way I think you mean.' He paused. 'Instead of threatening me, why don't you tell me what this is about, Simon? I can help you.'

Perfectly reasonable, Simon thought. But anyone who spent his life in court was an actor. Justice was a performance of masks and pretence.

Jordan would be ruined if what he did at Lizzie Henry's house became public knowledge. His clientele would melt away. He'd lose everything. And he knew it all too well.

'I'm sure you can help me anyway, Lawrence.' Simon smiled. 'That's why I'm here.'

The lawyer sat and weighed his choices.

Simon offered a sop. 'They'll never know who gave me their names.'

'You might want to talk to Joseph Nicholson and Henry Barraclough.' There was no anger or bitterness in his voice. This was nothing more than business, a negotiation where he'd come off worse. 'Nicholson's a widower. He has a weaving mill. The Luddites wrecked it back in '12.'

'I remember that. The council had to call out the dragoons.'

'He spent a lot replacing the machinery. When the war with France ended, the army didn't need uniforms any more. That was most of his business. I know for a fact that he's in debt.'

'What about Barraclough? I'm not familiar with him.'

'He's young. Struts around Leeds like he could buy the place, but he's living on credit and that's likely to be cut off soon. He inherited, but he made stupid investments.'

'Where does he live?'

'He has a house on the other side of the Square.' Jordan tilted his head. 'A brass knocker in the shape of a lion's head.'

Would it be possible to hide Hannah Milner in a place like that? No, he decided. Too many people around. And servants; Jane had that right.

'Does he have any other property?'

'There's a farm.' The lawyer shook his head. 'His father always fancied himself as a gentleman farmer. But he never made a go of it. It's for sale.'

'Close to town?'

'On the far side of Holbeck.' Jordan's eyes narrowed. 'What's going on, Simon? Why do you want to know?'

He ignored the question. 'Does the farm have a name?'

'Long Hill Manor. The fields are rented out, but I doubt anyone's been in the house since his father died.'

'Thank you.' Simon stood. 'Your secrets will stay hidden.' He had what he came for, places to look. The men shook hands. All forgiven, if not forgotten; nothing more than a deal. Jordan would have done the same thing.

In the square, lights twinkled as evening began to fall. They made the place seem welcoming and safe. But that was just another lie, he knew that. Nowhere was ever safe.

Another fruitless evening spent in the inns and the taverns. Down at the Wellington they'd been holding a wake for the Vulture, a dour, drunken affair. Simon had left quickly, and the hours since then hadn't brought him anything worthwhile.

In the morning they'd look at Nicholson and Barraclough. For now, he simply wanted to sleep, to feel Rosie's body warm against his own. He smiled at the thought, then a noise caught his attention. Just something small, the rattle of a stone kicked down the street.

He reached into his sleeve for the knife he kept hidden. The night was quiet, only a faint hum of sound carrying across the streets. A heel caught sharply on a cobble. About twenty yards behind, he judged. Just one person.

Then there was another, coming round the corner in front of him, a darker shape against the shadows. Simon stopped, putting his back against the wall. He pulled another blade from his boot.

Let them come to you. That was what an old street fighter had taught him when he was starting as a thief-taker. Make them work for it. Half the time they'll back away; footpads want an easy mark, not a battle.

But this was more than robbery. These men moved silently, purposefully. They were here to kill. Not a word, not even a look as they came towards him. Hats low to hide their faces.

He was ready. One of them lunged, and he parried, feeling his knife cut deep into the man's arm as he backed away. Simon was breathing hard. His gaze shifted from one man to the other.

Watch out of the corners of your eyes. He could almost hear the voice from the lessons. Keep yourself loose. Keep yourself steady. Let them commit, then make your move.

The other attacker was cautious, moving slowly, ready for any opening, for the tiniest lapse of concentration.

Simon felt a bead of sweat edging down his forehead. In a moment it would drop into his eye. The man would take his chance then. He tightened his grip on the knife hilts and breathed in. Be prepared.

Then everything changed. The wounded man gave a harsh, shallow gasp and collapsed to the ground. Simon looked. He couldn't stop himself. Jane was standing over the body, a blade in her hand, no expression at all on her face. Like a ghost bringing death.

The other man ran. Simon stood, waiting until the echo of his steps faded to nothing. He slipped his knives into their sheaths and flexed his knuckles.

'I was coming home and saw him following you.'

Simon pressed his hands against the wall to stop them shaking. The brick felt cold against his skin.

'Thank you.' He didn't trust himself to walk yet. Another minute. He stared down at the corpse.

'Do you know him?'

'No. He's been behind you since Vicar Lane.'

'I should have noticed.'

'They won't be back.'

'No,' he agreed. 'These two won't.'

They'd had their chance and they'd failed. But there might be others. Stronger, quicker. Finally Simon felt able to move. He was alive, he was unwounded. Thanks to Jane.

'Come on.' He tried to sound light, as if nothing had happened. 'Rosie will be worrying about us.' He noticed she still had the knife in her fist. 'You can put that away now,' he said softly.

Jane looked down at the weapon as if she hadn't realized it was there.

'He wasn't the first, was he?' Simon asked as they walked.

'Him?' She glanced over her shoulder, then shook her head.

SIX

The twins were asleep upstairs. In the kitchen, the shutters were closed, the jug empty on the table. Lamps lit the room, casting deep shadows into the corners.

'Are you sure it has to do with this case?' Rosie asked. She had a heavy shawl gathered around her nightgown, hair hanging free and uncombed down her back. Simon had woken his wife as soon as they returned. They needed to talk about this, all three of them together. 'You've made quite a few enemies over the years, Simon.'

The same subject, going round and round for more than an hour.

'Who could have told them?' she asked.

'Milner's servant?' Jane said.

'I don't think so,' he answered, then sighed. 'Well, maybe it's possible.'

'Who else could it be?'

Jane hadn't given another thought to the man she'd knifed. No regrets, no guilt. Kill or be killed. Did this make up for her mistake with Lizzie Henry? Was the slate wiped clean now?

'Someone could have been watching Milner's house after the kidnap and followed the servant here,' Rosie said.

That made sense, Simon realized. But it meant that the man who'd taken Hannah Milner wasn't working alone. He had a web of people.

'And someone employed a pair of killers.' He finished the uncomfortable thought and turned to Jane.

'Tomorrow I need you to go out to this Long Hill Manor place and look around. It's supposed to be empty.'

She nodded. 'As soon as it's light.' A glance towards the shutters; not too long until dawn, two hours at most.

'After that, see what you can find out about Nicholson. Go to his mill, talk to some of the women. Find out where he lives and take a look at the place. As much as you can discover.'

She nodded. It was straightforward enough, but a full day's work.

'What about you?' Jane asked.

'I'm going to ask questions. Someone will know the name of that man you killed, and who his friends are.' He curled his hand into a fist and tapped it against his chin. 'I don't take it well when people try to murder me.'

Jane lay curled on the bed, asleep as soon as she closed her eyes. No bad dreams that she remembered. Up with the first breath of day, before everyone else, washing her face and hands in cold water. Bread and cheese from the kitchen.

The air was like balm against her face. Cool, with just a hint of dampness. She raised the shawl over her hair and began to walk. The early workers were already out; she was one more face, quickly lost in the crowd. Across the bridge, out along Water Lane, the river to her right, and fewer people around. Past Camp Field, Kellett's Lane and Silver Street, where the first fingers of new buildings slowly edged out from Leeds. Houses, two or three small manufactories. Soon they were all behind her and she was the only person on the road. The only sounds came from cattle and sheep, and a breeze that rattled the tree branches. A quarter of a mile ahead, Holbeck village.

Jane recalled the satisfaction she'd felt as her knife cut through cloth and flesh, the way she'd put all her strength behind the blow. Men who made their living like that needed to die. Anyone would kill a rat without a second thought.

Simon had been right. He wasn't the first. Not even the second. But those others would have left her for dead and walked away smiling. She knew exactly how fragile life could be.

A question or two in the village and she was climbing the slope to Long Hill Manor. Off to the west a farmer was building a drystone wall in a field. She stopped for a minute, catching her breath on the hill as she watched him work. Picking out one rock from a pile, then another. Miles of them snaking in lines across the hills. How long had that taken? she wondered. More time than she could begin to imagine.

The farm lay along a rutted track. She stood at the head of the lane. The place felt abandoned. Still, she was cautious, circling

around to come at it from the wood on the other side. Appearances
could deceive.

She had no sense that anyone was watching her. Not a soul to
be seen, just a pair of rooks on a tree branch; loneliness and the
wind were their only companions.

Birds had made their nests in the rafters of the house. Cobwebs
grew thick in the corners, clinging to her dress as she moved
through the rooms. It didn't look as if anyone had been here in
years. Across the yard, the barn was slowly folding in on itself as
the roof gave way, and the byre held nothing more than a family
of mice.

A pity, Jane thought; the farm would have been an ideal place
to hide someone. But the answers to this were all in Leeds. She
felt certain of that.

The kind of men he needed to see didn't rise early. They preferred
the darkness to the light. But he'd kick them out of their beds if
he had to. There was more going on than he understood. It was
beyond a kidnapping and ransom. Someone had ordered his death.
Luck, and Jane's skill, had kept him alive. Find the man behind
it and he'd be able to take Hannah Milner home. After he had his
revenge.

First, though, he spent an hour on the tenter fields, flying a kite
with Richard and Amos, smiling as they chased back and forth.
It was what he needed, some joy to take away the brooding blackness running through his mind. Simon watched the boys run and
laugh, relishing life and loving his twins. Had he ever enjoyed a
childhood like that before his parents died? He couldn't remember
now. Clouds covered everything. The first clear picture in his mind
was the workhouse door opening and the sour stink as he was
pulled inside. Everything before that was blurred and muddled.

He'd made sure that his sons would never end up there. If he
died, there was money for them, and a carefully worded will to
see they were looked after. They'd have better lives ahead of them.

Fat Jack Dommerty was up when he arrived, drinking beer in his
parlour and picking at a plate of eggs. He made his money
connecting people with each other. He knew the right men for the
violent jobs, for broken bones and murder. Give him the victim's

name, pay the proper fee and it would be done. There was no shortage of clients in a town like this.

Now he sat at the table, flecks of food caught in his thick beard. He was big and bluff, with warm blue eyes and cheeks ruddy from years of drinking. He didn't look like a man who could arrange a killing with a snap of his fingers. But if a hard man was dead, word would have reached Dommerty's ears.

'Don't often see you at this hour.' He took a swig of ale. 'Want some?'

Simon shook his head. 'Someone died last night.'

Jack belched and opened his eyes a little wider. 'I daresay a few did. Anyone in particular?'

'A man who tried to kill me.'

The man picked something from his teeth with his thumbnail. 'He didn't succeed then, unless I'm talking to a ghost.'

'There were two of them. The other ran off.' He'd keep Jane out of it. The fewer that knew, the safer she was. Dommerty carefully laid his knife and fork on the plate and looked at him.

'What do you want me to say, Simon? You're alive. One of them isn't and the other one's gone. You've survived.'

'What do you know about it?'

'I haven't heard a thing.' That was surprising. He should have heard by now.

'Who else would be likely to know?'

Jack reached for an engraved silver coffee pot and poured himself a cup.

'You could try Will Cain. He might be able to tell you.'

Dommerty's competitor. It said so much about Leeds that two men trading in death could both make a good living. Like his namesake in the Bible, this Cain had killed his brother. Many years before. Expensive, crooked testimony helped him escape a guilty verdict.

'It wasn't him. I'd have been able to tell.' And Simon would probably have been dead.

'Never said it was,' Dommerty told him. 'But he'll probably know.'

'Where's he living these days?'

'The bottom end of the Head Row.' He chuckled. 'His house has a red door. That's what they tell me, anyway.'

The Milner business didn't sound like Cain's work, Simon thought as he walked through the people thronging Vicar Lane. It was too elaborate, too considered. Cain liked easy targets, work that was done quickly.

The door had been red once. Now it was spattered with mud and covered with dust, the colour muted, dulled.

Cain had a thin, feral face, with large, stained front teeth and dark, curling hair that fell over the tops of his ears. A good coat, caught at the waist and flaring over his thighs, tight trousers with a wide, loud check: every inch a dandy.

His rooms filled the ground floor. The furniture probably came with the place, old and heavy, dark wood that seemed to draw away all the light.

'What it's worth, Mr Westow?' Cain asked as soon as they were seated. 'You're here with a question, I can see it in your eyes.'

Simon took Milner's sovereign from his waistcoat and slapped it on the table.

'You can't be expecting much of an answer for that.'

'The truth will do.'

Cain looked down at the coin. 'Well?' he asked.

'Someone was stabbed last night. He died.'

'Go on.' He hadn't taken his eyes off the money.

'Another man was with him. He ran away. I want his name.'

'The dead man was called Turnbull,' he answered immediately. 'I'll have to sniff out the rest.'

'How long will it take?'

Cain shrugged. 'Come back in an hour. But it'll cost you another one of these.'

'Done.' To have the name would be worth every penny.

He was as good as his word. Nothing written, just a name whispered after the money changed hands.

'Should I expect to hear of his passing, too?' Cain asked.

'People live, people die,' Simon said, and closed the door quietly as he left.

Jane perched on the wall, waiting for the flood of women to come out on their dinner. Across Mabgate, a man was seated on the ground, his back again a wall. He was so thin he might have been bones tossed into a sack of flesh.

She waited as an overloaded cart lumbered past, then crossed the road and put a ha'penny in his hand.

'God bless you, miss.'

'What time do they finish?'

'Noon.' He didn't look at her. But he didn't seem to look at anything. Maybe he had a glimpse of a better place than this; she hoped so.

Nicholson's mill was as forbidding as a prison. The windows were set high in the walls, the heavy doors firmly closed until the bell tolled. A few seconds later, women emerged like a roaring flood, shouting, laughing, blinking in the light. For half an hour they were free.

Jane picked a girl around her own age, standing apart, a dazed expression on her face.

'Are they hiring on in there?'

The girl stared as if she'd spoken in another tongue. 'Are they—?'

'Don't waste your breath,' a woman said as she pushed past. 'She's simple, that one. Can't hear a thing.'

Jane glanced at the girl again. She was watching them carefully.

'Are they hiring on, missus?' she asked.

The woman snorted. 'Getting rid, more like. At this rate we'll all be gone in three month.'

That was news to take back to Simon.

'But the owner will still be rich, eh?' Jane said.

'Oh aye,' she snorted. 'He'll still have his big house when we can't pay us rent and we're out on the street.'

'And I bet he lives somewhere clean and posh, doesn't he?'

'Chapel Allerton.' She spoke the words like acid and pushed away.

The girl had crossed the street and hugged the man. His face seemed to come alive as she tenderly helped him to his feet. Jane stood, gazing at their backs until they turned the corner to Argyle Road.

She'd found her information quickly enough. Chapel Allerton. And it sounded as if Nicholson had urgent need of a thousand pounds.

* * *

One attacker dead and Simon still alive sent a message to whoever had ordered him dead. Both of them gone and Simon still walking the streets would make it even stronger. No magistrate would come after him; he was certain of that. The bodies would quietly disappear, stripped of everything they owned, as if they'd never existed. This was Leeds.

First, though, he'd discover who'd given the command to kill him.

The entrance to the court stood across Kirkgate from the Fleece, an arched opening barely wide enough for a man to pass. Inside, it opened up, ramshackle buildings crammed together around a small yard that reeked of shit and piss. And at the far end, almost hidden, was the place he wanted.

He climbed the stairs, careful to move silently, a knife already in his hand. At the top, another door, ajar and inviting.

Simon waited, listening for the tiniest sound – a scuff, the creak of a floorboard, even the sense of someone breathing. Beneath him, the house was alive. Soft noises rose, a man cried out from a drunken dream. But up here there was only silence.

He edged towards the door, reached and pushed it open.

The man was lying on the floor. His arms were flung away from his body. Light from a broken window showed the bloody wound on his back. Simon knelt and touched his neck. No pulse of blood, but the skin was still warm; he'd still been alive an hour before.

The price of failure was high.

Who? he wondered, watching faces as he walked up Briggate. Who was behind it? Not just the kidnap, but hiring a pair of killers, then murdering the survivor for not completing the job. That required knowledge, a ruthless mind and a deadly arm. The only way to win was to understand what was happening. And he was groping in the dark.

Simon knew the criminals in Leeds. From those at the bottom who picked a pocket and tried to survive from day to day to the ones at the top, feasting on the profits and rubbing shoulders with the council and the gentry. But he could think of no one with the will to organize this.

*   *   *

Simon bounced Amos lightly on his knee as the boy gnawed on a piece of bread and dripping. On the other side of the kitchen table, Rosie held Richard on her lap, his body curled lazily against hers.

Jane bit into a meat pie from the stall on Boar Lane, chewed, and swallowed.

'I couldn't talk to anyone at Nicholson's house. I tried to get in twice and they chased me off.'

'It doesn't matter,' he told her.

'We're no further on and Hannah's still missing,' Rosie said. 'Can you imagine what she's feeling?'

He couldn't afford to think about that. It didn't help the search.

'No one followed me today.' Jane said it with absolute certainty.

'I haven't felt anyone behind me, either.' He grimaced. 'But then I didn't last night.'

'If we're not finding any candidates, we must be looking at the wrong men,' Rosie said.

Simon stared at her, still jiggling Amos on his knee.

'Perhaps we are,' he agreed. 'We've gone after the obvious ones and we've found nothing.'

'Except two dead men,' Jane said.

In his head, he'd gone through every name he could imagine. Examined and discarded them all, one by one.

'They want their money tomorrow,' Rosie said.

'I know.' He wasn't likely to forget. He was aware of every minute that passed. And unless he had a stroke of fortune, he wasn't going to find Hannah Milner in time.

'What happens then?' Jane asked.

Simon gave a bleak smile. 'We lose. And we don't earn our two hundred guineas.'

'I'm not giving up on that money,' Rosie said. 'There must be a way to find her in time.'

Jane never wanted to remember. She'd forced all the old things away, shutting them away in the dark corners of her mind. But sometimes . . . it could be something as simple and innocent as a smell or the tone of a voice, and all the ugliness and pain spilled out again.

The man was on Bond Street, right on the corner of Albion

Street. He stood like a soldier, with his back straight and his head held high and proud. His right arm was missing, the sleeve pinned across his coat like the pictures she'd seen of Nelson. In his left hand he held an old tin mug. A dog lay at his feet, silently watching people as they rushed by.

'Help for a cripple,' he called out, and it was there, so plaintive, that for a moment Jane had to stop. In the pleading tone she could hear the echo of her father's voice as he crept into her bed that morning. For a moment, the world stopped.

She breathed, making herself swallow the bile that rose in her throat. Jane looked at the man again. His eyes were milky, unable to see.

Her father was part of the past. She'd burned it all, watched it catch fire and flame to ashes. Yet still . . .

People pushed around her with the ripe smell of unwashed bodies, jostling, almost knocking her off her feet. Then it passed, her head began to clear. She took a penny from her pocket and dropped it into the beggar's cup.

'Thank you,' he said, and the dog wagged its tail once.

Her thoughts were still roiling as she crossed Briggate. At Duncan Street she turned, passing the grandeur of the Post Office before turning on to Call Lane. The beershop was in a yard down from the entrance to the White Cloth Hall.

Men played dice or cards. One or two glanced up as she entered, then turned back to their games. Mrs Rigton sat by the barrels, watching her customers. The place smelt of smoke and stale beer. But the floor was swept clean, a fire burned in the grate each evening, and she sometimes allowed a little credit to the regulars.

Jane knew this place very well. She'd slept here every night for one entire winter; without it, she'd be dead.

She curtseyed to the woman. Mary Rigton smiled and patted the seat next to her.

'Sit down, child. You're growing so big, you're almost a woman now. Come on, tell me everything that's happening with you.'

'There's not much.' Jane looked around the room. 'Nothing changes here, does it?'

'Of course it does.' She smiled. 'It's different every day. You're just looking at the surface, that's all. Go a little deeper and it changes all the time. Are you still living with Simon and Rosie?'

'Yes.' It was Mary Rigton who'd urged her to go there when Jane wasn't sure.

'Are they treating you well?'

She thought of the hundred pounds she had hidden away. 'They are. But I'm here looking for some information.'

'I hardly thought it was a social visit, child.' Her eyes twinkled. 'You didn't send in your calling card. Who are you looking for?'

'A man died last night. Stabbed.'

'Catch-All.'

Jane cocked her head. 'Who?'

'Catch-All Turnbull. Or Turnwell, maybe. Something like that. I heard it this morning. He was in here a week or so ago, looking for work.'

'Who took him on?'

'I don't know. He only stopped by for two nights. A quiet man.'

'Could you find out, Mary? It's important.'

She considered the request. 'I can ask. No promises, mind.'

'Thank you.' She stood. 'I have to . . .'

Mrs Rigton waved her hand. 'You go, child. You're always so busy these days. Rush, rush – I suppose that's the way of the world now. Come back later, I might know more.'

SEVEN

When Rosie first told him she was going to have a child, Simon had stared at her, not certain what he felt.

'Are you sure?' he asked. It seemed impossible. She'd never caught before.

'I hope that's just shock on your face, Simon Westow.'

'It's . . .' He didn't know what to say. 'You're positive?'

'I am.' Her smile had been as wide as the world. She wanted children. He . . . a family would ground him. He'd take fewer chances.

Rosie had worked with him since he started as a thief-taker. That would have to stop. They'd need a better home than the room they rented. So many things.

He adjusted. He made the changes. Made arrangements to buy the house on Swinegate at a low price from a grateful client. He became a man of property; something he could never have imagined when he was young. And then the surprise – he became the father of twins. Suddenly life seemed to tower over him.

But he'd weathered it all. He loved his boys. His business had prospered, especially after Jane's arrival.

Until last night, no one had tried to murder him. He'd had his share of fights, he'd needed to use his knife to defend himself. Simon owned his share of scars. Yet never that.

Who wanted him dead?

Still no answer, no name.

'What if we don't find Hannah by tomorrow?' Rosie asked. 'What are we going to do then? Just forget about her?'

He could hear the reproof in her words.

'I told you what Milner wanted.'

'No. We don't give up on this one, Simon,' she told him. 'Even if we make no money.'

She was the one who looked after the books. Rosie knew to a penny how much they had in the bank account at Beckett's. Simon Westow, a man with a house and an account at a bank. It still seemed impossible.

She'd never suggested charity work before.

'If that's what you want.' She had a good head on her shoulders. Something about the Milner girl had touched her.

'I do,' Rosie said. 'I've been putting my mind to this. Whoever's behind it knows you. If it comes to handing over the money, you can't be there at the bridge. He'll spot you. Jane can watch from one side, and I'll take the other. We're women; he'll never notice us. Whichever way he goes from there, one of us can follow.'

He tried to speak, but her voice rode over his.

'Once we know where he's gone, we'll come back here for you.'

'No,' he said firmly. 'I don't want you taking the risk.'

'Don't you remember what you said?' Rosie asked.

'When?'

'Years ago. When we were just beginning.' She looked at him unblinkingly. '"It's you and me in this together now." Those were your exact words.'

'But—' he began. He'd said it, he remembered, and it was back to haunt him. He knew he was beaten. He never stood a chance against her. 'Who'll look after Richard and Amos?'

'Mrs Marsden next door will take them for a few hours. She enjoys having them.'

Rosie's eyes shone. Her face glowed with the excitement of the chase.

'We might still find her before that.'

'I hope you do. That poor girl must be scared out of her wits by now. And I'd like to feel the weight of two hundred guineas. But in case you don't . . . we'll be prepared.'

'Yes.' He picked up his hat, ready to go out again.

'There's something else, Simon.'

'What?'

'Even if you find Hannah, it's not going to be over for whoever took her. Or for us.'

The idea gnawed at him as he walked up Lower Briggate. Whores waited hopefully at the entrances to the courts and yards, caught in the murk of night. Someone opened a door and for a moment sound and light and laughter spilled out to fill the darkness. The London mail roared out of the King's Arms, the driver shouting to urge on the horses. In the far distance, someone was singing a drunken song.

He was alert, aware of people, shapes, all the sounds of the night.

The Bull and Mouth was busy. A table of weary coach passengers ate their meal as the driver tried to hurry them along. Noise echoed up from the stable in the cellar. A pair of musicians played in one corner, fiddle and concertina hammering away at a tune.

He saw the man standing at the bar. There was more grey in his hair than a year ago; it suited him. Clean-shaven, good clothes, he stood out among the battered travellers. Simon took a seat in the corner, off in the shadows, and waved for the potboy.

'Brandy. And a drink for that man over there.'

'I was just thinking about you this morning,' Barnaby Wade told him after he'd come over and seated himself at the table.

'Why's that?'

'A rumour at the coffee house. Someone was attacked by a pair of men last night.'

'I hadn't heard about that,' Simon lied. 'Why would that make you think of me?'

'You're the thief-taker.' Wade smiled, showing a set of crooked teeth. 'You're the one who ends up in dangerous situations.'

'Not too often. It wasn't me.'

The man shrugged. 'If you say so.'

Wade dealt in stocks and bonds. Nothing official, nothing *quite* legal. But enough to scrape him a living and sometimes pay a dividend or two. He'd been a lawyer once, before he was disbarred for offering bribes to the judges. Now he took advantage of men eager for quick money, and there was never any shortage of them. Wade knew how to write watertight contracts. No comebacks for fools in court. Over the years he'd proved to be a good well of information, one Simon returned to again and again. At times he almost seemed like a friend. For all that, though, he'd trust the man as far as he could throw him.

'I heard one of the attackers died and the other ran off,' he continued.

'Too many footpads around since the soldiers came home,' Simon said.

Wade shook his head. 'If it was me, I'd want to know who ordered it.'

'Why would anyone order a robbery?'

'And why would it matter, if you weren't involved?' Wade countered.

'Maybe I'm curious.' The smallest pause. 'It's my job, like you said.'

'I've heard nothing more about it.' Wade pursed his mouth. 'That's strange enough in a place like Leeds. You know what this town is like.'

Simon nodded. Leeds was always a sea of rumours. 'If you do hear something . . .'

Wade raised his eyebrows, then gathered up his hat and cane. 'You be interested? Of course.'

Nothing mentioned, yet everything said.

*   *   *

'Julius White,' Mrs Rigton whispered.

Jane nodded and left.

'That's not possible,' Simon said. He stared in disbelief. 'I don't know who told you, but they have to be wrong.'

'Why?' All she'd done was speak the name.

The table was littered with plates and mugs, the loaf torn half-apart. A single lamp hung from the beam, trapping them in a circle of light. Simon looked down, studying the grain of the wood. He could feel Jane and Rosie watching him.

'Because he was transported to Australia. How long ago was it?'

'Almost nine years,' Rosie answered. 'And good riddance, too.'

'He must have completed his sentence,' Jane said. 'A pardon or whatever it is, and come back to England.'

'Let's hope to God he hasn't,' Simon told her. He swilled the dregs of the beer around and drank it down. 'I was hired—' He glanced at his wife. 'We were hired to find a locket a maid had stolen when she ran off. White had it. When he was tried, he admitted he'd bought it. From a man, though, not the maid. That was what he said. Claimed he'd never laid eyes on the girl, but we couldn't find hide nor hair of the other man. White was sentenced to seven years' transportation.'

'I don't understand,' Jane said. 'Why are you so worried?'

'Before I tracked down White, I found the servant's body. She'd been raped and murdered.'

'But . . .'

'I never managed to find the evidence to see him tried for it.'

'He also swore he'd see us dead,' Rosie said quietly and looked at her husband. 'Both of us.'

EIGHT

'How could he have come back without anyone knowing?' Simon said.

'Do you think he has Hannah Milner?' Rosie asked. 'Could he have paid two men to try and kill you—?'

'And murdered the one still alive when they failed?' he continued.

'We both know the answer to that. It's the kind of thing he'd do. So is the kidnap. He's worked it well. If Milner caves in and pays, White's going to be a rich man. Milner came to me to find his daughter, so White's been able to hit two birds with one stone.' He shrugged. 'Perfect for him.' He reached across the table and took Rosie's hand.

'At least we know who we're fighting.' She tried to smile. 'What now?'

'We sleep,' he announced. 'There's nothing more we can do tonight. We'll start hunting for Julius White in the morning.'

Her body felt so familiar, curled against his in bed. The texture of her hair, the smell of her skin. But she was as tense as wire.

'What about the boys?' Rosie asked after a long time.

He looked into the darkness. 'I want you to keep the gate in the yard locked. And when I'm out, bar the front door and the back. Only open up for me or Jane.'

'I'm not going to be a prisoner in the house, Simon.' She sounded defiant, but he knew it was all bravado.

'If you go out, keep the boys on the apron strings. Do you still carry a knife?'

'Of course I do. Always.'

'Then make sure it's sharp and keep your hand on it.'

Eventually she fell asleep. He listened to the softening of her breath, sensed the way her shoulders relaxed. He needed to rest, to be ready. But his thoughts refused to stop swirling.

White had to be the man behind the kidnapping; he'd wager good money on it. The whole thing had his style. But to engineer it, he must have been back in Leeds for a while. The town had changed in the years he'd been gone. It had transformed itself. Industry had taken over.

How could he have returned without anyone knowing? Not a whisper had gone around. That made no sense. Someone must have spotted him, talked to him. He'd hired people. How could he do that and stay invisible for so long? It wasn't possible.

Simon was up early, standing in the doorway of the boys' room and watching them sleep before he left. A note for Jane and Rosie: meet at eleven.

There was still a crispness in the air, but underneath, a real hint of spring warmth. Already the streets were creaking to life. Sullen men and women on their way to the early shift, carts delivering and carrying away. Passengers staring out blankly as their coach trundled off towards Leeds Bridge.

He was aware of someone beside him, keeping pace, step for step. A small man with wild curly hair, his stock mis-tied, shoes dull and scuffed.

'I hear you gave your evidence to the commission, Simon.'

For a moment he had to think, to dredge it from his memory. His testimony about the workhouse and the factory. Three days ago. It might have happened in another lifetime.

'For all the good it'll do,' he said.

The man gave an encouraging smile. 'It all helps, it all builds. Eventually they won't be able to deny it.'

Martin Holden was a Radical. An honest man. It shone in his eyes and his manner. He wanted a better England for everyone, not just the rich. Children working no more than ten hours a day.

'I can't talk about it now,' Simon told him brusquely. 'I have too much to do.'

'Please, just a minute or two. To plan.'

It was impossible to dislike the man. He was so earnest, his manner always heartfelt and intense.

'Another time.' His voice was softer. 'I promise. Once this job I'm doing is over.'

Holden gave a reluctant nod and went on his way.

Simon tore from place to place, asking every familiar face about Julius White. None of them had seen him. No one had heard of his return. Finally, in a coffee house he saw Barnaby Wade again, smoking a cigar as he read the London papers.

'Did you find anything?'

'Not yet.' He paused and cocked his head. 'What is it, Simon? You look worried.'

'Julius White is back.'

'What?' Wade stared. 'He can't be. We'd have known.'

'That's what I've been told.'

'Dear Christ.' He exhaled slowly. 'Do you believe it?'

'I do,' Simon said. 'I want to know where he's staying, and who's hiding him.'

'I hoped we'd seen the last of him. Australia should have killed him.'

'Apparently it didn't. I need to know this morning. It's important.'

Wade pursed his lips. 'I'll do what I can.'

Other stops, more questions and no answers. Then finally, close to ten, a walk out to Black Flags Lane.

'Another early call, Simon,' Lizzie Henry said when she received him. He'd been forced to wait a quarter of an hour when he could have used the time elsewhere, prowling restlessly around her parlour as she dressed and preened. 'This is becoming a habit. I thought the list paid my debt to you.'

'I'm here to give you some information.'

A condescending smile. 'And what could you know that's worthwhile?'

'More than you want to imagine.' He waited until he had her full attention. 'Julius White is back.'

Lizzie Henry had been the one who prosecuted him for the theft that saw him transported. It was her locket that White stole. Her runaway servant he'd brutally murdered and raped.

He watched her face grow pale under the thick coat of powder. Suddenly she looked her age.

'How did you find out?'

'It was Jane. The girl—'

'I remember who she is. Is it true?'

'Yes,' he told her. 'I believe it is.'

'You know what people are like. They love tales.'

She was casting around for hope. But he couldn't give her any.

'I can't tell you. I haven't seen him. But I'm sure he's here.'

'I heard that two men went after you. Does that have anything to do with this?'

'Yes. And neither of them are still alive to say who hired them.'

Lizzie nodded then, finally accepting it was real. 'Thank you for warning me.'

'Be careful,' Simon said.

'I will, believe me. Very careful.'

*   *   *

Milner's servant was waiting outside his door as Simon returned to Swinegate.

'I knocked, but no one answered. My master instructed me to talk to you this morning.'

'If you want good news, I don't have any. Does he have the money?'

'He does.' The man's voice stayed smooth and unperturbed. 'But he told me to say he's not happy at your failure.'

'Then tell him that makes a pair of us. When I take a job, I like to complete it.'

'I shall.' The man never blinked, Simon realized. Just a constant gaze.

'And I'll finish this one. His . . . property will be returned, and his money. But he should keep the appointment.'

'I will inform him. He told me to say that, having let him down once, you'd better not do it again.'

Simon bristled. 'And you've heard me. Enough?'

'Ample.' That short, mocking bow again and he left.

Milner was the least of his worries now. It was less than an hour to the meeting on the bridge. No word from Wade about Julius White.

Jane stood on Pitfall, in the lee of a building. Deep in the shadows, no one would see her, but she had a straight, clear view of Leeds Bridge. It was still five minutes before noon but Milner was already there, pacing restlessly up and down, seven steps each way, carrying a leather bag.

It was difficult to believe so much money could fit into something so small, she thought. A thousand pounds. Enough to set anyone up in a comfortable life.

She'd never heard of Julius White before last night. But the look on Simon's face had told her all she needed. She'd never seen him scared before. This was different. This was real fear. Rosie had tried to mask her terror too, but it was plain on her face.

But that hadn't stopped her coming down the stairs in her best gown an hour ago, a dark blue muslin with embroidery on the neck and hem, with a softly-patterned woollen shawl and a hat that shaded her eyes. For a moment, Jane didn't recognize her; Rosie seemed so different, so elegant, wearing the clothes as if they were nothing, carrying herself with a straight back and an easy walk.

Now Rosie was somewhere on the other side of Leeds Bridge, keeping her own watch. The boys were settled at a neighbour's house, and Simon would be waiting anxiously at home. She turned, craning her neck to see the clock on the church tower. One minute to twelve.

Jane kept her eyes on the bridge, her right hand around the knife hilt, expectant, ready to move. She'd kill if she had to.

The first time . . . she'd been plagued for a year after that. She'd lurch awake in the night, on the bench in Mrs Rigton's beershop, sweat cold on her skin, the nightmare still galloping through her mind.

She'd knifed the man to save herself. And the second time she had to do it didn't weigh as heavily on her. The other night had felt like nothing. It was survival, nothing more.

A movement on the bridge caught her eye and she held her breath. A young man was running, glancing over his shoulder as if someone was pursuing him. He dodged between carts, making a horse rear in its traces.

But no one came after him. Jane pushed herself away from the wall. Something was wrong. The man leapt on to the pavement, speeding up. For a second he appeared to lose his balance, and knocked into Milner. Then he was speeding off again with the bag in his hand as the man shouted helplessly.

So easy. So fast.

Jane hurried away. He was coming to her end of the bridge. Which way would he go? She was at the top of Pitfall as he passed without noticing her. She followed quickly, quietly, walking, not running, always keeping him in sight. Another turn on to Call Lane and he slowed, clutching the bag close to his chest.

Simon came out of the kitchen as soon as he heard the key in the door.

'It was a lad. He ran into town,' Rosie said as she unpinned the hat and tossed it on the kitchen table. As she described what had happened, she let down her hair and shook it out. The words tumbled from her mouth. He listened, but for a moment all the sounds were meaningless; in her swift, innocent gestures he could see the girl he'd met at the mile marker.

'We'll have to hope Jane can keep up.' She reached for his mug of ale and drank.

'She will.' He had no doubt of that. Jane had the gift for it.

'I was scared, Simon.' She held her hand up. It was shaking. 'I kept thinking White would see me and remember.'

'He'll be staying far out of sight.'

White was clever. He was sly and dangerous. Simon doubted the money would buy Hannah Milner's freedom. Her father had plenty in the bank and he'd shown he was willing to spend it to save her. A thousand now, a demand for more tomorrow, maybe the day after, to let Milner stew and worry.

Unless Simon could find her first. But he knew he'd done a poor job so far.

There was only one way this could end. White would have to die.

NINE

By the time he reached the Post Office on Duncan Street, the boy looked casual and careless. Cocky. Outside the building he seemed to bump into a young man loitering there.

Jane saw it happen, far enough away not to be spotted. She smiled. It was exactly the way the pickpocket gangs worked. Hand off the loot in case you were caught. The new lad set off at a trot, down Kirkgate, and she stayed behind him. Halfway along the street he stopped and looked back.

By then she'd taken the shawl off her head and gathered it around her shoulders. If he saw her at all, she'd look like a completely different girl. Invisible. Then he was moving again, satisfied. Beyond the parish church, taking Timble Bridge across Sheepscar Beck, left on to Duke Street and another right to Off Street.

She needed to be careful. There were fewer people around here. The houses were brick, not too old, pushed and cramped together in long terraces, every one identical to its neighbour.

At the corner, Jane squatted, then moved her head just enough to see the street ahead. People rarely saw what they didn't expect; she'd learned that. The young man gave a glance around, knocked on a door and disappeared inside.

This was as far as she could go. The road was empty. Anyone watching would notice if she went by.

White had been careful, Simon thought as he listened to Jane's account. First, having someone snatch the bag with the money, then the switch later. But Off Street wasn't where this story was going to end. Hannah Milner wasn't there. It would be impossible to hold a girl in a place like that. Too many neighbours.

Still, he had somewhere to start.

'You did very well.'

Jane shrugged. 'It wasn't hard. What are we going to do now?'

'I'm going over there.'

'Where do you want me?'

'At my side,' he told her. Simon turned to Rosie. 'Keep the boys inside and the doors barred. When we're out would be a perfect time for White to try and pay a visit.'

The day had turned warmer and Simon was hot in the overcoat. But he needed it to hide the rifle he'd borrowed from Charley Press at the Wellington. The landlord has been dubious when he asked.

'You don't even know how to use it, Simon.'

'Then show me.'

Finally he'd given in. A quick lesson and now it was primed and loaded, covered from sight as he marched through the streets.

'I don't see what good something like that will be,' Jane said.

'It's mostly to scare them. But I'll fire if I have to.' He'd do whatever was necessary.

'Do you think this White will let her go?'

Around them, people strode along Kirkgate. No one was following them. Hardly a soul even seemed to give them a second glance.

'No,' he told her. 'He's going to milk Milner for money. And when he's done, he'll kill her.'

*   *   *

'I couldn't be certain which house it was,' Jane said. 'Has to be this one or next door, though.'

'It doesn't matter.'

He was already planning. These houses were back to back, only one way in or out. Small passageways led to a courtyard at the rear. The street was only five years old, built after the French war, all for the workers crowding into Leeds. But that was like trying to dam a flood with twigs. All these had been rented before they even had roofs. No matter how many they put up, it would never be enough.

Already the bricks were turning black as death, rough and pitted.

His choice, a green door or a blue one. Blue, he decided, hammering on the wood, then standing back and to the side, one hand on the rifle under his coat. Simon heard footsteps and the drawing back of a bolt. A young woman with a baby resting on her hip.

'Whatever you want, we can't afford it.' Her voice sounded too old for her body, weary as a woman ready for the grave. He tipped his hat.

'I'm sorry to have bothered you. I must be looking for your neighbour.'

'Them?' She almost spat the word. 'Been here two months and there's always someone coming or going.'

'Any women?'

'Not that I saw.'

'What about a lad, fair hair, looks like he might have lived rough?' Jane asked.

The woman eyed her sharply. 'Aye, I've seen one like that. Why, what's he done?'

'You should go back inside and lock the door,' Simon told her. 'For safety.'

She was gone before he'd finished the sentence.

He took a deep breath and knocked on the green door. As soon as someone turned the key he barged it open, bringing up the rifle. A young man lay sprawled on the floor.

'That's him,' Jane said.

'Who else is here?' He held the gun with the barrel trained on the boy's head. No chance of missing at this range. 'Who?'

The lad was close to tears. 'Just me. I swear.'

'Go and look,' Simon told Jane. 'And be careful.' He turned back to the boy. 'Where are the others?'

'Gone.' He tried to squirm away on his back. A jerk of the rifle stopped him. 'I brought the money like he told me, then he left.'

'He?' Simon asked. He needed to hear the name ring like iron.

'Mr White, sir. Please don't shoot me, please, mister.' He began to cry. 'Told me to stay here and he'd come back tonight. He said I'd be safe.'

'He lied. What did he do with the girl?'

'What girl?' Confusion filled his face. 'There's never been no girl here. All I knew is we was snatching a bag and bringing it to Mr White. He paid us.' His hand scrambled in the pocket of his trousers and brought out a few coins. 'Look.'

'Did White say where he was going?'

'No, sir. Just that he'd be back later.'

Jane came down the stairs. 'No sign she's ever been here.'

The boy was sobbing softly.

'Do you know what was in the bag you stole?' Simon felt his temper fraying. They were wasting their time here. White had outfoxed them.

'No.' He hung his head. 'What are you going to do to me, mister?'

'What about the other lad?' Jane asked.

'He took his money and went. Said there'd only be trouble if we waited.'

'Your friend was right.' Simon kept the gun aimed at the boy. Fear was a good way to spark honest answers. 'I want to know where to find White.'

'I don't know, mister. Honest, I swear I don't.'

A short nod from Jane; she believed him.

'Get up,' Simon told him. Clumsily, the boy rose to his feet, trying to hide the dampness on his trousers where he'd pissed himself. 'Now get out.'

He left the door hanging open as he went, the sound of running feet turning to silence as he turned the corner.

'Did you find anything at all?'

'It looks like the boys shared one bedroom.'

Simon raised his eyes to the ceiling. 'What about the other one?'

'Must have been White's. But there's nothing in it.'

He sighed. 'We might as well go home. I'm sure Mr Milner will be wanting a few words with me.'

'What do you think will happen to Hannah?' Jane asked.

He stared at her. 'I'm beginning to wonder if we'll ever find her alive.'

A stop to return Charley Press's rifle and they walked towards Swinegate.

'Someone's following us,' Jane whispered.

There were people bunched around them as they crossed Briggate.

'Who?'

'Just one man, I think.'

He couldn't sense anyone, but Simon didn't doubt her. He'd never met anyone with her ability.

'Slip around and get behind him. Find out where he goes.'

She was gone, as if she'd simply vanished into the air. Simon walked on, straight home.

An hour passed, marked by the steady, relentless ticking of the longclock in the hall. He paced around the house, head jerking at any loud noise out on the street. Still no information from Wade.

Rosie stayed in the kitchen, preparing food, making bread, anything to fill the minutes.

Where was Jane? Was she safe?

And finally, the knock. Two raps, then three, then one. He pulled the door open, then locked it again behind her.

'Well?' Simon asked as he followed her through the house.

She poured herself beer and drank. 'He followed you all the way here. Fair hair, thin, looks like he hasn't had too many good meals. He stayed for a minute or two, then left.'

'Where did he go?'

'The Bull and Mouth. He went in and started talking to Thomas Calverley. I couldn't get too close. Calverley knows my face.'

Calverley knew both of them. Many of the goods stolen in Leeds went through his hands. Some he sold on. Others found their way back to the owners through the thief-takers, in exchange for a cut of the fee.

Simon did business with him often enough. Everyone in the trade did. He was as inevitable as tomorrow.

'Where did he go after that?'

'Still with Thomas when I left.'

'I think we'd better pay Mr Calverley a visit, don't you?'

But before he could move, there was a sharp, businesslike knock on the door. Milner's servant; he'd wager a guinea on it.

Still no expression on his face, and the grave tone in his voice.

'My master wants to see you. Now.'

'Where?'

'Drony Laith again.'

'Tell him I'll be there in a quarter of an hour.'

'Wait here,' he told Jane, then turned to Rosie. 'I'll be back once I've had my skin flayed.'

Milner was waiting in the middle of the field. He was standing by one of the tenter poles, digging the tip of his cane into the ground.

'Well?' he said as Simon approached. 'Where is she?'

'I don't know. I'm sorry.'

'Sorry?' The man's face darkened. 'You took the job and said you'd bring her home. Did you see what happened on the bridge?'

'I know all about it. The boy who took the money handed it off to someone else. I found him at a house off Marsh Lane.'

'Then where is he? Where's my thousand pounds? Where's my bloody daughter?'

He was shouting, his voice echoing back from the hills across the river.

'The boy's gone,' Simon said calmly. 'I'm searching for the man who has your money and your daughter.'

'Gone?' His eyes bulged. 'What in the name of Christ were you doing? He should have been arrested and sent off to hang.'

'I let him go because there's nothing more to learn from him.' Milner wanted the truth; he'd give it to him. 'The man who took Hannah is called Julius White. He's spent the last nine years in Australia for theft. I was the one who caught him. He's clever. And he's deadly. He's killed before.'

'I don't care what he's done before, Westow.' His voice was tight, the anger barely tamped down. 'It's what he's doing now that's my concern. When I employ a man, I expect him to do his job. This White still has my daughter and now he's got my money. He's making me look like a fool.'

Simon wasn't going to offer excuses; the man wouldn't accept them.

'It's not over yet.'

'You're damned right it's not. It won't be until my lass is back at home and this man is hanging from the gibbet.'

If she ever comes home, Simon thought. If it's not too late.

'Now I know who he is, I can go after him.'

'You've put up a piss-poor show so far.'

No need to reply. He wasn't likely to change Milner's mind.

'He'll send you a letter. Maybe today, maybe tomorrow. Demanding more money.'

'He can do what he bloody well likes. He won't see another penny until my daughter's back with me.' Milner raised a hand and pointed. 'And don't you be telling me otherwise.'

'I need to see that letter when you receive it.'

'Tell me why I should trust you? You've managed to fail me once.'

'Because there's nobody else who can help you. Where else are you going to go? The constable? He's a joke; you know that as well as I do. He's nothing more than a title. And you'll be lucky if you can find the Watch sober or awake. I'm what's here, and I'll tell you this: I'm good at what I do.'

The man set his jaw. Rage burned behind his eyes. When was the last time anyone had talked to him like this? Simon wondered.

'Then you'd better prove you are. I warned you before that I'd destroy you. Fail again and I'll do it.'

Milner walked off with his shoulders pulled back, determined. A man fighting the world.

Simon had given him a dose of the truth. He *was* the only one who could help now. Yet Milner was right, too: he'd failed. He'd been stupid. He'd thought this job would be like finding any other piece of stolen property. And he'd underestimated the kidnapper.

But now he knew.

A few drops of rain began to fall. He turned up the collar of his coat and started for home.

TEN

Calverley wasn't in the Bull and Mouth, or any of the other inns along Briggate. A steady drizzle began as they trudged from place to place, turning the greasy cobbles slick.

'Maybe he's gone home,' Jane said.

Simon shook his head. 'Not before midnight. He spends as little time there as possible. Can't stand his wife. He'll be in one of these places.'

They found him in a dram shop on Guildford Street. Calverley sat with his back to the wall, a glass in his hand. He was a large man, with a prizefighter's body that had run to ruin, a broken nose, and a web of scars around his eyes.

He was a very small cog in the machine. Vital, but one that could slip through the fingers and be lost on the floor. For this short moment, though, he was the most important man in Leeds.

'You're a hard man to track down, Tom,' Simon said as he shook the rain from his coat and sat down at the table. Jane stood close, one hand in the pocket of her dress, silently stroking the handle of her knife.

'You found me.'

'I hear you were in the Bull and Mouth earlier.'

'What about it? I'm there every bloody day.' There was a dangerous edge to his voice. Calverley had reached the point in his drinking where anything could tip him into violence. Time to tread carefully.

'You were talking to someone there.'

'Probably to half the people in the place.'

Simon turned to Jane.

'Long fair hair, looks like he could use a lifetime of good meals,' she said.

'You mean the little weasel.' He hawked and spat on the floorboards.

'Who?'

Calverley shrugged. 'That's what I call him. Don't know his

real name. He wanted to sell me a watch.' He snorted. 'Said he'd found it earlier.'

'He was following me around today.'

'Yours, is it?' He reached into his waistcoat and tossed a pocket watch on the table. 'You can have it back for a tanner. Same as I paid.'

'Where will I find him?'

'How would I know?' He stared and began to bunch his left hand into a fist. 'You want the watch or not?'

'It's not mine, Tom,' Simon said calmly. 'What's his proper name?'

'Who bloody cares?' The words exploded out of him and he stood, heavy and bulking. The room was instantly silent.

Jane took a step back and drew her knife. Simon made a small gesture. Don't do anything.

'Sit down, Tom. We're just talking, nothing more.'

'Don't you bloody tell me what to do.'

'Sit down, Tom.' He raised his voice slightly, sitting back and trying to hide his fear. He'd seen Tom Calverley on the rampage. The man could destroy a place like this in minutes. But he could be calmed just as quickly, too. 'Sit down and have another drink.' Simon waved for the potman.

Very slowly, the man lowered himself to his chair. The moment had passed. No more trouble for a little while.

'Now,' he continued. 'This man. What do you know about him?'

'He's a little bastard. He'd fleece his own mother for three farthings.'

'I need to find him.'

'Try the old blacking factory, down by the river.' His voice had softened, the fury softening from his eyes.

'The one that burned down last year?'

'I heard he sleeps there.'

'Do you remember Julius White?'

The man turned his head, eyes slowly focusing. 'I do.'

'People are saying he's back in Leeds.'

'Can't be him.' Calverley shook his head as if it could never happen. 'He was sent to Australia.'

'Say what you like, Tom, but I think they're right. Better keep your eyes open.'

*　　*　　*

Only the shell of the factory remained. Jane remembered the blaze, burning bright and loud, the stink of boot black that hung over the town for days. Now there was just burned brick, twisted iron and charred, sodden wood. A ghost of a building. Soon enough someone would knock it down and put up something new; land was too valuable to leave as a ruin.

Rats skittered across the floor. Over in the far corner a piece of the roof hung down; it gave some sort of shelter. A small fire glowed.

By the time she came close, Jane was able to pick out the children. Twenty or more. The younger ones were huddled together, some already asleep, others staring with fearful eyes.

The adults sat around the blaze. Some looked more ghost than human, insubstantial, drained of life. Others were weary, but on their guard, staring at the stranger and ready to fight or flee.

Simon had stayed outside. Jane moved quietly among the men and women. She was a creature of the night now, just like them.

'I'm looking for a lad with fair hair. Someone said he looks like a weasel.'

'What's it worth?' a woman called out, and began to cackle. Jane came closer.

'He sleeps here,' she said.

'Not tonight.'

She couldn't make out most of the faces. Too dark, too hidden. But the man she'd followed wasn't here; she was certain of that.

'Where will I find him?'

'Maybe he'll come by later,' one voice shouted.

'Come here and I'll show you where he is.' A man. But it was empty talk. There was no threat in this place.

She saw a young woman staring into the fire and squatted beside her.

'Do you know where he is?'

In the light she began to pick out a few features on the girl's face. Sunken cheeks, rat's tails of hair. Two fingers missing on her right hand.

'Did you work in a mill?' Jane asked. The woman turned, blinking as if she'd just woken from a deep sleep.

'How . . .?' The sentence withered before it could form.

'The hands. I've seen it before. I was there once myself. Doffer girl.'

The woman nodded.

'Do you know the name of the lad I'm looking for?'

'James,' she replied vaguely. 'Or maybe it's John.' A quick, nervous smile. 'Something like that.'

'Where else does he go?'

She shook her head, small, jerking movements from side to side.

Around them, the others muttered or dozed. Jane was no threat; they could safely ignore her. She stood and wandered away, turning to look back from the broken wall. No one stared after her. She might never have been there at all.

The sound caught her. Scuffling, down on the riverbank. She hurried, pulling out the knife.

Simon. She recognized his shape. Kneeling over someone. He heard her and raised his head.

'He tried to leave right after you went in. Is this him?'

The man struggled as Simon dragged him towards a sliver of light. But his fight had gone; he knew he was caught.

'That's the one.'

The nickname fitted well; he had a rodent's sharp features, a long nose and deep-set eyes. Wiry, with bony wrists, as if he hadn't grown into his body yet.

'You certainly look like a weasel,' Simon said. He kept a tight grip on the man's jacket. 'Why were you following me today?'

'Paid me to.' The words came out in gasps.

'Who did?'

'A man.' His eyes were bulging with fear.

'What man?' She could feel Simon's anger building.

'He said he'd heard I was good at not being seen. He was brown. You know, like he'd spent a long time in the sun.'

'Name?'

'He never said. Told me to watch a house and follow anyone who went there. Then I had to go and see him.'

'Where?'

'Place by the old ferry. He promised he'd give me five shillings.'

'You didn't go there straight away, did you?' Jane asked.

He turned his head, trying to make out her face in the darkness. 'I nicked a watch. I thought Tom might buy it.'

'And after that?' Simon asked.

'I went down to the ferry and told him. He paid me.'

'Nothing else?'

'No. I came back here. Look.' A hand fumbled in the pocket of his trousers as he dragged out some coins. 'Didn't even have the chance to spend any of it yet.'

She watched as Simon let go of the man and stood. He was breathing hard. Rain ran down his face.

'Go on,' he said. 'Get out of here.'

The lad scrambled away and stumbled off into the night.

The old ferry. She'd been by it often enough, half a mile down the Aire and Calder Navigation, beyond Fearn's Island. It was quiet down there, she thought; a good place to keep a girl hidden.

'What do you want to do?' she asked Simon.

'We'll go in the morning,' he replied after a moment. 'It's too dark to see anything there now. We'll make an early start.'

ELEVEN

They left just before dawn, feeling the early chill off the water. The rain had stopped; dirty puddles filled the roads. The few people on the streets wore haunted looks. Simon hardly noticed them; he was trying to picture the buildings around the old ferry. A storehouse, he remembered that, and the ferry office. But the rest? It was all so faint in his memory.

No matter, he thought; they'd find out very soon.

And by the time they arrived, White would already have gone. He'd been ahead of them every step of the way. He'd anticipated each move Simon had made. As if White had been testing him, to see if he was good enough.

Jane walked beside him, not speaking, caught in her own thoughts. He was grateful for the silence. Before they left the house, he'd caught a glimpse of his face in the mirror. Pale, the skin drawn taut over his bones. Eyes that seemed sunk in his skull. He'd barely slept. Every time he closed his eyes he dreamt of finding a faceless girl who died in his arms.

When they arrived home the night before, a note from Barnaby Wade was waiting for him: *I've asked about White. No one seems to know. If he's here, someone is shielding him well.*

He was here. Simon could almost smell him. Who'd take in a man like that? Why? What hold could he have over someone after all this time?

The barge crews were beginning to stir as they passed. The boats were lined up two and three deep by the warehouses, loud creaks as they bobbed lightly in the water. Soon they'd be loading, unloading, setting off back to the coast.

He shook it all from his mind. The only thing to consider was what they'd find at the old ferry.

A few more minutes and they drew close. The track down to the riverbank was overgrown with weeds. The ferry boat had long since moved to the new crossing further downstream.

'Are you ready?' he asked.

'Yes,' Jane answered. Her voice gave nothing away.

Simon felt the tightness around his chest. Each breath seemed like an effort. The anticipation. He'd be fine once they arrived, as everything began to unfold. He took the knife from his belt, another from his boot as they left the road. No one was watching.

Just two buildings. No wonder he hadn't been able to picture more. The ferryman's hut and the old stone house used for storage.

'You take the hut,' he told her, and Jane moved off to the left, gliding over the grass. Close to the other building he stopped, looking around. Footprints in the mud, but that meant nothing; it was a good shelter. The door hung slightly open. The wood had rotted away where it met the ground.

Simon raised his boot and kicked it wide open, letting the daylight pour in. A few empty crates, a tattered sack or two in the corners. A large spider waddled across the ground. Cobwebs hung from the rafters. The dust rose in heavy clouds as he moved a stack of boxes, and the remains of an old fire lay in the middle of the floor. Someone had slept here, but a long time ago. Most people had probably forgotten it had even existed. But not Julius White.

'She's here,' Jane called out.

He ran across the open ground and ducked under the sagging lintel. Hannah Milner was in the corner of the small room, hunched

up, eyes bulging, trying to make herself small. Her wrists and
ankles were tied, a scarf pushed into her mouth to keep her quiet.

'It's all right,' Simon told her as he knelt. 'We're here to take
you home. Cut the ropes,' he ordered as he eased the gag out and
heard her gasp. 'It's fine. You're safe now, Hannah.'

He watched as she rubbed her wrists, then her ankles. The bonds
had been tight enough to leave marks on her skin. Then the tears
began, a river of them down her cheeks. At least she looked unhurt.
No bruises he could see. Her clothes weren't torn. Simon glanced
at Jane. She stared down at the girl, no expression that he
could read on her face.

Hannah had her face in her hands, still crying. He stood and
watched helplessly as her shoulders shook. Finally it subsided
and she wiped her cheeks dry with the back of her hands.

'I'm sorry,' she said in a small voice. 'I just . . .'

'You're safe. No one's going to harm you now. I promise. Can
you stand?'

He helped her up. She grimaced, and Simon steadied her as she
took a few awkward steps round the room.

It was a slow, aching walk back into Leeds. Hannah had her
arm through his, hobbling, staring down at the ground. Jane's
shawl covered her hair; no one would know her.

He needed to understand how it had all happened. But as he
asked his questions, all she gave were brief answers, tiny sketches
of memory.

She remembered a man approaching. Well-dressed, polite. He
claimed her father had sent him. A long silence as her words
faltered. Slowly, Hannah began again: she was in a room, hands
tied, mouth stopped with a dirty cloth. The man returned, warning
her not to scream, then giving her water and food.

'How long were you there?' Simon asked. 'What kind of house?'

She didn't answer him. The night before, after dark, she'd been
taken out to the ferry.

'I thought they were going to kill me.'

'They?' he asked, but she continued.

'They tied me up and left. I couldn't move. All I could hear
was the water.'

Close to Leeds, as the noise began to wrap around them, more
faces on the street, Hannah seemed to feel a little more at ease.

Simon glanced over his shoulder. Jane was three paces behind, alert, keeping guard.

He led her to Swinegate, seeing her panicked look as he opened the door to his house.

'Don't worry, you'll be fine. I live here. My wife will look after you. I need to tell your father we've found you.'

The back door, the familiar servant, a few muttered words, then instructions.

'We're going to meet your father's carriage in an hour,' he told her.

Hannah looked brighter, more alert. She'd washed and eaten and exchanged her dirty clothes for one of Rosie's gowns. Now she was sitting in the kitchen, and the boys pestered her with questions.

'I don't know how to thank you.' She seemed dazed by everything. But what else would she feel after being taken by a devil? 'All of you.'

'It doesn't matter.' Rosie shooed the twins away upstairs. 'It's Simon's job.'

He tried a few more questions, but she simply shook her head. Rosie glared at him. Perhaps it was best to let her start forgetting.

Then it was out to Drony Laith for a final time. Milner took his daughter's hand and kissed her cheek. The servant smiled to see her.

'I don't think she's been hurt at all,' Simon said. 'In any way.'

The merchant nodded. 'Her mother will be glad to have her home.'

'You should be gentle. She's had a bad time.'

'Yes. And no one will know what happened.' The words were a warning.

'No one.'

'What about the one who took her? He still has my money.'

'That's up to you,' Simon told him.

'What in God's name do you think I want?' He spat his answer. 'Get it back. Kill him if you have to. And you can take your fee out of what he stole from me.'

'That's not what we agreed.'

'Your money was for returning my daughter before I had to pay. You failed, Westow. You want that two hundred guineas? You know what to do.'

He turned his back and marched back to the coach.

'You've been very quiet.'

'We were meant to find her, weren't we?' Jane said. 'That was the plan.'

'Yes,' he agreed, 'we were.' White had left a trail of people to guide him there. Every step had been intended as a challenge to him: follow if you're good enough.

'It's like he's taunting us,' Rosie said. 'If we hadn't been able to do it, she'd have been left there to die.'

She was right. Hannah Milner had never mattered to White. She was simply a device to bring him money and weigh Simon's skill.

'And we still don't have any idea where he is.'

'Or what he's going to do next.'

'I can tell you that,' Simon said. 'He's going to have his revenge. He's a rich man now.'

'He might be. We brought Hannah home and we don't have a penny for it,' Rosie reminded him.

'We're not going to see one until we find White and get that thousand pounds back.'

'That's what he really wants, isn't it? This is where it's all been leading. Him against us.'

Simon stopped and looked at her. The battle was still to come. He turned to Jane.

'This isn't your fight. He doesn't have a grudge against you.'

'He wants his revenge on you. You and Rosie.'

'He does. Not just us, but yes, that's why he's come back. Unfinished business.'

'Then it's my fight,' she said.

He smiled. It was as close as she'd ever come to saying she was one of them.

'I'll be glad to have you. But it's not going to be easy.'

Jane shrugged. 'That doesn't matter.'

*   *   *

Rosie slammed a pan down on the stove.

'Milner didn't even thank you?'

'No.' Clients were usually grateful. They might bargain over the fee, but they were glad to see their property returned.

'Then he should have seen his daughter when you brought her here. The poor girl was terrified. I could hardly get any sense from her at first. This is going to stay with her for the rest of her life.'

'Milner said I hadn't done the job I promised.'

'And I suppose he could have gone out and brought her back himself.' Her tone was withering.

'He said to take the two hundred from the money when we recover it.'

'We'll take a sight more than that. Two jobs, two fees,' Rosie said. 'I'll give him an accounting and he'll be lucky to get his two sovereigns back. I'm going to bleed him for it.'

'First we have to find White. We need to do something he's not expecting,' Simon said.

'What?' Rosie asked. 'Look at it. He's done a very neat job of leading us by the nose so far.'

'I don't know.' Silence filled the kitchen.

TWELVE

T he sun had appeared, shimmering and muted through the smoke rising from the chimneys. It lit up the colours on women's dresses and caught in the water of the potholes and puddles. Weather was weather, Jane thought; dry was better than wet, she liked the warmth more than the cold. But you couldn't change it. You survived.

Out here, lost in the shouts and the noise and the bustle, caught in the haze and the stench, she could think. There were places she could run if she needed, one or two who'd hide her if she asked. She knew Leeds in a way White never could, better even than Simon. He'd been respectable for too long.

A thought kept pricking at her. How had White managed to stay hidden since his return? He'd been able to find people, to select his victim, rent a house, all without anyone seeing him. But Australia hadn't turned him into a ghost.

Nine years since he'd been convicted; that was what Rosie had said. A long time to be away. She'd had a family then, a mother and father she believed she could trust. A lifetime ago.

Only two kinds of people were able to hide themselves well: the very rich and the poor, and no man without money could have done what White had achieved. He had a thousand pounds more now. Enough to purchase any number of lives and deaths, and build thicker walls around himself.

She crossed Quebec Street, along Eyebright Place, by the Infirmary, the roads outside Park Square, then back along Park Lane and Merry Boys Hill, before she entered the yard behind the Green Dragon.

A dog dug into a midden, growling as she passed. At an opening between two houses, Jane turned again, following the passageway into another court where flagstones covered the ground and the small houses were neatly tended. A few plants were poking out of the soil in an old barrel under one of the windows. The glass sparkled clean in the light.

It had the calmness of a country lane. The houses all around cut off the sounds of the town. Jane tapped on the door, happy to see the old woman who answered. She was spry, dressed in a style that had been in fashion well before the French wars. Her grey hair was carefully tucked under a cap, she wore a dress with a high waist and square neck, the sleeves puffed out over her small shoulders. A pair of spectacles perched on her nose and she held a book in her hand, one finger marking her page.

'Oh my,' Catherine Shields said with pleasure. 'Jane. Jane. Come in, my girl, it's lovely to see you again.'

Mrs Rigton had been the one who'd first sent her here, delivering a bottle of tonic. As soon as she set foot in the tiny court, Jane had felt her heart ease a little. After that visit she came back often, just for the pleasure of being here. She brought little gifts, flowers she picked, a glass bottle she found, and Mrs Shields accepted them all as if they were the most beautiful presents she'd ever been given.

There was a radiance about her, a serenity that Jane loved. For one long summer, it felt as if she'd been here every day, cleaning things, running off to shop for Catherine at the market, planting seeds in pots and tubs and watching them grow. Mrs Shields had talked: about her husband, a man who'd died before Jane was even born, the children she'd birthed, all dead before they'd been alive for a year. Plenty of sorrow, but she was content. She was happy.

It had taken time, but eventually Jane had talked, too. She'd remember the things she had when she was part of a family. Some of the things she'd seen since then. Not all; never all. But this place, this house, this woman, took her outside all that. It was a haven.

Jane had grown; life had changed. She'd drifted away. She had her work with Simon and she didn't come to visit as often. Yet as soon as she entered the yard, Catherine's gentle magic seemed to lift her. Once, she'd brought Richard and Amos. The woman had fussed over them like a grandmother, finding treats tucked away in cupboards to give to them.

They sat with the door open, letting sunlight warm the room, drinking the sugared water Catherine loved.

'You look like someone with too much on your mind.'

'I want to find out about something,' Jane told her, then corrected herself. 'Someone.'

'Who's that?'

'A man called Julius White. Who was he?'

'Oh my,' Catherine said as she pulled a small handkerchief from her sleeve. 'My, my. That is the past, isn't it?'

Simon lay on the floor and let the twins climb on him. Soon enough they'd be too big for this. Already, their little knees and elbows jabbed sharp enough to make him wince. But he was reluctant to let it go. He loved the contact. To see the joy on their faces, hear their laughter as he tickled them; it seemed to replenish him.

Tonight, he vowed, he'd go nowhere, do nothing except wear out his sons. Hannah Milner was home, White could wait until the morning. The man wouldn't be going anywhere until his business was finished.

Rosie was studying the accounts, her foot tapping out a rhythm on the floorboards. Finally she put down her pen and sanded the page.

'We're doing well enough for now. But that two hundred from Milner would have seen us sitting very pretty.'

'Work will come,' Simon told her. 'People are never going to stop thieving.'

'Thank God.' She sighed. 'What are we going to do about White? I don't want to spend every day scared he's going to come.'

'I'll find him. I did it before.'

'Don't be too cocky,' she warned. 'He's led us a dance. It looks as if he learned plenty when he was Bayside.'

'I daresay he did.' He placed his hands around Richard's chest and lifted the boy into the air, swinging him from side to side until he squealed with pleasure. The old White had just been brutal. This new one was cunning. Nine years could ring plenty of changes.

In 1808, England had looked bleak. The war with France was going badly. Napoleon ruled most of Europe. The year before, he'd taken Portugal; now he was marching in Spain. At home, the government was terrified of revolt that simmered just below the surface. And well they might be. When a man could barely earn enough to live, food prices kept rising, and the enclosures by landlords drove people out of the countryside to try and earn something in the towns, the poor were going to feel like a threat. The manufactories were bringing in new machines that let one man do the work of ten. A skilled trade meant nothing any more.

People stole in order to live. What justice could there be when a man worked all week and still saw his family starve? The owners had their fine houses, their servants. They wanted for nothing.

Simon retrieved the things they took. But he'd never taken a man to be prosecuted for trying to feed his children. The law was a crooked system, everyone knew that. It was rigged for the rich; steal a few loaves and you ended up on the far side of the world in a penal colony. Take a fortune and they made you a lord.

Simon was still young then, but he'd already earned a small reputation in his work. He had the nose for it, a natural gift. He knew who to ask, the places in Leeds to go in order to hear things. He scuffled out a living. He and Rosie made enough to keep themselves. They were young, they could survive on next to nothing. Finding Lizzie Henry's locket and arresting Julius White changed all that. It had been the making of him.

Lizzie began praising him to her clients and the people she

knew. Soon notes arrived, asking him to find things that had been
. . . lost. And to manage it with speed and discretion. He did work
for the wealthy, the people he despised, and made sure he charged
them stiff fees for his services.

And now . . .

Now he was comfortable. A businessman. He had a house for
Rosie and the children, money in the lockbox. An account with
Beckett's Bank. He'd become just like the people he loathed. Julius
White had been the foundation of it all. Now he could be the end
of it, too.

'What are you thinking?' Rosie asked.

'Nothing. Just memories.' He turned his head to look at her.
'We'll find him.'

'You'd better kill him this time, Simon,' she said. 'Make sure
he can never come back again.'

That thought was lurking, hiding at the back of his mind. Could
he do it? He'd never needed to discover that about himself. He'd
wounded men before, but to kill? Better to hand someone over
for the justices.

Finally, he sat up, rolled the boys off him and sent them to bed.

'Whatever happens can wait until morning. We found Hannah
Milner. I'll call that a fair day's work.'

They were eating breakfast when the sharp knock came. Simon
glanced at Jane. She followed him into the hall, closing the kitchen
door behind her. He had his knife in his hand as he drew back the
latch.

George Mudie stood there, a piece of paper waving in his hand.
Simon exhaled slowly and slid the weapon back into its sheath.

'What's dragged you out so early?' he asked. 'You're rarely
about before ten.'

'This.' He pushed the paper towards Simon's face.

'You'd better come in.'

It was a discussion for the parlour, away from his family.

'You look worried, George. What's the trouble?'

'Read it.'

A letter. He scanned it quickly, then raised his head to see Mudie
watching him.

'When did this arrive?' Simon asked.

'This morning. Damn fool doesn't know the *Gazette* doesn't exist any more. I was cleaning the press when a boy brought it.'

This notice to be in your next edition. A shilling enclosed to pay for the advertisement.

There are people in Leeds who might well recall the name Julius White. I was transported to Australia for the theft of a piece of jewellery. There, I served my seven years under the hot sun, with good masters and bad. I received my pardon and now I have returned to England. My conviction was unjust, as all honest folk should know. I've come back to seek redress, to find justice. Those who saw me convicted and sent across the world for so long know who they are, all of them still alive and in Leeds. Let them be warned.

The same shaky hand as the notes to Milner.

'Has he sent to it the *Mercury* and the *Intelligencer*, too?'

'I don't know,' Mudie said. 'I came straight here. But it's a fair bet that he has.'

'Do you think they'll publish?'

'Not if they have an ounce of sense. The council would ask too many questions.' A half-smile flickered. 'Of course, if anyone at the *Intelligencer* had a brain, they'd never have got rid of me. Is it true, though? Is White really here?'

'He is, and he's already doing what he promised.'

'Did you know that when we talked the other day, Simon?'

'Not then, no.'

A suspicious frown crossed Mudie's face. 'You were asking me about John Milner, too. Does all this have anything to do with him?'

'No,' Simon said. As far as things went, it was true. Milner's part was done. His only importance to White had been the money. 'That was business.'

'If you say so,' he replied doubtfully. 'I remember when White was in court. I thought he'd hang.'

Simon had believed that, too, until he saw the guarded looks between defendant and judge and knew something had been arranged. The charge of murder had already been dismissed. It made him wonder if White had some powerful friends. Now the letter brought the idea back to him. It was a declaration of intent. Of war.

'What do you make of it?'

'It's obvious who he means,' Mudie said. 'You're the one who arrested him. Lizzie Henry paid for the prosecution.' His eyes flickered and his brows drew together. 'Didn't he say back then that he'd have his revenge?'

Simon nodded. 'When they led him down from the dock. Spoke it like a preacher.'

'And none of us believed him.'

'Why would we, George? We knew where he was going. How many come back from there? Name one.'

Neither of them could.

'You know chapter and verse on everyone in Leeds, George. White's been in town for a while.'

'Has he?' The man looked startled. 'Nobody's mentioned him.'

'I know. And he came back with money. Who could be hiding him? Who owed him enough favours for that?'

'There were always rumours . . .' Mudie began. 'You must know that.'

Simon shook his head. 'I'd come across his name. The first time we met was when I found him with the locket he stole.'

'He goes back a long way here, Simon. Before you started working. He helped people when they ran into some trouble. Important people.'

'Who?'

'I've tried to find out often enough, but it's like clutching fog. One thing's certain. People owe him favours, and when he wants to collect, they daren't say no. White knows where the bodies are buried in town.' He gave a dry bark of a laugh. 'Probably literally, in some cases.'

'Do you know who he's killed?'

'No, and nobody's going to start naming names. He might have been away a long time, but that doesn't mean people aren't scared of him. Especially if you're right and he's back in Leeds.'

'He's here. There's no doubt about it.'

'There was a rumour once . . .' Mudie began.

'What?'

'That someone with influence had murdered a man and paid

White to get rid of the body and cover things up. But it was never more than words. I never managed to find anything. People just went silent when I started asking.'

'It's not like you to give up,' Simon said.

'Sometimes you realize you're never going to get anywhere, however hard you try.' He shrugged. 'Then another story comes along and it all becomes history.'

'Do you think you could find a name?'

'After all this time? I can try, but don't hold your breath. I doubt I'll be any more successful than I was before. What are you going to do?'

'Find him and finish this business.'

He read the letter to them. Rosie stared at the table and stayed silent. Jane sat and listened without speaking.

'His idea of justice is to kill us,' Rosie said when he finished.

'He's careful enough not to say that, though.'

'He doesn't seem to know about me,' Jane said.

Simon shook his head. 'He knows, right enough. You can bet on that. He's planned all this very well. But you were never a part of it. And he doesn't have any idea how good you are.'

'Where do we start looking for him?' she asked.

'We ask questions, same as ever.' He drank, wiped a hand across his mouth, and stood. 'The sooner we begin, the sooner it'll be over.'

She heard Rosie lock the door behind them. In a moment they were simply two more faces among all the people on Swinegate. A man with a crutch limped by. Two children played in a puddle. A woman cried out, the words slurred together, madness in her eyes.

'Where are we going?'

'I want you to talk to everyone you know. We need to find someone who's seen him.'

'I asked someone about White yesterday,' Jane said. 'What he was like.'

'Leeds was safer when he was on the other side of the world.'

'She said people believed he'd murdered more than that servant.'

'Six,' Simon answered. 'That's the guess. But no one's certain. Maybe it was none. He never said.'

'Why did it take so long to put him in the dock?'

He shrugged. 'No evidence. If White really killed them, he hid it very well. People were unwilling to take him to court and testify. He had powerful friends.'

'Who?' Jane asked.

'Councilmen, landowners, probably. He did their dirty work.'

Jane frowned. 'If he knew all those people, how did you manage to get a guilty verdict?'

'Because Lizzie Henry brought the prosecution, and she wields some influence, too. He had the locket that was stolen from her. We had the evidence for that, at least.'

'You're the one who got him convicted.'

'Seven years was the lightest sentence the judge could give him.'

Jane nodded. 'What about Lizzie Henry?'

'I've warned her.'

'I didn't like her.'

'Don't be too quick to judge. She has her uses.'

'Do you think he still has important friends after all this time?'

Simon exhaled slowly. 'We'll find out.'

She began where she'd first heard the name. Mrs Rigton. The woman didn't appear surprised to see her again.

'I wondered how long it would take you.'

There were no more than a handful of drinkers in the place, men with no work to fill their days. One had his head down on the table, snoring quietly. Two others played cards. Jane sat on a bench opposite the woman.

'Who told you White was back?'

'Found out all about him, have you?'

'More than enough.'

'Keep your distance, that's my advice.' Mrs Rigton reached out and placed a hand on the girl's wrist. 'Be careful, girl. He's a dangerous man. I don't want to see something happen to you.'

'I need to know. He's after Simon and Rosie.'

The woman stayed silent. Finally she sighed. 'I shouldn't tell you. I want you safe.'

'If we can get rid of White, everyone will be safer. Catherine told me all about him.'

Mrs Rigton nodded sadly. 'I'm sure everything she said is true.' The woman seemed to come to a decision. 'Maybe you're right. We'd all be better off without his type. I heard it from Sam Crookshank.'

'I don't know who he is,' Jane said.

'No reason you should, child. He's a businessman, very respectable. Does work for the council. He has an office at the top of Kirkgate.'

'If he's so respectable, why would he know someone like White?'

'Because money doesn't care if it gets its hands mucky.' Mary Rigton shook her head and sighed. 'It can always wash them clean again later. Business is a strange world. Right and wrong don't mean much when there's profit to be made.'

Jane had watched a preacher once, calling people out for their sins as he stood on Briggate, bellowing at the top of his voice. If you make money your God, he warned, you'll stand in filth. At the time it made no sense to her: people needed money to live. They chased it – they had no choice. But later she began to understand what he meant. There was money and there was wealth, and a sea divided them.

'Thank you.' She started to rise.

'You can't go marching in there, child.' She tempered the warning with a tender smile. 'His clerks will throw you straight out. Wait until he goes for his dinner. Find him on his own and tell him I sent you.'

'How will I know who he is?'

'He's easy enough to spot, girl.' She rubbed her cheek with a knotted old hand. 'He has a mark the colour of port wine right here.'

Jane didn't have to move. She could follow Crookshank with her eyes as he walked the short distance from his office to the alehouse in Turk's Head Yard. Back again half an hour later. No chance to talk to him.

She'd come back after the business locked its doors for the day. She'd find her opportunity to approach him then.

As she began to walk away, Jane felt the familiar prickle down her spine. Someone was watching her. She didn't turn, just drifted slowly up Briggate. He followed. Soon she could pick him out in the reflections from shop windows. A young man. Nervous, to judge by his face. Inexperienced.

Time to find out what he wanted.

She slipped into Bay Horse Yard, and behind a wall, drawing her knife as she waited.

The footsteps were hesitant. One, two, then stop. Another, and another, until he was in the yard.

Suddenly Jane was behind him, with the blade at his throat, patting his coat with her free hand to feel for weapons. Nothing. He stood absolutely still, looking ahead.

'Why are you following me?'

'I'm not.' His voice quivered with fear. She could smell it on him. Jane pressed the tip of the knife against his skin, just hard enough to bring a drop of blood.

'Don't lie to me,' she warned.

'The man I work for told me to see where you went.'

'And who's he?'

'Mr Crookshank.' The words came in a flood, almost tripping over each other. 'Someone saw you from the office window and told him. I'm just the junior clerk. He said I had to watch you and follow, then tell him.' Very carefully, he held out a hand with ink on the fingers. 'See?'

Jane took the knife from his neck and stepped back. The young man began to rub the spot where she'd jabbed him.

'If he wants to know, he can ask me himself. Go back and tell him Mrs Rigton sent me. What time does your office close?'

'Eight o'clock,' he answered without thinking.

'I'll be outside then, waiting for him.' She took another pace backwards. 'Go on, go and let him know what I said.'

He turned and ran, boots echoing loudly in the passageway before he vanished.

Jane stood and thought. She was angry with herself for being spotted; she needed to be more careful. But she'd been able to deliver her message to Crookshank. At eight she'd discover whether he was willing to talk to her.

With the knife safe in her pocket and the shawl over her head, she moved back down Briggate.

* * *

Julius White. Simon said the name so often during the afternoon that he could taste the soot whenever he spoke it. A few had heard he was back, but no one admitted they'd seen him.

The man hadn't turned into a spirit on the other side of the world. He didn't know any magic. He was flesh and blood and bone, the same as everyone else. He'd hired people, he'd written letters. He was somewhere in Leeds.

By six, Simon felt as if he'd spent the hours hitting his head against a wall. He felt frustrated. He was good at this work; he'd proved it over the years. But the last few days had shown him that he wasn't good enough.

He'd go out again later and see what the night brought.

'Sam Crookshank?' Simon spooned up more of the soup with one eye on the boys, watching that they didn't spill too much on the table. 'So he was aware that White had come back,' he said thoughtfully.

'Do you know him?' Jane asked.

'He has that stain on his face. We've never talked, but I know he has dealings with the council.'

'A mark?' Rosie looked up sharply. 'On his right cheek, the colour of a plum?'

'That's him,' Simon said. 'Why?'

'He's the one who pulled Richard away from that cart.' She tousled her son's hair.

'Then I owe him some thanks.' He pursed his lips. 'I don't remember him having anything to do with White before he was transported.'

'He set someone to follow me,' Jane said. 'One of his clerks. I sent him back with a message that I'd be outside the office at eight.'

'I'd like to be there.'

She nodded. He kept looking at her face for any sign of resentment. He knew that Jane preferred to work alone. She rarely revealed who gave her information, and he'd learned never to ask. Three years of working together, two with Jane living under his roof, and so much of her was still locked behind doors. Sometimes he wondered if they'd ever open.

The meal was over, Amos and Richard shifting restlessly on their chairs.

'Right,' Simon said, 'I have time to get this pair to bed before we leave.'

Julius White might want his blood revenge, but at home he was determined to live as if nothing was happening.

With the sun gone, there was a bite in the air. Simon huddled into his coat, glad of the extra warmth. Jane never seemed to feel the cold; she still wore her thin old dress, the shawl gathered around her shoulders.

A woman with a baby on her hip searched a pile of rubbish for anything useful. People walked home from work, heads down. Lights still burned in offices and shops. Couples strolled arm-in-arm, lost in each other.

Finally, the door across the street opened and Crookshank came out on to Kirkgate. Blinking behind his spectacles, he glanced around before strolling away slowly.

Simon started at a quick trot, Jane at his side. In just a few yards they caught up to the man, one on either side of him. He was tall, half a head above Simon, towering over most of the people around. He glanced down at Jane.

'My clerk said Mrs Rigton told you to come and see me. What do you want?'

He sounded terse, annoyed by her company.

'Julius White,' she said.

'What about him?'

'You knew he was back in Leeds.'

'What if I did? He served his sentence. He was free to return.'

'We want to find him,' Simon said.

Crookshank turned his head. 'You're the thief-taker.'

'I am. And I believe I need to thank you for saving my son from a cart.'

It caught the man off guard; he knew it would. The man blushed a little. It made the mark on his skin stand out even more.

'I hope he's fine.'

'He is. And very well chastened. I'm curious, Mr Crookshank – how do you come to know White?'

'We did some business before . . .' He let silence fill the gap. 'And he trusted me to look after his affairs while he was away.'

As if it had been a trip for pleasure, a Grand Tour. But Simon smelled the wariness coming from Crookshank. He could use that.

'When did he return?'

'About three months ago, I believe. That was when I first saw him.'

Three months, and a shadow all that time. 'Where is he living? Who's hiding him?'

'I didn't know anyone was,' Crookshank replied calmly. 'He served his sentence in full.' A small hesitation. 'I don't know where he's staying. He visits me at my home.' It was a reluctant admission.

'Where's that?'

Crookshank drew himself up. 'Little Woodhouse. Beech Grove.'

An impressive address. The man had done very well for himself.

'But that's in the other direction.' Simon smiled at him.

'I'm well aware of that, Mr Westow. I have to meet someone.'

'White?' Jane asked.

'A gentleman,' he replied after a moment. 'His name is none of your concern. We have an appointment.'

'I understand Mr White came into some money very recently,' Simon continued.

'Did he?' Crookshank's confusion sounded genuine. 'I don't see how.'

'He did. Very definitely. A small fortune. You can take my word on that. When you see him, pass on a message from me. Tell him it won't stay in his hands for very long.'

'I don't know what you mean.'

'That's fine. He will.' He stopped, and Jane was still, too, leaving Crookshank to keep walking and glancing back over his shoulder.

'Do you think that did any good?' she asked.

'Maybe. The question is what will White make of it?' Simon shrugged his shoulders. 'We still have work to do tonight.'

THIRTEEN

So Crookshank had been looking after White's affairs. The way he'd said it, the man might have been any client or friend. But the words meant more than he realized, Simon decided. Julius White had always known he'd return. He'd left things worth saving. And it confirmed those looks he'd seen in court, from dock to judge. Everything had been worked out beforehand.

Simon sat in the beershop, the drink untouched in front of him. Another evening that brought nothing. Nobody had seen White. Half of them had never heard of him. He was looking in the wrong places. The man wasn't hiding among the criminals and the poor. That was why they hadn't even had a sniff of him yet.

And if he wasn't with them, he had to be sheltered and out of sight among the rich. What had he entrusted to Crookshank? Money? Valuables? Property? And those influential friends . . . Simon had believed they'd abandon him with the trial and try to forget they'd ever known him. But maybe they hadn't all blown away with the wind that took him to Australia.

He needed to begin searching elsewhere.

By midnight he was home. Rosie was asleep, tossing and thrashing in her dreams. The boys were in their beds. And Jane . . . not a sound from the attic. She might be there, or still out and around.

He stood on the landing, listening to the small creaks and sighs of the house. In the morning they'd start fresh.

Jane listened. Simon could see the doubts cloud across her face. She ate as he talked, the pobs she liked for breakfast, bread in warm milk.

'You'd think people with money would have better sense than to hide someone like that,' Rosie said.

'He must have a hold over them,' Simon said. 'Something he knows.'

'Then it would have to be something bad. Something important. It's nine years since he left. Things change.'

'Not as much as we think, it seems.'

'Perhaps the rich have deeper secrets than the rest of us,' Jane said quietly. She tore off a piece of bread and began to chew it.

'Maybe that's true,' he said. He didn't know, didn't care. As long as he found White, they could all carry their secrets to the grave.

'We know a few wealthy people, too,' Rosie said. 'There's Emma Hart.'

Four years earlier, they'd found some plate and lace handker-chiefs that burglars had taken from the woman's house on Park Lane. She'd been grateful for their return. She must be in her late forties now, he thought, a widow with a brassy, vivacious voice and a teasing smile.

She wasn't the only one. He knew a small scattering of the well-to-do around Leeds. How many of them would help him, though? How many would even give him the time of day any more? A thief-taker was just another tradesman. Useful when you needed him and then forgotten.

Rosie looked him up and down and shook her head. 'If you're going to call on the quality, you'd better wear your good suit and get a yourself a shave. One look at you like that and they'll never let you through the door.'

Jane had never known anyone rich. She never would. They inhab-ited a different world, somewhere that was always clean and bright. But she did know a few of their servants: a kitchen maid in a house out along North Street. A washerwoman in a grand place on Park Square. A groom for a man who liked to play at being a farmer.

That was the place to begin, she decided. Josh always seemed willing to find a few minutes for her. He was a pleasant lad, shy, willing, happier with animals than with people; working in the stables was the perfect job for him.

Half an hour's walking, up past Richmond Hill, the climb along Spital Field and beyond Star and Garter house. The suggestion of spring warmth growing every day. Up on the peak, she turned around to see Leeds below.

Down there, when she was moving along the streets, the town felt so large, every inch as big and choked as she imagined London would be. From here it looked small. Everything was pushed and crammed together, so tight it might burst. The chimneys poked up, throwing out a haze of smoke to shroud the place. If she reached out her hand she felt she could pick it all up, squeeze it in her fist and put it away in her pocket.

You're not a child, she thought. Stupid ideas don't do any good. With a grim, serious face she turned back to the track.

Josh was in the hayloft, tossing straw down to the stable floor with a pitchfork. He'd been ten and thin as a wretch when she first met him as they looked for food after the market one Saturday. Even then he'd loved horses, spending time at the ostler's gate, face breaking into a smile when he was allowed in to groom one of the animals. Some nights they let him sleep in the stables and gave him a meal. Finally they took him on, and he couldn't have been happier if he'd inherited a fortune.

He'd done well. Horses scared her, so large and threatening, but he'd handled them as if he'd been born to it. He worked hard, he relished every hour of the job, and the beasts responded to him. Then last year, Mr Warner had offered him a position in charge of the stable out here. It wasn't big, just three horses and a gig to keep running. But for him it was a dream that had become real.

A long way from sorting through the rubbish and trying to fill their bellies. Josh had security now. He had a future.

Jane stood at the entrance to the stable, watching him work. He'd grown into a young man. Still thin, but he'd filled out with all the labour. The muscles bulged on his arms as he shifted load after load. He finished, wiping the sweat off his face, and climbed down the ladder.

'They work you hard here.'

He turned in surprise, his mouth curving into a smile when he saw her. Half his teeth had fallen out, a memento of those years of hunger.

'How long have you been there?'

'Long enough.'

He'd been a brother to her once. A little older, watching out for her when neither of them had anything. Now, in their different ways, they were both settled.

'You haven't been to visit in a while. The last time you were here there was snow on the ground.' He poured a mug of beer and offered it to her. Jane shook her head.

'You look happy,' she said.

'Me?' He glanced around and she could see the joy in his eyes. 'I suppose I am. Mr Warner's pleased with the way I look after the animals. What about you?'

She shrugged. 'I'm fine. I'm looking for someone.'

'You found me.' Josh grinned.

'Does Mr Warner have any guests staying here?'

'Him? No. He hasn't even been here much himself this year. Too busy, that's what he said when he was out last time.'

'What about the other places around?' After the walk up here, she wanted to return with something.

He drank as he wandered round the stable, patting a horse's flank before picking off a piece of straw.

'I thought I saw a stranger over at Hawley's farm. Why?'

'What did he look like?'

He pushed his lips together. 'This job of yours. A girl shouldn't be doing things like that.'

'It's work.' That was all anyone needed to know.

'But . . .'

He started this argument every time she came to see him. Sometimes teasing, occasionally with a sharper edge. Today she wouldn't let him distract her.

'The man. What did he look like?' she repeated.

'I only saw him from the back. But it wasn't Hawley or anybody who works for him. He didn't walk like any of them.'

'How long ago was this?' Jane asked.

'Four or five days.' He stared at her. 'Why?'

'Where is the farm?'

He opened his mouth to speak, closed it again, then led her to the stable door and pointed.

'You see those trees up on the ridge? It's just down from there.'

A dark, weathered box of a building on the hillside, exposed to the wind. A third of a mile away, she judged. At that distance it would be impossible to see how burned a man's skin might be.

'Is he still there?'

'I don't know. I only saw him once.'

She could wait here all day and not catch a glimpse of the man. It might not even be White. And there was no way to approach the place without being seen.

'I'd better go back,' she said.

'I know someone over there.' A blush crept up from his neck. 'I could go over later and ask, if you like.'

'I'd be grateful. Be careful, though. Just say you happened to see someone.'

'Come back tomorrow and I'll tell you.'

Jane started back down the track, holding the shawl tight as the wind began to blow. She could never live out here where the cold penetrated to the bones. Up on the hills life seemed too fragile, like nature could pick it up and end it in a second.

The man at the farm was no more than a faint possibility. But even that was better than going home empty-handed.

'You know people.'

Barnaby Wade put down his coffee cup and dabbed his mouth with a handkerchief. Around them, the coffee house buzzed with conversation. Men with soft faces and intent voices discussed business, shook hands on a quick deal.

'I knew people, Simon,' he said slowly. 'I was barred from the law a long time ago, remember? Now I gull fools and take their money.'

'It's legal.'

'Yes,' he agreed slowly. 'I make money. A few of them do, too, sometimes. But it doesn't make me welcome in the best houses. You already know that.'

He did, but asking cost nothing. And it was still too early to call on Mrs Hart. Never before ten, that was the etiquette.

'Is this to do with White?' Wade asked.

'Yes.'

'I've heard he wrote a letter to the newspapers, but I haven't seen it in the *Intelligencer* or the *Mercury* this morning.'

'No one's going to print it. He says he's back to demand justice.'

Wade took out a cheroot and lit it from a spill. 'I can imagine the kind of justice he wants. You'd better watch out for yourself.'

'I will, don't worry.' He gathered up his hat. 'I am. Let me know if you do hear anything. I want to know where he's staying.'

In the distance he heard the toll of the bell as it rang ten o'clock. Simon took a breath, crossed Park Lane and knocked on a door. He was wearing his good black suit. Rosie had adjusted his stock until it was sat just right at his throat. The barber had given him a shave so close that his skin shone pink in the mirror. He looked quite respectable enough to call on a rich widow.

The maid in the apron believed he was, at least. She escorted him through to the parlour, bobbing a curtsey as she announced him, then quietly closing the door as she left.

Emma Hart look amused. She was dressed in muslin the colour of bilberries, a silk shawl around her neck, hair neatly dressed, just a few strands of grey to give away her age. A small dog nestled in her lap, and she stroked it as she spoke.

'You're in your finest get-out, Mr Westow. Are you on your way to a wedding or a funeral?'

'I'm here on business.' That was enough to pique her interest.

'Business? I've had nothing stolen.' She raised a carefully painted eyebrow. 'Or do you know something I don't?'

'I'm looking for information.'

She smiled. 'I see. Well, I hear gossip from the ladies, but I don't know if that's *information*.' She emphasized the word gently. 'More like defamation, usually. What kind of things do you want to know?'

'About a man who returned to Leeds a few months ago.'

'Then perhaps you'd better sit down and tell me about him.'

By the time he finished, he had her promise to listen carefully and pass on anything she heard.

'But there's a price, Mr Westow.'

Wasn't there always? In one way or another, life was filled with debts and obligations.

'What is it?' he asked.

'When it's over, you come back and tell me the whole story. There's more to it than you said, I can tell.'

'I will.' If he was still alive then.

'One last thing,' Mrs Hart said as he was leaving. 'When you do return, present yourself like this. You're a handsome young man. Dressing well suits you.'

He was planting seeds, he realized as he walked out over Quarry Hill. Now he had to hope they'd grow soon, without drought or flood. He wished the Vulture hadn't died; he always had information to peddle. Still, Jane was right, someone would replace him soon. But now was when he needed to know things.

The house on Black Flags Lane was quiet. But all the trade here came with the night. The doors leading off the corridor remained shut. He'd never seen any of the girls who worked here. That privilege was reserved for the paying customers to make their choice.

Simon had to spend ten minutes waiting in Lizzie Henry's parlour, gazing out of the windows at the ground coming into bloom.

'Have you found him yet?' she asked as she swept into the room. There was a brittle edge to her voice. Under the powder, her face looked drawn and haggard.

'No.'

'Someone was saying last night that he's sent a letter to the newspapers.'

'He did.' Simon handed it to her and waited as she read.

'We both understand his idea of justice.'

'Then I need to find him before he dispenses it. He had influential friends before, you remember?'

'Of course. But even they couldn't stop his transportation.'

'Seven years was the lowest sentence the judge could give.'

Her expression hardened. 'What are you trying to say, Mr Westow? Spit it out.'

'I believe it was arranged. Money probably changed hands to make sure White had an easy time over there. He had someone looking after his affairs while he was gone.'

That made her pay attention. 'Who?'

'It doesn't matter.' Crookshank's name hadn't been on the list of clients she'd given him. 'But that doesn't sound like someone who never expects to return, does it?'

'No,' she agreed.

'And he's visited this man a few times since he's been back in Leeds. His important friends didn't all desert him after his arrest.'

She cocked her head. 'Why?'

'He has a hold over them.'

'Then you'd think they'd be glad to see him go.'

'Maybe they were,' Simon said. 'But he's back now and he's staying with one of them, out of sight.'

'I see.' She began to pace about the room, arms folded tightly around herself. 'Then what do we do now?'

'I need you to ask the men who come here if they've seen him, if they know where he might be.'

'You've no idea at all?'

'I'd hardly have come otherwise,' he said quietly.

She stopped and stared at him. 'What will you do when you find him?'

'I'll see that he hangs.'

'It would be better to kill him. Make sure there's no escape.'

Simon shook his head. 'He's a kidnapper and an extortionist. That's enough to see him on the gallows.'

'Has he done that?' she asked in surprise, then pursed her lips. 'It's strange I never heard about it. Was that why you wanted my list?'

'Yes. Before I knew who was behind it.'

'But you won't kill him.'

Simon shook his head. 'Not unless I have to.'

She gave a bitter smile. 'Principles and morals. They don't seem to belong in your profession.'

'That's who I am.'

'If ever he comes here, I'll murder him myself.' She nodded towards the fields beyond the window. 'Bury him out there.'

'You'll ask your clients about him?'

She nodded. 'I will.'

Simon heard the servant bolt the door behind him. Lizzie Henry was a woman terrified for her life.

There was one other person to see while he was dressed in his good clothes. The constable. It was a name rather than a job. A position. All the ceremony and the money that went with the post, but none of the work. Cecil Freeman had been part of the council long enough to earn the sop, a nest to gild his retirement. He supervised the watch, old men who covered the different wards of Leeds and hobbled a mile rather than risk a fight. It was no wonder a thief-taker could make a good living.

He found Freeman in his office at the Moot Hall, dictating to a clerk.

'Go,' he said as Simon entered. 'Write that up in a good hand and leave it for me to sign.' Once they were alone, he said, 'What brings the honour of a visit from Mr Westow? It must be something important if he's deigning to see the law.'

'Julius White.'

The constable leaned back in his chair and steepled his fingers under his chin. He was an old man, a face of sagging jowls with fine, wild hair on his head, more sprouting from his ears and his eyebrows.

'What about him?'

'He's back in Leeds.'

'What of it? As long as he received a full pardon in Australia for his crimes, there's no reason he shouldn't return.'

Simon placed the letter on the desk. 'Read that.'

Freeman looked at the letter. 'I'll ask you again, Mr Westow, what about it? From anything in here, he might well be starting proceedings in court.'

'You know better than that.'

'I know what I can see.' His voice was cold. 'If you have a complaint against Mr White, swear it out with a magistrate. If you don't, I have more pressing business than talking to a thief-taker. Good day to you.'

There'd never been any love lost between them. Freeman loved his title and the small trappings of office. He was pleased to serve out his time and pocket the bribes and offerings that came his way. Weak, venal and useless.

Outside, on the street, he gazed around. People going about their business, a pickpocket moving slyly among the crowds and trying his luck. As he passed the Leadenhall abattoir off Vicar Lane, he heard the rhythmic thud of cleavers and smelled the iron stink of blood. A butcher's boy came out, weighed down by a flank of beef.

Time to go home and into his proper clothes. He wasn't made to be a dandy.

FOURTEEN

'You have another note,' Rosie said as soon as he stepped into the kitchen. She lifted the lid on a pan. Steam rose in a cloud around her. 'Milner's man brought it.'

Simon broke the seal. It was terse, written in a firm, sure hand, the signature an illegible scrawl.

> *To date, I've heard nothing from you about White or my money. I had higher hopes of you after your initial failure, but you have let me down once more. Time is running out for you to achieve a result that satisfies me.*

'He's not pleased with my work,' Simon said.

Rosie wiped her hand on her apron and pushed a strand of hair off her face. Her skin was pink and shining from the heat.

'Let me see.' He heard the anger bubble in her face. 'A result that satisfies him? Who does he think he is? We haven't made a penny off him.'

'He believes it's my fault he lost his thousand.'

'Next thing, he'll be blaming you if it rains.' She tossed the letter on the table. 'I notice he didn't mention his daughter.'

'Did you honestly think he would? She's a commodity. People only bother about them if they're damaged.'

'He'd better not show his face round here.'

Simon laughed. 'I don't think you need to worry. He'd never lower himself.'

'He threatened to destroy you. Don't forget that.'

'I haven't. It's just words. What can he do? Things will always be stolen, and people are going to pay to have them back.'

'I daresay.' She pressed herself against him and sighed. 'I'll still feel better about everything when White's on the gibbet.'

'So will I.' He kissed her forehead. 'We'll see if Jane's friend has a good word tomorrow. I need to be out again tonight.'

'Mam,' a voice called from the yard. 'Richard's got his foot stuck in something.'

She rolled her eyes. 'If I were you, I'd go now.'

Jane caught the smell of roasting meat as she entered the old blacking factory. Whatever they'd caught sizzled in small strips on the fire.

'You were here the other day,' a woman said, looking up. 'I remember you. You were looking for someone.'

'That's right.'

She sat next to the woman, feeling the cold ground beneath her. Soon enough it would penetrate her flesh and leave her chilled. But at least there was a roof of sorts here. A covering, even with some of the tiles missing. When Jane glanced up she could see tiny squares of night sky.

'Did you ever find him?'

'Yes. But I'm after someone else now.'

'Who's that?' The woman wore a dazed look, as if she saw the world through a veil. When she turned her head to ask the question, Jane smelled the gin on her breath.

'Someone who might have been here. He was looking to hire people.'

The woman snorted. 'Don't be daft. No one's going to come here to do that.'

'Maybe someone did.'

The woman shrugged and licked grease from her fingers. Jane wandered around the fire, asking her questions. The people were tired and dulled. Hunger did that. Scrabbling to hold on to life wore you out. Existence drained you.

Finally she found an old man with milky eyes who nodded at her question.

'I remember.' He scratched what remained of his hair. 'A man came. A few nights back. Three? Four? I don't remember.'

She pounced on his reply. 'What was he like? Did you see him?'

'I don't see anything too well these days, luv.' He offered a gentle smile. 'Not like I did. Used to be I could pick out a hawk on a hill a mile away . . . I heard him, though. He had a strange voice.'

'Strange?'

The man thought before he answered. 'It were like he were from Leeds but there was something else in it, too. Summat I didn't know.'

'What did he want?'

'He were looking for that lad as looks like a weasel. Seemed to know he was often here.'

'Did he ask for him by name?'

'He did. But the lad weren't around. Sorry, luv, that's it.'

'Never mind.' She pressed a penny into his palm and wrapped his fingers around it.

'There was summat else,' he added slowly. 'It's just come back into me head. He said the boy could leave a message for him at the Old George. To talk to the landlord.'

Another two pennies in his palm, and it was worth it.

'Find yourself a bed for the night,' Jane told him. 'Somewhere warmer than this.'

'I'll be fine, lass,' he said. 'I'll be reet. But thank you.'

She had a link. Jane smiled to herself as she walked. From the Calls, she turned up Briggate. The whores stood at the entrances to the courts, looking bored behind their fans. The Old George stood halfway up the hill, windows brightly lit, voices and laughter spilling like a stream on to the street.

She paused at the door then walked on. The landlord would take one look and order her out. Better if Simon talked to him. It would wait for the morning.

By the time she turned on Boar Lane she knew someone was behind her. He was trying to tread lightly, but she could tell. Her hand slipped into the pocket of her skirt, fingers tight around the knife hilt.

She heard him speed up, drawing closer as she reached Alfred Street. She vanished round the corner, then turned to face him, the blade hidden in her hand.

He was dark-haired, wild-eyed and dirty. A big man in a tattered coat.

'Don't you know it's dangerous for a girl to be out on her own at this time.' His voice was low, the menace lurking behind his words. 'You need someone to walk you home.'

'I can look after myself.'

'You ought to be careful. Bad things might happen.'

'You've said your piece. Now you can go.'

'I don't think so.'

He reached out and gripped her arm. Jane's hand darted forward and suddenly he let go, as if his skin was burning. His fingers moved to his cheek, staring at her in horror as he felt the warm blood.

'What d'you want to do that for?'

'Touch me again and I'll kill you.' No anger in her voice; it was a statement of fact. He started to back away, still holding the flapping skin on his face.

'Bitch,' he shouted. 'Whore.' His boots echoed off the buildings as he ran.

Maybe he'd think twice in future. But probably not. There were too many men who believed every girl owed them pleasure. She wiped the blade on her skirt and slid it back into her pocket.

Simon saw her face in the light from the lamp. Pale, full of something he didn't quite understand.

'Are you all right?'

'Just tired,' Jane answered as she sat on the bench. Rosie took brandy from a cupboard and poured a small glass.

'Drink that,' she ordered, and stood over her, hand on hips, until it was gone. 'Better. There's a little more colour in your cheeks now.'

'I found something.'

Simon listened, nodding his appreciation.

'You've had a good day,' he said when she finished. 'Better than mine. It's Zack Cartwright who runs the George. I'll go and see him tomorrow.'

'I want to go with you,' Jane insisted.

'After you've been up to that farm?' he asked.

'I'll get an early start.'

'Something's wrong with her,' Simon said. He could hear Jane's footsteps on the stairs to the attic.

'Shock,' Rosie replied. 'That's why I gave her brandy.'

'Shock? Why? What happened?'

'I don't know.' She shrugged. 'There's not much we can do if she doesn't want to tell us.'

'By now, you'd think—'

'No, Simon. It's up to her. You know what she's like. You can't force it.'

He sighed and nodded. 'Come on, we might as well go to bed, too.'

But first he made sure the doors and shutters were properly barred.

Rain had swept through during the night, and the wind felt more like February than April. Her hair whipped around her head. Jane had goose pimples on her arms as she climbed the hill, hugging the shawl close. Mud from the path clung to her boots.

It was warmer in the stable. Josh was sitting in the corner, close to a small brazier, eating something from a steaming bowl.

'You look perished.'

'Chilly outside,' she said. 'Worse up here.'

'Sit down.' He pushed the bowl at her. 'Eat this, it'll warm you up.'

The small warmth of the fire began to seep into her bones and the porridge filled her belly.

'Did you talk to your farm girl?'

'I told you I would. I rode over.' He glanced towards the horses. 'They needed exercising, anyway. She said the master had someone staying, but he left the day before yesterday.'

'What he was like?'

'Emily only saw him twice. Just in passing. But he had dark skin, like he'd been in the sun for a long time. Years, maybe.'

White. It had to be. She felt a quickening in her blood.

'Where was he going? Did she say?'

'Emily said he rode down towards Leeds.' He looked at her, his gaze serious. 'You need to watch yourself. She said there was something about him. It scared her.'

'No need to worry about me.'

'I know, but . . .' He stared down at his feet.

'And there's Simon.'

Before she left, he took an old riding coat from a peg.

'Take this,' Josh said. 'It'll keep you warm. You might as well have it. No one wears it, anyway.'

The coat was big, far too large for her, and smelled of horses

and straw. There were rips and patches, the hem swept close to
her ankles and she needed to turn the sleeves back twice over her
wrists. As she walked back to town, at least the wind didn't cut
through to her skin. Better than before, she thought with a smile.

'So White's probably back in town after staying with that farmer
– what did you say his name was?'

They walked down Swinegate towards Leeds Bridge.

'Hawley.'

'Maybe I'll go and have a word with him later.' Simon turned
the corner and they strode up Briggate, crossing the street to the
Old George Hotel. Around them, the town was alive with shouts
and cries, the carts and coaches that pushed relentlessly along the
roads, and the perfume of soot in the air. 'Pay attention in here.
You need to watch Cartwright. He's as oily as they come.'

'What do you mean?'

He looked at her. The new coat Jane had found was little better
than a rag, still with the strong stink of a stable. It hung down
near her feet and she was almost lost in it, but she wore it proudly.

'He'll tell anyone what he thinks they want to hear. Don't believe
a word he says unless he can prove it.'

The kitchen was noisy, a clatter of pans, steam rising from a
pan. A patch of grease shone on the floor. Simon talked to
a sweating man in a shirt covered with stains. He pointed down
a corridor.

Zack Cartwright was in his office, a ledger open on the desk.
It was a barren room, in need of a scrubbing, a dirty window
showing the yard behind. Everything looked worn and weary, as
if only habit held it all together. But the entire hotel had seen
better days.

'Mr Westow,' the man said, smiling as he put down his pen and
carefully closed the book in front of him. A doubtful nod to Jane.
'Miss. What can I do for you?'

'You keep messages for people here.'

'We do,' Cartwright said. 'Show me a hotel that doesn't. You
know that.'

'I hear Julius White has been using this place to receive mail.'

'Julius White?' The man's face clouded. 'Wasn't he transported
years ago?'

Simon's voice was filled with disappointment. 'Zack, I can see the lie in your eyes.' He shook his head. 'I know you can do better than that. You've got to be capable of a few honest answers.' He slammed his hand down hard on the desk. The pen and ledger jumped. 'Even if I have to drag them out of you.'

Cartwright flinched. Simon had dealt with him before. He was a weak man, a coward, too ready to please everyone, to find some favour. A show of force and he wilted.

'He came in here two months ago and said he needed a place people could leave messages for him. I was surprised to see him.'

'How much did he offer you?'

'Two shillings a week.'

'Zack . . .' Simon warned.

'Three shillings.' The man corrected himself quickly. 'That's what I meant. And he warned me that if I told anyone he was in Leeds, he'd come and slit my throat.'

That sounded closer to the truth.

'Has he received many notes?'

'A few.' Simon said nothing, staring at him. 'Honest, Mr Westow. Not many.'

'When was the last one?'

'Two days back. He collected it that afternoon. Nothing since then.'

'And I don't suppose you happened to read the contents of those notes?'

The man shook his head. 'I didn't dare to look. Really, I didn't. He'd know.'

Simon weighed what he'd heard. Cartwright was scared; he could almost hear the man's heart thumping. Most of what he'd said had the taste of believability.

'If he comes back, I want to know about it straightaway. Agreed?'

He waited for the nod. Acceptance. Defeat. Maybe Cartwright would do it, maybe not. But he'd put the fear of God in him.

As they walked out on to Briggate, Simon began to laugh. Even Jane was grinning.

'Now we'd better go and talk to some ostlers. White left that farm on a horse, you said. He has to be keeping it somewhere.'

* * *

Too many of them, Jane thought. She'd spent the afternoon trudging from stable to stable all through Hunslet and Holbeck. The larger ones served the coaching inns; the smaller ones often had no more than two or three beasts, spavined hacks for hire.

By four her feet ached and she was sick of seeing horses. But in Josh's coat she was warm. She'd slit the pocket so she could quickly reach through to her knife; now she felt safe again.

Six o'clock and she'd visited the last place. No one resembling White had left a horse on this side of the Aire. She crossed Leeds Bridge, watching the carts and coaches make their way in and out of town.

On Swinegate, Jane stopped so suddenly that the man behind bumped her aside as he strode past. She crept back to the corner, hiding in a ginnel. A man was watching Simon's house. Not White. This one was pale, with a thick moustache and a high-crown hat, staring at the building as if he wanted to imprint every detail on his mind. Two minutes later he thrust his hands deeper into his pockets and started to amble away. She followed.

'He went into the Boot and Shoe,' she said. 'There were only a few drinking inside, and it's impossible to stand in the yard there without being seen. There's a back entrance, too.'

'Interesting.' Simon rubbed his chin. He had no idea what it meant, but there was nothing he could do about it for now. 'At least I found the stable White's using. It's out near Bean Ing Mill.' He glanced at his wife. 'Rosie's come up with a plan.'

'Tomorrow I'm going to dress up in my best clothes and go there,' she said. 'I'll tell the stable owner that's my horse. Someone stole it, and I want to know where to find him.'

'If we can find out where he's staying, we can go after him.' Simon continued with a grin. 'We're going to turn the hunter into the hunted.'

'What are we going to do tonight?' Jane asked.

'Nothing,' he told her. 'We're going to rest and sleep and be ready for the morning. Don't you think you've earned it?'

He heard small feet dashing down the stairs, the shout of one boy, then another, voices trying to climb over each other.

'Enough,' Simon cried. 'If you've got something to say, come in here and do it properly. You're not a pair of animals.' A few

seconds later they came into the kitchen, heads down, trying not
to giggle.

'Let me see those hands,' Rosie said, examining them as Richard
and Amos held up their palms. 'How could you get so mucky upstairs?
Over by that bowl, now. I'm going to scrub the pair of you clean.'

'Do you think it'll work?' Jane asked quietly.

'It might,' Simon replied after a moment. 'We need to do
something.'

'I'm not sure. Someone watching this place . . .' She shrugged.

'We'll look into it tomorrow,' he promised.

FIFTEEN

Jane stood by her window, staring down at Swinegate. The street
was dark, the only light coming from cracks in shutters or a
night walker holding up a lantern. She stayed in the shadows,
out of sight.

The man wasn't there. She couldn't spot him, couldn't feel him.
But something about him worried her. The way he took his time
and studied the house, then wandered easily away. It meant something, she was sure of it. But she didn't know what.

It was a bad dream, a nightmare. She woke, gasping for breath as
she sat up in the bed. But it clung to her, little shards hooked in
her mind. No details, just images, fragments. A feeling like a
shroud. She knew if she closed her eyes again it would return,
and she'd plunge deep into it once more.

Still the middle of the night, blackness outside. She picked out
footsteps running hard along the street. One man, no one behind
him. A small pause and then a hammering on the door. Jane slid
out of the bed and stood, watching out of the window.

He was warm, Rosie was twined around him, but the knocking
woke him instantly. Gently, Simon untangled himself, pulled on
his trousers and crept downstairs, making no noise, the knife ready
in his hand.

He took hold of the handle and pulled the door wide, ready to strike. But he knew the man on the doorstep. Lizzie Henry's servant. Her guard. A big, brutal man. Now his eyes were wild with fear.

'What is it? What's happened?'

'She's dead.' He had to place a hand on the frame to steady himself. His voice was shaking with grief. 'Someone got in and killed her.'

'How?' She knew White was after her; Lizzie had been so scared she'd have kept her rooms secure.

The man tried to collect his thoughts. 'I found her . . . I don't know . . . not long. She was already dead.'

No question who'd done it.

'Go back there,' Simon ordered quickly. 'Get all the customers out. Give them some story, it doesn't matter what. Send them home, and make sure the girls are safe.'

The man nodded. He craved instructions, someone to make the decisions.

'I'll do that.'

'After that, wait for me. I'll be there in a few minutes.'

Simon locked the door and took a breath. He saw Jane at the top of the stairs, coat gathered around herself, the blade tight in her fist.

'Did you hear all that?'

'Yes.'

'Let me dress and we'll go.'

A clear night. Even the haze that hung over the town couldn't block all the stars in the sky. Enough of a chill in the air to bring a bloom to their breath as they walked quickly through the streets. The town was almost silent, eerie, just the snuffle of a dog in a midden, the bark of a fox off on a hill somewhere. No human sounds. A time for all good people to sleep or stay out of sight.

On Black Flags Lane, the door to the house stood ajar. The mistress was dead, the men with money gone; no reason to lock it any more. No noise inside; the man must have done what he'd ordered. A lamp burned in Lizzie's parlour, casting a soft glow over her corpse. She was sitting in her chair, head back.

'She looks like she's asleep,' Jane said from the doorway.

'She won't be waking up again.' Simon crouched by the woman, examining her face. 'Someone's broken her neck. Snapped it.' He glanced around the room. Nothing disturbed. No sign of a fight. He tried the back door: locked. The windows were all closed, the shutters barred tight. The only way in and out was the door to the corridor. From her chair, Lizzie would have been able to see anyone who entered.

He kept prowling until he heard the servant. The man hurried in, then stopped. A few tears began to fall down his cheeks as he gazed at Lizzie. He breathed deep and wiped his face with the back of a hand.

'The clients left quickly and quietly,' he said after a moment. 'No fuss.'

'What about the girls?' Simon asked.

'I've put them all together in one of the rooms upstairs. They won't try to go anywhere.'

Simon looked at him, but he was still staring at his mistress.

'Where were you when it happened?'

'We had a disturbance. A gentleman was beating a girl. That doesn't usually matter too much, but she was screaming loud enough to interrupt everyone. I had to go up and take care of it. I threw him out.'

'Who was he?'

The man shook his head. 'I don't know. It was the first time he'd been here.'

'And what happened after that? Did you come back here?'

'Yes.' His eyes hadn't left the body. 'I wanted to let Miss Henry know. She was . . .' He extended his arm in an empty gesture. 'She was like this.'

'What about the front door? Was it unlocked?'

'No. In the evenings I'm in the hall. When a gentleman arrives, he knocks and I let him in.' Simon saw Jane ready to speak, but made a small motion with his hand.

'Was it always that way?'

'No. Miss Henry changed it a few days ago.'

'When you escorted the gentleman out tonight, was the door locked then?'

It took the man a minute to answer.

'I don't know,' he admitted finally. 'He'd been drinking and he didn't want to leave. I had to force him out. I don't remember. I never thought . . .'

'No reason you should,' Simon assured him. 'You didn't hear anything?'

'No.' He hung his head. 'Nothing at all.'

'Why did you come to get me?'

The man drew himself up. 'Miss Henry told me that if anything happened I should go and find Mr Westow. She said you'd know what to do.' He brought a key from his waistcoat, walked over to a bureau, unlocked it and picked up a letter from the blotter. 'She said I should give this to you.'

Simon broke the seal. Just a few words written on the page in a rounded, girlish hand.

You and the girl. Find him and kill him.

Folded in with it was a draft for one hundred pounds, drawn on Beckett's Bank. He put everything in his coat.

'Did you see anyone strange outside tonight?'

'No.' He sounded certain. 'Miss Henry had told me to keep my eyes open. I never saw anyone besides the customers.'

'Right.' Simon took a final glance around the room. Perhaps something was missing, after all . . . 'Her locket. Where is it?'

The servant stared at Lizzie's neck.

'It's gone. I know she was wearing it tonight. I remember seeing it.' He looked lost and helpless. 'He must have taken it.'

'Yes,' Simon said. 'He did.'

Outside, the night wrapped around them.

'White must have arranged it all,' Simon said. 'Paid someone to go in and create a disturbance so he could pick the lock and slip inside while the servant was busy.'

'Why didn't she scream?' Jane asked. 'She must have seen him.'

'I don't know.' Simon sighed. Fear? Resignation? 'I really don't know.'

'What was in the note?'

'She wants us to find him and kill him.' A small hesitation. 'She's paying us a hundred pounds.'

'Why did you ask about the locket?'

'That's where it all began.'

Their footsteps rang off the buildings as they reached town. Somewhere close by, the bakers were already hard at work, bread in the oven ready to sell in the morning. The familiar smells of Leeds.

'Are you going to do it? Kill him, I mean,' Jane asked.

'Everyone keeps asking me that,' Simon said with regret.

'Are you?'

'No,' he answered finally. 'Not unless he doesn't give me any other choice. I'm not a killer. I'll make sure he dies at the end of a rope. By law.'

'I'd do it.' She was so certain, so casual about it, she might as well have said she needed to tie a shoelace.

'First we have to find him,' Simon reminded her. 'Let's hope Rosie can discover something at the stables.'

'I still don't really understand why he came back,' Jane said.

'He always intended to return. He's had years to savour his revenge. That's a long time. Now he wants to taste it and discover how sweet it is.'

'Why, though?'

Why. He didn't know the answer; the best he could offer was guesses. Maybe White couldn't accept that he'd been caught, that he hadn't been able to pay or lie his way out of the sentence. He'd been a criminal long before Simon had found him with the locket. An untouchable man who'd taken a very swift tumble from grace. Or perhaps it was hate and anger that drove him.

Simon understood hatred. He'd known it, he'd nurtured it since he was a boy. Hatred of the people who ran the workhouse, the factory owners who only cared about their profits, the overseers who revelled in their cruelty. Hatred was a knot in his belly. A fire that burned and never went away. It never would.

Or maybe White simply needed to prove he was still better than all of them. But pride was a stone tossed in the water. It vanished and sank.

The only one who really knew why he was doing this was White himself. And the only certain thing was that he was a very dangerous enemy to have.

'Go back to bed. We might as well have a little more sleep while we can. It's going to be a busy day.'

Jane didn't rest. She sat by the window, watching the street, seeing people start to move around with morning, ready in case the man returned. And he definitely would come back, as sure as breathing. His gaze was too intent, too set. When she saw him, she'd follow and find out exactly what he wanted.

The boys became quiet as soon as they saw their mother. She glided down the stairs wearing a deep red dress, an elaborate design in lace on the hem and at the neck. Her hair was up, gathered under a hat, rouge colouring her cheeks, her lips a bright, brilliant red.

The twins had never seen her like this before. They stared, open-mouthed and astonished, as Simon escorted her to the door.

'Good luck,' he whispered in her ear. A few seconds later, Jane slipped out too, almost hidden inside her coat.

'Well?' He turned to Richard and Amos. 'What do you think of your mother? Surprised?'

It was easy to keep Rosie in sight. She moved along the street as if it belonged to her. People parted around her. At the stable Jane stayed back, finding a space that let her see into the yard. No one had followed them, but she still kept her eyes sharp; there was one man she wanted to spot.

Five minutes and Rosie made her way out again, delicately raising her skirt above the muck and treading carefully. At the gate she looked around, winking as her gaze slid over Jane. Back towards home.

Dressed that way, everything about Rosie changed, Jane thought. She held herself differently, walked with all the confidence of money and position, as if she didn't have a care to bother her. The only thing she couldn't alter was her face, but the cosmetics tried hard.

She was still trying to puzzle it out, to understand why and how, as they turned on to Swinegate and she caught something – a small movement, a glimpse of a face – from the corner of her eye. Him. Back again. He was trying to look invisible, but he didn't possess the knack of it.

His eyes were fixed on the house. He hadn't noticed Rosie yet. Another ten yards, though . . .

Jane sped up until she was just behind her and hissed: 'Don't go in the front. Someone's watching.'

The smallest of nods. Rosie didn't break stride. The man saw her, kept his gaze on her as she went past the house and along the street. It gave Jane time to find a place to watch the watcher.

'Why did you use the back door?' Simon asked as Rosie came in, pulling the hat off her head and letting down her hair.

'Someone's outside. Jane told me.'

'Did he spot her?'

She started to laugh. 'Come on, Simon. You know better than that.'

The boys were sitting at the table, drawing in chalk on pieces of slate. She bent over them, asking what each picture was, praising them, ruffling their hair before she turned back to him.

'I did what we said. Told him my horse had been stolen, and someone had seen it in his yard. At first, he didn't know whether to believe me or not. But he did say someone called Black had brought it. Mr Black.' She repeated the name. 'Recently returned to England from a spell in the Indies, it seems.' Rosie raised an eyebrow. 'He's paid for a week, hasn't been back since. The poor stable lad was almost falling over his feet to help. He showed me the animal as soon as I asked.' She grinned as she recalled it. 'About all I could do was keep nodding and hope I looked as if I knew what he was talking about.'

'What did you do when he finished?'

'I gave him a penny and told him to give Mr Black a message from me. To tell him that Miss Henry desires the return of what was taken from her. He'd know where to find me.' She grinned with satisfaction and twirled around the floor. 'What do you think?'

'Lizzie Henry?' Simon stood and wrapped his arms around her. 'That was an inspired touch. The dead visiting our friend, Mr Black.'

For a fleeting moment he could see the woman in her parlour, eyes wide, fixed on nothing. Wanting him to make White pay for her death.

'I even made him repeat the name so he wouldn't forget it.' She sighed and pulled away. 'I'm going to change. I never feel like myself dressed up like this.' At the door she turned. 'What are we going to do about the one outside?'

'Leave it to Jane. She'll take care of it.'

One hour of standing, then another, until her legs ached the way they had when she was a doffer girl in the mill. The man hardly moved, more like a statue than a person. But if he could do it, so could she.

SIXTEEN

I t was easy enough to leave the back way. Through the
ginnels, one leading to another, then out to Briggate along
the yards. Simon gave a small grunt of satisfaction and
crossed Leeds Bridge into Hunslet.

The houses were grim, the factories grinding as he marched
along the streets. He hadn't wanted to come over here. He and
Gerrold Peters had stood on opposite sides of the law for too long.
But needs must, and the devil was driving him across the river.
The man might be able to help. For a fee.

Peters was a sneak thief. He'd spot an open window, an unlocked
door, then slide quietly into the house and carry away every small
item of value he could cram in his pockets. He'd sell them on to
a fence, or back to the owner through a thief-taker.

The man was careful. No single thing he stole was worth much,
not enough to make a householder pay for a prosecution. Still, he
managed to make enough to sketch a life, not rich but not poor,
either. Middling.

And Peters knew a few things about Leeds better than anyone
else. Who lived where, what guests they had, when they were
likely to be out. Everything was stored away in his head. It was
his business, and he took care of it scrupulously. His freedom
depended on good information.

He had a small, tidy house, close to the pottery on Jack Lane. The
garden was his pride, always carefully tended. Shoots were poking
through the dark, rich soil. By summer he'd have a fine display of
flowers, colourful and brilliant.

Peters answered the door himself, looking down his long, straight
nose and snorting as soon as he saw his visitor.

'If you're here looking for something, you're out of luck. I've
been poorly.'

'You won't have been earning, then.'

Peters shrugged. He was tall, elegantly thin, his hair combed
forward to hide the way it was receding up his forehead.

'Not any concern of yours, is it?'

'It might be. I could put some money in your pocket.'

He spat. 'Is that right? And why would you want to do that, *Mister* Westow? Concerned about my welfare all of a sudden, are you?'

'Information,' Simon told him. 'I'm looking for someone.'

'Then good luck to you.' He began to close the door. Simon stuck out his boot and leaned his weight against the wood.

'I'm not here to pass the time. You can help me and I'll be grateful. Or the next time I catch you with something stolen, I might swear out a complaint myself with the magistrate and pay for the prosecution. Imagine this garden of yours growing wild for seven years.'

'You couldn't afford it.'

Simon smiled. 'Are you sure you want to wager on that? I'm a man who cherishes his grudges.'

Peters shook his head. He was bright enough to know when he was beaten. 'What do you want, Westow?'

'You know who's staying where.'

'I told you, I've not been well the last few days.'

'But you can find out.'

'I suppose so.'

'You can,' Simon insisted.

'Don't beat around the bush. What do you want to know?'

'Do you remember Julius White?'

'Hard to forget, wasn't he?'

'He's back. I want to know where he is. He's staying somewhere in town.'

'No.'

'I'll pay you five pounds.' It was far more than any working man could earn in a month. More than generous, and Peters knew it. His eyes shone with greed.

'That's all you want, to know where he is?'

'And to make sure it's true. I'll pay when I know you're not lying.'

After a moment, Peters nodded. Simon knew the man too well: given half a chance he'd pass on a false address and pocket the money.

'I need to know today.'

'It'll take me a while. I told you—'

'I know what you said. And you heard what I'm offering. I'll come back at six.'

'Make it seven.'

'I'll be here.' He glared at Peters. 'You'd better not let me down.'

Simon wasn't going to put all his faith in Gerrold Peters. White had to be showing himself in order to hire people. Yet nobody admitted they'd seen him. The bastard wasn't invisible, unless he'd learned some trick from the natives in Australia. And whatever magic they might have wouldn't work in England.

There were too many beershops and gin palaces in Leeds to ask in every one. But wherever he went, no one remembered seeing a man with a face burned by the sun.

He went home frustrated, eyes moving along Swinegate until he picked out the man watching the house. At least he'd be surprised.

Jane saw Simon walk along, unlock his front door and disappear inside. For a moment, all the watcher could do was stare. Then he scuttled away and she began to move, glad to work the ache out of her knees.

Following him was easy. He never even glanced round to see who was behind. He didn't seem to notice much at all as he tried to push his way through the crowds on Briggate. Market day and the place was thronged with women hunting for bargains and the cheapest prices. None of them paid attention to a girl in an old coat and a shawl over her head. She might as well not have existed.

He was stupid, she thought, keeping to the main streets when ducking through the courts and ginnels would have been quicker. Jane stayed well back, never letting him out of her sight. Down the Head Row, across Vicar Lane. Along to Mill Garth, and finally Lady Lodge, close to the rickety bridge over Sheepscar Beck. He knocked. A moment later he was gone.

'That's excellent work,' Simon told her. 'No one saw you?'

'Why would they?' Jane replied. 'There was nobody behind me.'

'Who lives there?' Rosie asked. 'I know I've seen the place. Whoever owns it must have some money.'

He didn't know. But Peters would, and he'd be seeing the man in a few hours. Lady Lodge wasn't far from Black Flags Lane; White could have walked back there in five minutes, before anyone discovered Lizzie Henry's body.

The hands on the clock always moved more slowly when he was waiting. Time seem to take forever to trickle away. Finally it was twenty to seven and he pulled on his coat and hat.

'Is anyone watching?' he called up the stairs.

'No,' Jane shouted back from the attic.

He was ready to go.

Even down on Jack Lane, he could hear the parish church tolling the hour. Peters was waiting for him.

'Well?' Simon asked.

'He's at Lady Lodge.'

At least he could be certain the man was telling him the truth. No point asking how he'd found out; Peters would never tell. Sources, secrets, information. They were the real gold in this business, and people guarded them closely.

'Whose house is it?'

'Belongs to Mr Madeley.'

'I don't know him.' He'd never even heard the name before.

'Rich man.' Peters shrugged. 'Someone told me he has a stake in a mill. Put up a lot of the money, but kept it very quiet.'

'Which one?'

'Milner's.'

That was interesting. Worth five pounds all by itself. Milner's daughter kidnapped and White a guest of his business partner. Something was wrong there. Very wrong.

'What's the best way to get into the Lodge?'

The man snorted. 'Don't want much for your money, do you? You've got what we agreed. You'll find out I was telling the truth.'

'I already know you were. Maybe it'll become a habit.'

Jane had followed him. He hadn't asked, and she'd stayed far enough away that Simon would never even know. She'd had her own dealings with Peters, and knew better than to trust him.

But no one hid in the shadows. As Simon left the house she melted away. No need for him ever to know she'd been here.

*   *   *

'We need a proper look at the house.' He chewed the last of the tripe and pushed his plate away.

'I could go over tonight,' Jane said.

'No,' Rosie said. 'If White's had that message from the stables he'll be on his guard.' She was silent for a moment. 'You know, it makes sense now. White wants to lure us out to Lady Lodge. I started to wonder about that lad watching this place. He was standing outside, plain as day. We couldn't have missed him if we'd tried. Then he went straight over there.'

'Why would he do that?' Simon asked.

She rolled her eyes. 'For God's sake, Simon, think about it for a moment. It's a trap. You break in, you're caught. The owner of the house claims you've stolen something, prosecutes, and that's it. You'll end up where White was for seven years and he'll be sitting here laughing.'

As soon as she said it, Simon could see it clearly. Stupid. He should have known better. Instead, his mind had been concentrated on finding the man. This had every hallmark of White. Devious as the devil himself. Thank God Rosie's brain was working properly; his certainly wasn't.

'What do we do, then?' he asked. 'How do we catch him?'

'He has to come out sometime,' Jane said.

SEVENTEEN

Nobody spying on the place as he left home. Simon marched briskly all the way to Milner's house, his anger rising with each step, and hammered on the front door until the servant answered.

'Is he home?'

'Mr Milner is here.'

'Tell him we need to talk. It's important.'

He waited in the small library. It was a man's room, dark and heavy, looking out over a small back garden. Not too many books on the shelves, authors with strange names that Simon didn't recognize: Tacitus, Herodotus. Cicero, Bede. He was studying the spines when Milner entered, his face like thunder.

'You'd better have a good reason for coming here.'

'I do. You'd better sit down, Mr Milner.'

'And to the front where people will see you—'

'I said sit down.' He barely raised his voice, but it was enough to shut the man up.

'What do you want?'

'You own a mill. That's right, isn't it?'

'Of course it is.' Milner glared. 'Everyone knows that. Why have you come to—'

'Who else owns it with you?'

'No one,' Milner snapped. 'Don't be a damned fool.'

Simon took a pace forward. He was younger, bigger, stronger. 'I said who else?' he asked quietly.

'A gentleman named Madeley.' His look could have burned Simon on the spot.

'Just him?'

'Yes. My name's on it, and I own one third of it.' Milner seemed to have to drag the admission out from deep inside.

'Has your partner tried to buy you out?'

'He's suggested it once or twice. I've always said no.'

'I think he's stopped taking that for an answer, Mr Milner. Where are your wife and daughter?'

'What does that—?'

'Where are they?' Simon spoke slowly, a careful emphasis on each word.

'They're in York, staying with some relatives of my wife. She thought it would help their nerves.'

Out of the way. Good.

'Where did you get the money for Hannah's ransom?'

'From the bank.'

'How much do you have left in there?'

'That's none of your business.'

'If you want it back, it's very much my business, Mr Milner. The man who took your daughter is staying with your business partner.'

For a few seconds, the room stayed silent. The colour rose in Milner's face and his eyes began to bulge.

A decanter stood on the desk. Simon sniffed it, poured a glass and placed it in Milner's hand, making him drink.

'Bastard,' he said finally. 'How did you know?'

'I guessed. How long has he been trying to buy you out?'

'A year or so, I suppose.'

'Is the factory making money?'

'It gets by, but it needs more investment. New machines.' He turned and looked at Simon. 'I don't have the money to put into it.'

'Does Madeley know that?'

Milner shook his head. 'No.' A small hesitation. 'I didn't think he did.' He sighed. 'Maybe I was wrong.'

'When did he last approach you with an offer?'

'The day after Hannah . . .' He corrected himself. 'After you brought Hannah home.'

He'd expected something like that. The timing was right. But Milner's new humility was a bonus. Now the bluster had gone, perhaps they could find something useful.

'How much money do you have?'

The man gave a wan smile. 'Nothing. Two hundred, maybe. The thousand took almost everything.'

Two hundred was hardly nothing. It could keep most families alive for years.

'You own property.'

'It's all mortgaged.'

'Does Madeley know?'

'No.' He considered his answer. 'I don't know; maybe he does. Did he really arrange my daughter's abduction?'

'I think it's likely that he had a hand in it,' Simon said. 'And he had the perfect person to carry it out.'

'This Julius White man?'

'Yes. White wants money. More than that, he wants his revenge on the people responsible for his transportation. He's already begun.'

'What?' Milner blinked. He was looking dazed, stunned by what he'd learned. Hardly surprising. The whole world was crashing down around him and there was nothing he could do to stop it. 'What do you mean?'

'Did you hear about Miss Henry?' The man nodded. 'Years ago, she prosecuted White for the theft of a locket. That's why he was sent to Australia.'

'Then why don't you go in and take him? You said you know where he is.'

'Tell me, is your business simple and straightforward?' Simon asked.

'No. Of course not.'

'Neither is mine.'

He needed proof, something so solid that a good lawyer couldn't tear it apart in court. And so far he had nothing at all. White's letter to the newspapers was artfully phrased. He could argue he meant justice by law. And there was nothing at all to show he'd been out on Black Flags Lane. If he tried to find the men who'd followed him on White's orders, Simon knew he'd discover that they'd vanished or died.

'What are you going to do? I want my money back.' Milner gazed at the floor. 'I need it.'

'I have an idea.'

A walk out to a silent house, and a quiet word.

'Do you want revenge for your mistress's murder?'

'Yes,' the man said. 'I do.'

'I might be able to give you that chance soon.'

'Just tell me where and when.'

'Milner's going to send a letter to Madeley suggesting they meet at the factory tonight to discuss things.'

'What are we going to do?' Rosie asked. Simon had brought a pair of wooden toys home from the market, and the boys were playing noisily in the front parlour as the three of them sat in the kitchen and talked.

'I'll be at that meeting.' He turned to Jane. 'I want you to see who comes with Madeley and waits outside.'

She nodded. 'Do you think White will be there?'

'He's not going to show his face that easily. He'll stay at Lady Lodge.'

'Then how does that help us?' Rosie said.

Simon smiled. 'We're going to do something he doesn't expect and see what happens.'

The machines stood idle, dozens of them lined up on the factory floor. What would it be like in here during the day? Simon wondered. An ocean of noise. It would be impossible for the workers to speak. People learned to read lips, he knew that; it was the only way they could communicate. Twelve hours of standing and they went home each night half-deaf, worked to the bone.

The air was heavy with a mix of scents: wool, lanolin, oil, and the stale sweat that seemed to have soaked into the building.

In the offices, things were different. Sparse and cold for the clerks, wooden desks and hard benches, then a plush, decorated office for Milner, with a carpet over polished floorboards, a large desk and a window that looked out towards the river and the hills off to the south.

Simon picked up a chair and moved it to the corner. Madeley wouldn't see him when he entered. Milner sat behind his desk, but he couldn't settle, no sooner down than he was up again. Pacing to the window, staring for a few seconds, then back again.

The longclock ticked off the minutes to seven. Finally the hour began to strike, and the chimes faded. A short while later, Simon heard footsteps along the corridor. The door opened and Madeley came hurrying into the room.

'John, I'm glad you finally want to talk about this.'

He wasn't an imposing man. Small, stout, a full head of curly brown hair revealed as he removed his hat. There was nothing menacing about him, not even a single thing that was memorable. There were hundreds just like him around Leeds. He was better-dressed, but otherwise he would have faded instantly into a crowd.

Milner swallowed. His gaze darted around the room. 'We have to discuss it sometime.'

'And why not now, eh?' Madeley sat, crossing one plump leg over the other and placing the hat in his lap. 'We need to spend capital on this place. You know that.'

'We're doing well as we are.' His voice quavered. Still Simon stayed perfectly still, not a word, not a movement, listening and watching.

'But we could do better.' Madeley was full of enthusiasm. 'We could do so much better. If we spend money on these new machines, we can let a quarter of the employees go. Think of the savings in wages, man. By itself, that will pay for everything in two years. We'll be able to produce more cloth, and sell more. You know it's sensible.'

'You don't understand the business,' Milner said.

'I know how to make money. And I'll have you to advise me; I'll pay you well for your services.'

'Is everything money to you?' Simon asked as he rose from the chair. Madeley jerked his head round in surprise, then turned back to Milner.

'Who's this? I thought it was just going to be you and me.'

'Let's say I know the man who's staying with you at the moment.'

'What?' He tried to stand, but Simon placed a firm hand on his shoulder.

'You're here and you want to talk, so why don't we do that? We can talk about Julius White.'

'I don't know who you mean. I came here in good faith—'

'You came here because you smelled money,' Simon corrected him. 'You see the chance to grab all of Mr Milner's business and you're happy to take it. What kind of terms did you propose?'

'Fair ones. Very fair.' All the heartiness had vanished from his voice. Simon leant close enough to smell the fear.

'A good gesture would be to return the thousand pounds your guest stole from Mr Milner.'

'I told you, I don't have anyone staying with me.' What did he believe? Simon wondered. That if he said it enough he'd be able to convince everyone?

'I know the truth, Mr Madeley, so let's take that as understood, shall we? And also that you know your partner here doesn't have a great deal of money at present. A thousand less, in fact, thanks to Julius White.'

'I don't—' He shut up as Simon's fingers pressed down on tender flesh.

'We have an interesting predicament,' he continued. 'You have a guest who's a kidnapper, a thief and a murderer.'

'He's not.'

Simon smiled. 'You see, we're beginning to get somewhere already. You're admitting that he's staying with you. But you keep dangerous company.'

'He's—'

Simon cut him off. 'A thief, a kidnapper and a murderer. I know exactly who he is. But I couldn't understand why he'd chosen to snatch Hannah Milner until I learned about you and that you wanted to buy out your partner.'

'I didn't know he'd done that,' Madeley said.

'No? I'll be very interested to hear you prove that in court. I don't think it'll take a jury long to understand the connections. And it's a very short trip from the cell to the noose.'

'It had nothing to do with me.' The sweat stood out on his face.

'I've already told you, we'll see about that. After all, we have you here, and it won't take long for Mr Milner to go and swear out a warrant with the magistrate. Have you ever been in the gaol?' All the man could do was shake his head. 'You won't like it, believe me. No comforts and plenty of low company. And you'd be surprised how long it can take for a case to come to trial.'

Milner had kept silent, staring at Madeley with eyes full of fury. Leave the pair of them together and one could end up dead.

'I think you'll agree that we have a dilemma,' Simon said. 'I don't know you, it's nothing to me whether you dance for the hangman or not. I want Julius White.'

'And any attempt to buy me out stops immediately,' Milner added.

'Yes, yes.' The man couldn't speak quickly enough. 'Of course.'

'That's a start. You see, it's easy once we all agree. Now, let's move on to the big question. How are you going to deliver your friend to me?'

'Me?' He looked up at Simon. 'I can't do that.'

'Then you don't seem to understand. You can and you will. It's as simple as that. It's either that or your life. I don't know what kind of hold he has over you, but I'm sure putting it this way makes your choice easier.'

'He'll kill me.'

'No, he won't,' Simon said. 'He won't have the chance.'

'How?' Madeley asked. 'You can't protect me.'

Simon brought his face close enough to smell the man's breath.

'You'd better pray that I can.'

By the time they left the factory, Simon had the information he needed. Madeley had sketched the layout of his house, marking the room where White was staying and the ways in and out of the place.

'Was he there when you left?' Simon asked.

'Yes. Him and the cook.'

'Now come with me. I'm going to make sure you're safe.'

That was the easy part. Jane was waiting outside. With her on one side and Simon on the other, they walked to the house on Swinegate. The children were in bed. Rosie was waiting for them.

'Let me warn you,' Simon said to Madeley. 'You need to stay on your best behaviour. If I were you, I wouldn't try anything stupid. My wife used to work with me. She's far deadlier than I am.'

The man looked at her as if he couldn't believe a woman might be dangerous.

'He's right,' she said with a cold smile, slipping her knife from its sheath. 'And I've a much shorter temper.'

'I need your keys,' Simon said.

'My keys? Why?'

'Why do you think? To get into your house.'

Meekly, he handed them over.

They hurried along Vicar Lane. Leeds was alive with people. Saturday night and the beershops were full. Payday, and men hoped to find oblivion for a few hours. A group of them staggered down the middle of the road, laughing and singing, oblivious to the horses and carts nudging around them.

When Milner's servant first came to him, Simon had never expected any of this. He'd never been asked to find a person before, but Hannah was legally her father's property. It was his job. It was what he did. It had seemed straightforward enough, to find the girl who'd been taken and deliver her home.

And all along, White had been the puppet master, pulling the strings to make them all dance. But he couldn't have known that in the beginning. White had led them all along a path, then that road had turned. Left, right, back on itself, until all the twists dizzied him.

Once he learned about the connection between White and Madeley, everything started to make sense. Yet even now, Simon wondered how much he still didn't know. There had to be more. All the relationships were tangled and knotted. Business, obligation, strange friendships and enemies. But there'd be time to slice through them all later, once White was in jail and waiting for his trial.

Simon didn't turn by the workhouse at the top of Lady Lane. From the corner of his eye, he saw Jane looking curiously at him. But she stayed silent, keeping pace as he started out along Black Flags Lane.

'How are we going to take him?' she asked finally.

He patted the keys, hearing them jangle in his pocket.

'We're going through the front door, just as if we own the place.'

'Someone needs to cover the back.'

'Don't worry about that.' He nodded towards Lizzie Henry's house. 'I've taken care of it.'

The servant was waiting. His face was grim as he marched stiffly beside them, listening closely as Simon gave his orders. A sword clattered against his leg and the handle of a pistol protruded from his pocket.

'Don't kill him,' Simon said. The man simply stared and gave no answer. 'I mean it. He can hang for murder.'

A lamp burned in one of the rooms at Lady Lodge, the shutters still open, casting a faint light out into the garden. Simon stayed in the shadows, Jane close behind him. There was no sign of White through the window.

The key turned easily in the lock, and the door opened silently. Stepping into the hall, Simon took out his knife. He gestured, and Jane moved toward the rooms upstairs.

There was no reason for White to expect them. A little luck and they'd take him swiftly and cleanly.

The map Madeley had drawn was clear in his mind. Simon felt his heart thumping, the knife hilt slick in his hand as he tested each door until he came to the lit room.

A fire burned invitingly in the grate. The lamp stood on a small, delicate table, and next to it, a glass of wine. A book lay open, face down, on a chair. But no sign of Julius White.

Simon felt the prickle of fear rise up his spine. The man knew. He was prepared. He was waiting somewhere in the house for them.

He climbed the stairs, testing each tread before he put his weight

on it, then along the hall. Turned the handle of White's room. In
the faint light through the window, he could see it was empty.

From door to door. Nobody.

He couldn't hear Jane moving around.

Finally, only one door remained. It was ajar, a faint light inside.
Simon took a deep breath and pushed it open.

EIGHTEEN

The low glow of a banked fire. Just enough to make out
the shapes in the corner. One large. The other smaller,
with the shine of steel at her throat.

'Drop the knife.' It was a rough voice. Definitely Leeds, but
there was something else, something strange overlaying it. At first,
Simon didn't move. Then White tightened his grip on Jane's hair,
pulling her head back to show more of her neck.

Simon let the weapon fall to the floor.

'Good. Now the one in your boot.'

He had no choice. White had already killed Lizzie Henry. He
wouldn't give a second thought to murdering Jane.

Simon took it out and laid it on the carpet. White had said
nothing about the knife hidden in his sleeve. Maybe he didn't
know it existed. That offered him a chance . . .

'It's a long way to come for revenge, Julius. A long wait, too.'

'Makes it all the more pleasurable when it happens.' A dark
smile that didn't reach his eyes. They were cold, hard, glittering
in the firelight. 'I've enjoyed watching you run around, acting like
you knew what you were doing.'

'And now you've got me here.'

'It was always just a matter of time. When I was ready for
you.'

'You've done a fine job of preparation.'

White bobbed his head at the compliment.

'Don't worry, Westow, your part in this little play will soon be
over. After that, there's just your wife, then I'll be on my way as
quietly as I came.'

The voice, Simon thought. It was almost an Irish lilt over the local accent. A voice that was impossible to miss.

'You think it'll be that easy?'

'I know it will be. You really should have learned by now, Mr Westow. I'm always three steps ahead of you. I always intended to come back and do this. You were never going to come out on top.'

Simon's chest felt tight. He wasn't going to let anything happen to Rosie or the boys. He couldn't afford to let White win.

He had Jane. Simon daren't risk her life. He could see a mix of faith and fear in her eyes. The belief he could get them out of this alive. The hint of a chance, and he'd do that. White's body looked hard and muscled, still brown from all the sun in Australia. But he'd have spent half a year on a ship coming home, then a few more months in Leeds. He'd have softened, slowed.

'Do you think you know the truth about everything that happened nine years ago?'

'I'm certain I do,' Simon said.

White raised an eyebrow. 'But what if you don't? Just because you're so sure doesn't mean you're right. Lizzie Henry could have had that servant killed as revenge for stealing. It wouldn't be the first time.'

'She was raped, too.'

White shrugged. 'The murderer could have done that.'

'He did. It was you. And the man you claimed you bought the locket from never existed.'

'But what if he did? Consider that.'

Suddenly White pushed Jane away, a hard shove. He meant her to crash into Simon, to send them both sprawling to the floor. The words had been a distraction, nothing more. But Simon was quicker. He slid to the side and pulled the knife from his sleeve.

'Perhaps you're not as far ahead as you think.'

Jane fell. She rolled, then sprang straight back on her feet. The weapons Simon had placed on the floor were in her hands, grim fury on her face.

'Two against one,' Simon told him. 'Things change very quickly. Not really three steps at all.'

White's eyes darted from one of them to the other.

'You can hurt one of us,' Simon told him, 'but the other will kill you. And I don't think you came back here to die.'

White smiled. 'What's my choice?'

'This afternoon Milner visited the magistrate and swore out a warrant on you for taking his daughter.'

The man nodded slowly. 'I'm not a fool.' He dropped his knife.

'Search him,' Simon told Jane.

She was thorough. Pockets, boots, sleeve. The edge of her knife rested against his cheek. As she finished, she slid it down and stood back to watch the blood begin to form and trickle over his flesh. White just stood, impassive. Nothing to read in his eyes.

'You should tell the judge what you did for all those rich men in the past. It might save you from the noose.'

White stared. 'I don't peach.' He spat and smiled. 'No need.'

Bravado, Simon thought. It was over for him now.

'It's time to go, Julius. After all, it won't be the first night you've spent in a cell.'

He didn't resist. The only time he hesitated was on the step, as Simon locked the door. Lizzie Henry's servant stood there, waiting for them.

'Mr White is going to the gaol,' Simon said. 'Perhaps you'd like to escort him.'

'I'd be very happy to do that.' The man's mouth twisted into a crooked grin.

'Remember what I told you. I want him alive to stand trial,' he warned. 'Don't let him escape. The rest is up to you. He's not armed.'

'Wouldn't matter much if he was. He won't be getting away. You can trust me on that.' Casually, as if it was nothing, he kicked White between his legs, smiling with satisfaction as he crumpled. 'On your feet,' he ordered. 'We've got a way to go, and you're not going to enjoy the journey.'

Jane watched them go. The servant dragged White along. The anger spat and burned inside her. She'd let herself be caught. She'd let herself be taken.

'We should have killed him,' she said.

'I told you I wouldn't do that unless I had to,' Simon reminded her. 'He surrendered. It's better this way – everything will be legal when he hears the hanging psalm. It won't be long now.' He looked at her. 'I will say this: if he'd hurt you, he'd be dead already.'

'I was stupid.'

'You're alive. Just be glad of that.'

But it didn't seem like comfort. She'd cut White, she'd felt the knife slice through his skin. It wasn't enough. She wanted to watch the last breath leave him, to see the blood boil from his throat.

She'd been careful entering the room. Alert for any sound, any movement. She hadn't even had a sense of anyone in there. No smell, nothing at all. He'd appeared behind her like a ghost, grabbing her hair in one hand and putting the knife to her throat with the other. No chance to fight back. No chance to do anything.

He'd made her weak. She could never forgive that.

'Do you think he'll really deliver White to the gaol?' The pair had vanished into the blackness.

'Probably.' She knew it was as much as Simon was going to say. If White vanished, he wasn't the one responsible. His hands would be clean.

They began the walk back into town. Soon enough they were surrounded by the abandon of Saturday night. Raucous laughs and bloody faces. Wild eyes and men shouting. A woman's wild cackle. She'd never understood it. For her, it was no different from every other night of the week. People would die, people would be born. Folk would spend their money and wake the next morning with nothing to show for it but a sore head and an empty purse. It didn't seem to be much of a way to live a life.

'Did Milner really take out the warrant?' Jane asked.

'He did. Once we go through White's things, I daresay we'll find Lizzie Henry's locket, so we can add murder to the charges.' He let out a low breath. 'He won't be able to escape that.' He turned to her. 'How do you feel?'

'I'm fine.' She hadn't been scared. Just resigned. Angry at her own failure. He'd been better than her. She'd been helpless, overpowered. Exactly the way she'd felt with her father on top of her. The way she swore she'd never feel again.

She'd have done the world a favour if she'd slit White's throat instead of his cheek.

Two men lay head to toe, passed out on the gutter at the edge of Briggate. Jane could hear the sound of a fight somewhere, the roar of men urging each other on. Leeds was alive on drink.

As Simon closed the door behind them, it all receded. Rosie hurried through from the kitchen, anxious, mouth opening with relief to see them both alive and unhurt. Jane stood aside as she embraced her husband, running her fingertips down her cheek.

'Is he . . .?'

'He should be in a cell now.'

Rosie closed her eyes for a moment, then exhaled. 'It's over?'

'Yes.' As much as it could ever be over until White was on the gallows with a rope around his neck.

Without a word, Jane left them, climbing the stairs to the attic room. She wouldn't cry. She didn't cry. By now she knew how to keep it all inside, never to let the world see a single thing.

Madeley sat with a glass of wine in front of him, the bottle half-empty on the kitchen table. He looked up as Simon came in.

'You don't have a guest any longer,' Simon said. 'It's safe to go home now.' He took out the keys and tossed them to the man. 'I appreciate your help.'

He gave a snort. 'I didn't have much choice, did I? Where is he?'

'In gaol.'

'We've had an interesting talk while you were gone.' Rosie's voice sounded too bright for the room. For the night. 'Mr Madeley definitely won't be pushing to buy his partner out of the factory any more. He even signed a document to say so.'

Simon nodded. He knew it wasn't even worth the cost of paper and ink. The man could always claim he'd been forced to sign. But it was something.

'It's Sunday tomorrow. Court won't sit until Monday. I'll come and search White's belongings in the morning. Did he bring much?'

'No,' Madeley answered. 'Hardly anything at all.' He hesitated. 'Are you certain it's safe?'

'I am. What hold did White have over you?'

The man held his gaze for a moment, then looked down at the floor.

'Ten years ago I had some problems. A man was trying to blackmail me. Someone told me about White. I went to see him and the man never came back.'

'Did White murder him?' Simon asked.

'I didn't ask. The man never returned, that's all I know.'

And what he didn't know couldn't weigh on his conscience.

'How much did you pay White?'

'Enough.'

'There's no such thing for a man like him,' Simon said.

'Maybe not. He turned up three months ago. He must have just come back from Australia. He said he needed somewhere to stay for a few days.'

'You could have refused.'

Madeley shook his head. 'You don't say no to someone like that.'

Not when he knew so much that you didn't want out in the open.

'How long did those few days become?'

'A week. Then he was back six weeks later. He needed some ready money, he said.'

'And you had the idea of putting pressure on Milner by kidnapping his daughter.'

'Yes,' Madeley admitted quietly.

'Never mind. It's all over now.'

The man stood, and gave a small bow towards Rosie. 'I can't say it's been pleasant to meet you, Mr Westow. But it's been instructive.'

'I'll be there in the morning.'

Simon needed to sleep. His body was exhausted, muscles aching after the night. His mind was drained, thoughts swirling emptily. Rosie was curled up against his chest, his arm around her shoulders.

'What happened tonight?'

He was warm, comfortable, starting to drift.

'I'll tell you when it's light.'

Jane sat on her bed. She'd failed. Again and again, she went through every single detail, sifting the pictures in her head, trying to understand how White had taken her by surprise. But she couldn't find an explanation. He wasn't there; she knew she was alone in that room. And then, before she even knew it, she felt his hand and smelled his breath and the pressure of a blade at her neck.

The candle flickered, throwing shadows around the attic. She pushed up the sleeve of her dress. Took the knife, forcing it down slowly against her skin. A thin line. The dark bloom, looking as deep as the night. She felt it. The release, the guilt. Once, twice, three times. She watched as the blood trickled down her arm. She'd failed. She deserved this. She needed to be punished.

Simon woke rested and calm, and stretched in the bed. Rosie and the boys were downstairs, bustling round the kitchen. Sunlight leaked through the shutters. By the time he left the house, the day was mild, just a few light clouds hanging in the sky.

Sabbath morning, and Leeds was quiet. Soon enough, the bells would begin to peal for service. The parish church, St John's, Holy Trinity, a clamour of them for the faithful. For now, though, there were few people around, nothing more than a carriage or two on the road. By afternoon, couples would be promenading up and down Briggate. Groups of young men would gather to flirt with girls. Probably the way it had been since the town was first here.

But for him, it was a day of business.

Jane had left the house before he'd even risen.

'She was very quiet,' Rosie said. 'Hardly said a word.'

'She's always that way.'

'This was more than usual. She looked as if she hadn't slept. And she kept rubbing her forearm. I asked if she'd hurt herself, but she just drew back like she'd been scalded.'

Simon didn't know. He couldn't begin to understand. She was a strange one. She took some things so deep to her heart while others flowed over her. Everyone made mistakes. He accepted his. He learned from them. But in this trade, he knew, any mistake could be the last.

White had gambled. The way he pushed Jane, he was so certain she'd send Simon tumbling. He'd failed, too. He didn't know about the knife on Simon's arm. And so he'd lost. It could so easily have gone the other way. Dwelling on it wasn't going to help. You took the good fortune that came.

'Did she say where she was going?'

Rosie snorted. 'Does she ever? Ate some bread and left. The boys weren't even up.'

*   *   *

Lady Lodge looked bonny in the sun. Peaceful. The grass around it was a brilliant spring green, and the light fell flatteringly on the stones. Beyond it, Sheepscar Beck burbled and sang over the rocks. He could almost have been in the middle of the countryside.

Turn around, though, and the truth stood stark. The manufactories loomed like castles. Houses were packed tight against each other. Chimneys stabbed at the sky. No smoke, a day of rest today, but tomorrow it would all return, as dark and awful as ever.

Madeley looked as though he'd spent a restless night. His clothes were clean and fresh, a sober, churchgoing suit, white stock carefully tied at the neck, trousers tight in the fashion, and boots with a glistening shine, but he seemed anxious, eager for Simon to be done and gone, as if that might erase everything that had happened.

'I'll take you up to his room.' No small talk, not a smile.

The windows gave a view over the slope down to the water and the hills rising in the distance. The bed was neatly made. A bureau, a small table with a basin and ewer. A worn pannier lay over the back of a chair. Simon tipped out the contents. A purse with a few coins. Some letters that he pocketed. And there, fastened behind a small flap, Lizzie Henry's locket. With that, and her servant's testimony, no jury could fail to convict, on top of the kidnapping charge. And no judge dare give less than a death sentence. All the influence in Leeds couldn't buy him out of it now.

But there was more. He knew there was more. The ransom White had taken from Milner. His eyes searched around the room. Two minutes later, he had the leather bag in his hand. Hidden behind the carving on top of the wardrobe. Simple, obvious. Inside, more bank notes than he'd ever seen in his life. At home, he'd count then, take out the two hundred guineas of his fee, and return them to Milner.

Madeley was waiting impatiently by the door, hat in his hand, ready to leave for church.

'Did you find what you wanted?'

'I did. You can rest assured. Julius White is going to swing.' Simon saw the relief on the man's face and leaned closer. 'And if you're lucky, he won't implicate you.'

He left before Madeley could say a word. Let him think about that as he sat on a pew. Maybe it would make his prayers more fervent.

*   *   *

Simon strolled back along Vicar Lane. He felt satisfied – he had everything he needed to see White face justice. And he'd earned every penny of his fee. Last night he'd come closer to death than he'd ever known in this work. Jane had stood on the brink and stared over the edge of it. But they'd both survived. They were here. They'd see tomorrow and the days that came after.

He raised his head as someone called his name. George Mudie was hurrying along in his fat man's waddle, waving his stick and shouting.

'You want to be careful, George,' Simon said. 'You'll do yourself an injury.'

'I've been looking for you. Have you heard the news?' he wheezed as he came to a stop, hands resting on his knees as he caught his breath.

'About White? He was arrested last night.'

Mudie's eyes widened and he shook his head wildly. 'No, not that. He was up before the magistrate a few minutes ago.'

'What?' That was impossible. No court sat on the Sabbath. He'd never heard of it. 'Which magistrate?'

'Hardisty.' Mudie had caught his breath. 'I don't know who arranged it, but they opened up the Moot Hall.'

'It can't be. You must have heard it wrong. Who was there to prosecute?' Simon asked. Someone must have been. Milner had brought the complaint. His lawyer must have known.

'No one,' Mudie answered. 'Just White and the judge.'

'That's . . .' It couldn't be legal, he was certain of that.

'It's what I heard.' He hesitated a moment. 'Hardisty said that since the prosecution hadn't put a case, White was free to go. He walked out of the courtroom.'

It couldn't happen. Not in England. This wasn't the law. But Mudie was serious. Someone had given the magistrate his orders or a bribe, and he'd done as he was told. But now Julius White was back on the streets. Now he understood what the man had said the night before. No need to peach. Not when things could be arranged.

'Where's Hardisty?' He turned back, ready to run to the Moot Hall.

'He left Leeds straight afterwards. A relative who's ill, he said. I saw him ride away myself.'

Sweet God, he thought. Rosie. The boys. Jane. Milner. Madeley. Too many people were in danger.

'I need to go.' He shook Mudie's hand. 'Thank you, George. I'm glad you found me.'

'Did you find—' Rosie began. Then she saw the look on Simon's face. 'What is it? What's happened?'

'White's been released.'

She stood, stunned. Exactly the way he felt.

'But . . . how?'

He told her the little he knew.

'I want you and the boys out of Leeds until this is done.' Simon slapped the bag with Milner's money on the kitchen table. 'Our fee's in there. Take it and go somewhere safe.'

Rosie looked down at it, then raised her head to him.

'No, Simon. I'm not leaving. I'm not going to let him force me out of my home.'

'Amos, Richard,' he said. 'Get them out of here, at least.'

She nodded. 'I can send them to stay with Mrs Burton in Kirkstall. She's always said she'd like them to visit.'

'And what about you? I want you safe, too.'

'I'm staying here.' She held up her left hand. The wedding ring caught the light. 'You see that? I haven't forgotten what it means.'

She wasn't going to back down. Not on this. She was here, with him, the way she'd been since they first met. He smiled at her, then counted out two hundred pounds from the bag and another ten for himself.

'I'll take the rest to Milner. He can use it. And he needs to know. I'll tell Madeley, too.'

'Be careful.'

'I will. Keep the house secure. And make sure Jane knows as soon as she comes home.'

'She'll probably have heard by then.'

The news had spread quickly. Jane was sitting with Mrs Rigton when a man dashed in to tell them. The old woman's face showed nothing. Once the man had rushed on to pass the word, she said, 'You need to watch out for yourself, girl. He's going to be especially dangerous now.'

'I told Simon we should have killed him.' Jane's voice was quiet, thoughtful. She remembered the way he'd held her, the steel cold on her skin, the feel of his body pressed against hers.

'Maybe you should have. But today's too late for regrets. I daresay Simon thought he was doing the right thing.'

'Now we have to do it again.' Without thinking, her hand slipped through to her pocket for the reassurance of her knife.

'I wonder what kind of hold he has over them,' Mrs Rigton said. 'I've never heard of a magistrate sitting on a Sunday in my lifetime. It takes power to arrange that, child.'

It needed the kind of men she'd never know. Men who had no need to shout, because every whisper was obeyed. The ones who really ran everything.

She should be scared. Somehow, though, the news hardly touched her. He'd beaten her once. He'd had her helpless. She was never going to let that happen again. Never.

'I'd better go. Simon . . .'

'He'll know,' Mrs Rigton said. 'You have to look to yourself.'

'I will.'

The woman patted her knee with a bony hand. 'Make sure that you do. If I hear anything, I'll get word to you.'

In the distance she could hear voices raised in a hymn from the Methodist chapel. Maybe God helped them, but in her world He'd turned his face away from every plea. Or perhaps He'd just never seen or heard them at all. In their corners and crevices, the poor were easy to miss.

She kept looking around every few moments. But Jane didn't sense anyone behind her. Nobody watching. Not a soul lurking near Swinegate as she made her way home.

Inside, Rosie was busy packing two bags with clothes and a toy or two for the boys.

'You've heard,' Jane said.

'I have. I'm sending the twins to stay with someone.'

She nodded and began to help. Enoch, the coachman at the ostler's yard down the road, would take them.

'I can go with them,' Jane offered. 'Make sure they're safe.'

A moment's hesitation, then Rosie nodded her agreement.

* * *

Milner had turned pale at the news. He hugged the money close to his chest and didn't say a word.

'Are your wife and daughter still in York?'

The man nodded dumbly.

'If I were you, I'd go and join them for a few days. One way or another it'll all be over soon.'

Madeley was still at church. The news would be flying around him as he left the service.

One more call to make.

Even from a distance, Lizzie Henry's house seemed deserted, dead. As Simon approached, the feeling in his belly grew. A sense of dread. The front door hung open. Something bad was inside.

He called out once, twice, but there was no answer. Simon moved from door to door. Every room was empty. The same upstairs. Just silence. Only the attic left. He climbed the stairs warily, knife in his hand. Halfway up, the smell hit him.

A chair lay on its side, tipped over. The noose had been tied over a beam. The window was open. In the breeze, the servant swung slowly, to and fro, like a pendulum. A pool around his feet, and the stench of soiling himself.

He hadn't been dead long; his skin was still warm when Simon reached out to touch him.

It could have been suicide. Who was to say anything different? But he knew the truth.

NINETEEN

He cut the body down, caught it like a sack before it fell and laid it on the floor. The man deserved that much at least. He'd been devoted to Lizzie; at least he'd be with her again now.

In heaven. That was what the master of the workhouse had always told them. Every Sunday at service, every morning at prayers. Drummed into them all, into their heads and their backs. A better place than this earth, and their suffering here would help them find a place with Jesus.

Even when he was young, Simon had never believed it. All he needed to do was look at the hopeless faces all around him. Why would any God let them hurt?

He was thinking too much. Sometimes memories could help. More often, they were vicious and cruel and painful.

Simon left the house, pulled the door to and walked back into Leeds. White was somewhere out there, waiting.

Enoch's cart rumbled over the cobbles. Jane had rarely ridden in one before. She'd forgotten how different the world could seem from up here. To look down at people as they marched along, so caught up in their own worlds that they never glanced up to see her.

Back in the ostler's yard, she climbed down to reality. Invisible in a different way. No one had followed them to Kirkstall. The boys were both safe with Mrs Burton and her husband, ready to have adventures out at the ruined abbey.

White had to die. If they'd done it last night . . . but Mrs Rigton was right; what ifs had no currency in this world. Regret never changed a single thing.

With the boys gone, Rosie would worry about them. But it was better this way. And it wouldn't be for long. Jane could feel it in her blood. Things would boil over quickly enough. After last night, White would be eager to complete his revenge.

Where could she start to look? The old blacking factory was empty. No one would gather there before dusk, not while there was the chance to find a penny or two in town. Begging was better on a Sunday. A day of rest, a day of church, when people's rusted hearts creaked open to charity. It had helped keep her alive once or twice when she was younger.

White would want to kill her, too. To complete it all. As she walked, Jane kept her right hand in the pocket of the old coat, reaching through to keep her fingers tight on the hilt of her knife.

She ducked into the passage by the Ship Inn. Behind a door in the wall lay a rickety old stair up to a platform, and a hole in the wall that let her see over Briggate. No one was waiting below, no one searching. Maybe White wouldn't be trusting anyone else now, and doing everything himself.

Jane sat and thought, her back against the wall. All she needed was one glimpse. Just one. White had to hunt down three people.

They were only searching for him. A single glimpse and she'd be behind him. This time she'd make sure he didn't take her by surprise. And when they were alone, she'd make him pay for everything he'd done to her. A cut for each one she'd given herself.

There was only one way to face her fear. To take her blade, tear through it and make it disappear. Up here, out of sight, she was safe, but being hidden away wasn't going to bring an end to all this. She needed to do something.

By dinnertime, the news about White was common knowledge. It grew in every telling. Simon heard that White had killed four men, that he'd held off a group baying for his death. That the magistrate had offered him a complete pardon.

In the space of a day he'd gone beyond flesh and blood. He'd become a tale, a myth. Someone claimed that in Australia he'd learned to walk through walls, to cast spells so he wouldn't be seen.

No. He knew better. The man bled. He felt pain. He was as real as any of them.

The only sure thing was that no one seemed to have seen him since he left court. Julius White had vanished. And Simon knew that wasn't possible. He wouldn't leave Leeds until his job was done. He'd travelled ten thousand miles to carry it out. He still had the loyalty of some very influential people in Leeds.

Those were the ones he needed to find. To discover what hold White had over them and break it.

Mudie's rooms above the old newspaper office were shabby. Old furniture, books and papers lay all round, gathered in dusty piles and tied with string. No fire burning in the grate, and only a dusting of coal left in the scuttle.

The man was poor. The loaf of bread on the table looked as if it had lasted him for days. A shilling or two would go a long way here. But Simon knew Mudie; he was too proud to beg for charity.

'You said that Hardisty was the magistrate who held the hearing this morning?' Simon had a faint image in his mind of a man with a cold, stern face.

'Convened the court at eight. The hearing lasted five minutes. As soon as it was done, he left Leeds. I already told you all this.'

'Hardisty didn't arrange this by himself, George. Someone pushed him. Who's behind it? Who gave him his orders?'

Mudie raised a pair of thick eyebrows. 'I don't know. I tried to find out when I heard.'

'I'll pay for the information.' Simon reached into his pocket and dug out a florin. 'That's on account. And I need to know as soon as possible.'

He saw Mudie eye the coin hungrily.

'I'll do what I can.'

Park Square was almost silent. Trees coming into leaf, a sense of peace and calm. No coaches rumbling around, only a nanny and two children on the pavement. He thought about Amos and Richard. By now they would be out in Kirkstall, and Rosie would be on her own in a quiet house.

Soon enough the boys would be back and the place would ring with noise again. He'd make sure of it. But this way was best.

At Mrs Hart's house on Park Lane, the servant eyed him doubtfully. The other day he'd worn his best clothes to visit, the fashionable jacket with the swallow tails and the tight-cut trousers. Today he was dressed for work, and half the garments had seen much better days.

'She'll see me,' he assured the girl. But still she closed the door and made him wait on the step. Finally, he was allowed in, escorted through to the parlour. Emma Hart sat in her Sunday best, a gown that cost more than he wanted to imagine. She was standing by the window, staring out at a garden just beginning to come alive for spring. As he entered, she turned, looking amused.

'Hettie thought a tramp had come to the door. I told you last time, Mr Westow, you look so much more handsome when you dress well.'

'Needs must.' He shrugged.

'Well.' She eyed him. 'I suppose you must have a reason for arriving like this. I'd imagine it has something to do with Julius White.'

'It does.'

She glided across the room and poured two glasses of wine from a decanter, handing one to him. Did money teach grace? he wondered. The way she moved, her ease around everything . . .

'Court on a Sunday? I've never heard of anything like that before.' Mrs Hart shook her head.

'No one has,' he said. 'And White was released. There wasn't a lawyer in the room to make the case against him.'

'What have you come to ask, Mr Westow?'

'You know who's powerful in town, Mrs Hart. Who's pulling the strings? Someone gave Hardisty his orders. Someone told him to get White out of the gaol.'

'A man who can do that carries plenty of weight,' she said thoughtfully, tapping her index finger against her chin. 'There aren't many who could arrange something like that. Not in a few hours on a Saturday night.'

'Who?'

'The mayor, of course.' She shook her head. 'No. He's a venal little man, but he'd never flout the law so obviously.' Her eyes stared at nothing as she weighed the faces in her head. 'I can think of two possibilities,' she said after a while. He waited. 'Do you know Councillor Atkinson?'

'I know who he is,' Simon replied. He'd seen the man, but never met him. Tall, haughty, with thinning ginger hair and a sharp face. The type who exuded power and took wealth as his right. Yes, he could be a good candidate. But what hold would White have on a man like that? 'Who else?'

'Robert Fairfax.'

Simon shook his head. 'I've never even heard of him.'

'You won't have. That's how he prefers things.' Emma Hart gave a brief smile. 'I know his wife a little. We sit on a pair of charity committees together. She's pleasant enough but she's . . . cowed. Always flustered.'

'What does he do?'

'Do?' She raised an eyebrow. 'Not everyone needs to *do* things. Really, you ought to know that by now, Mr Westow. He has money. A fortune. He inherited it. That's what he does. And he enjoys moving people around as if they belonged to him. Like toys.'

'Why would he help Julius White?'

'I couldn't begin to tell you. I've no idea if he did. You asked me for names, that's all. You can't expect me to know their motives as well.'

'Where does Fairfax live?'

'Out in Chapel Allerton, I believe. I've never been to visit.'

Another hurried smile. 'I've never been invited. But I'm not sure anyone has. He's very private, I understand.'

'And those are the only two you can think of?'

'Don't you think that's more than enough for a place like Leeds? Two men above the law.'

'Honestly?' he replied. 'I expected more. All I want is for this business to be over, and White where he belongs.'

Her eyes sparkled. 'Where's that, Mr Westow?'

'At the end of a rope.'

Jane walked. It was the best she could think of, to wander around town, to make herself a target. Her body felt tight, tense, every sense on edge. She wanted White to come after her, to hunt her. She knew Leeds better than he did. The tiny ways, the hiding places. The best spots to ambush.

Let him come and then she'd have her revenge for the night before.

All afternoon she moved around. Up and down Briggate. The Head Row, Vicar Lane. Boar Lane, Park Row. Mile after mile, feeling the pale sun on her face, on her back. Twice men had followed her for a short distance, then turned away. But no White.

By five, her legs ached and her feet were sore. Slowly, she made her way home to Swinegate, cutting through the courts and the ginnels and coming out close to the house, where she could stand and spy on anyone watching the place. But there wasn't a soul to be seen.

'He thinks he's above the law,' Rosie said. She slammed her hand down on the table in frustration. The strain showed on her face. Missing the boys, Simon thought. Worrying about them.

'He's already proved he *is* above the law,' he said quietly. He unfolded the piece of paper in front of him on the table. 'I've been given two names. People who have the power to tell the magistrate to hold his session today and free him. Robert Fairfax and Councillor Atkinson.' He ran his finger down the list, stopping briefly, then moving on. 'Lizzie Henry gave me the names of her clients,' he explained. 'Atkinson's here. No mention of Fairfax.'

'I've never even heard of him,' Rosie said.

'I hadn't, either. He's a very rich man, apparently. Reclusive.'

'Why would someone like that help White?' Jane asked.

'We don't know that he did.' He ran a hand through his hair.

'It's just a name I've been given. I need to find out. He certainly has the power.'

'Since Atkinson's on that list, we should go after him first,' Rosie said. 'We have a lever.'

'Not quite. We have a name.' Simon sighed. 'That's all. Lizzie's dead.' He paused for a moment. 'So is her servant.'

He heard Jane suck in her breath.

'You didn't say anything about that,' Rosie told him.

He gave a slight shrug. 'What was there to say? I didn't want to scare you even more. I went there this morning. The place was empty. He was up in the attic, hanged. It looks like suicide, but . . .'

'But it was White,' Jane said.

His voice was solemn. 'Paying him back for the beating last night. And we don't stand a chance of proving it.'

'One more reason he needs to be caught,' Rosie said quietly.

'I know. Believe me, I know.' He pointed at the list again. 'In the morning I'll go after Atkinson.' He took a breath. 'He's not going to know what Lizzie wrote about her customers. A few threats might bring something.'

'What do you want me to do?' Jane asked.

'The same thing you've been doing today,' he told her after a moment. 'It's a good idea. Sooner or later, he's going to be tempted. And start asking again, if anyone's seen him.'

Simon couldn't think of any other way she could help. But he doubted that White would be lured quite so easily; the man was probably hiding somewhere out of sight, making his plans. Still, it was worth trying, and he couldn't take Jane along to confront Councillor Atkinson. She knew that, too. With her alongside him, they'd simply be turned away. Alone, in his best clothes, he might have a chance to talk to the man.

She nodded. 'I'm going to bed.'

He heard her feet on the stairs, then silence. Simon reached across the table and took his wife's hand.

'Missing them?'

'Every second. I keep worrying that they're all right.'

'So do I.'

She gave a weary smile. 'You'd think we'd be happy to have some peace and quiet here, wouldn't you?'

'There won't be any peace until White hangs.'

She nodded. 'He will. But that's what we thought last night, remember?'

'This seemed so simple when we started.' He kept hold of her hand, squeezing it lightly. 'All we had to do was find Hannah Milner and take her home. Now I can hardly believe she was involved. It seems so long ago.'

'That was before we knew White was behind it.'

'True.' His voice was bleak. He sighed, then smiled. 'He's good, but he can't beat the three of us.'

'He came close.' Rosie's reminder was stern. 'Don't you ever forget that.'

'No.' He raised his head, as if he could see through the ceiling. 'I don't think Jane will, either. You were right, she's been even quieter than usual today.'

'She blames herself,' Rosie said.

'Why? Nobody's perfect.'

'You don't understand. She expects everything from herself, Simon. She doesn't give herself an inch. Look at her: she's lived here for two years, and as soon as she steps out of the door you wouldn't know she'd ever been in the house.'

'That's just how she is. It's her way.'

'But two years?' Rosie shook her head. 'She's hardly changed in that time. I know she likes the boys, and they love her. But, honestly, Simon, sometimes I believe she could walk away and never give another thought to anything here.'

'No. She'd still think about it,' he said. She might go, and maybe she'd never return, but it would remain there in her mind. 'That's Jane, and we can take it or leave it. Nothing we can do or say is ever going to change her. She's very good at this job. She was born for it.'

TWENTY

Monday morning. Already he could taste the smoke in the air. The manufactories were working, the constant thumping of machines and the noise of the people out on the streets. A cacophony.

Simon was in his good suit, and fresh from the barber. His hair was cut short and oiled, his shave sharp and clean and smooth. There was no rush. Atkinson would be at the monthly council meeting. He'd find the man once it was done.

Carts filled Briggate. A man came out from Rose and Crown yard, arm raised to halt traffic as the mail coach veered out into the street, sending people scattering out of its path.

Simon stood in front of the Moot Hall. The building sat right in the middle of the road, an island with the town flowing briskly around it. In front of him, the old wooden stocks stood soft and rotting, the metal hinges brown with rust. They'd never been used in his lifetime. As he studied them, Simon became aware of a movement, someone coming closer. He turned quickly, starting to reach into his sleeve for the hidden knife. But it was only Martin Holden, the eager Radical who'd arranged his testimony about the workhouse and factories to the Commission.

'Simon . . . good day.' He bobbed his head nervously.

'Hello, Martin.'

'You promised we could talk more.' The man always seemed fretful, as if he was unsure of himself and how people might welcome him. It was an odd trait in someone so dedicated to finding justice for children. But this wasn't the right time for a conversation. Holden could talk for hours. He was full of facts and numbers. He overwhelmed with them, too many for anyone to take in.

'I did,' Simon agreed. 'Once my work was done, I said. It's not over yet.'

'Oh.' The man looked bewildered. 'When . . .?'

'I don't know. You've heard about Julius White?'

'Who?' He frowned, then his face cleared. 'Oh, yes. I have.'

'Once he's caught and sentenced, then we can talk.'

'I see.' He pushed his hands into his trouser pockets and nodded. 'Another time, then.'

He watched Holden walk away. So earnest, just one thing in his head. Perhaps the man really could bring some changes, but Simon doubted they'd happen in his lifetime. The world only moved quickly when there was money to be made. On anything to help the poor, it was as slow as treacle.

Half an hour of standing and pacing around, watching dulled

faces, lost in the raw sounds of Leeds. Finally, the councillors began to emerge. Two of them hurried down the steps, late for their appointments; the others followed in dribs and drabs and began to drift away. Two minutes later, Atkinson emerged, tapping his hat down on his head, casually surveying Briggate before sauntering towards the Head Row.

He lived out along North Street, in a large house close to Sheepscar Beck. Simon didn't hurry; there was ample time. He caught up with the man near Brunswick Place, just as the sprinkling of small dwellings dwindled away to become fields.

'A word, if I might, Councillor.'

Atkinson turned, curious. He stared down his nose, as if every man he saw was below his concern.

'Do I know you?'

'No.' Simon smiled. He didn't offer his hand; Atkinson would never have taken it, anyway. 'Not yet.'

'Then what do you want?' He fussed with his gloves, pulling them tighter over his hands. His skin was pale, a few freckles scattered across his cheeks.

'Lizzie Henry.'

Atkinson didn't even glance up. 'I heard she was dead.' His tone dismissed her. She was history, no longer any concern of his.

'That's right. And the man who murdered her was in the gaol until yesterday morning.'

'I still don't see what any of this has to do with me.' He started to walk away.

'She left a list of the customers who enjoyed her girls, and what they enjoyed. Your name is on it, Councillor.'

He continued, but his stride faltered a little.

'You're a gentleman of influence in town.' Simon pitched his voice a little louder, letting it ring over the grass. 'The kind of man who could give orders to a magistrate to fix a trial.'

Atkinson halted. 'Why would I want to do that?'

'Perhaps you should tell me, Mr Atkinson.' Five steps and he was close enough to see the man's chest rise and fall.

'And if I choose not to?'

'Then I daresay the *Mercury* would enjoy publishing some scandal. It's interesting how quickly a reputation can crumble once secrets start to come out. Turned away from society, not welcome in many places . . .'

'Plenty of people used Mrs Henry's establishment.' Atkinson tried to keep his voice steady, but Simon could hear a tiny quaver. The first small crack in the façade.

'That's very true,' Simon agreed. His bluff might work. 'But I'm not interested in them. Only in you, Councillor. Think about it for a moment: you'd become quite the centre of attention. Even if the papers didn't publish, a few hints would be bound to leak here and there. That can be very effective.'

'Some people might call that blackmail.' He began to walk again, but more slowly now, with Simon keeping pace, staring ahead.

'They can call it what they like. All I'm interested in is the truth. Tell me that and no one will ever know about your . . . tastes.'

'And how could I trust someone like you?' A sneer in the words. Keep going, Simon thought, and I'll let everyone know for the sheer pleasure of it.

'You can't,' he replied. 'But then again, you don't have the power here. I do.' Let the man feel what that was like for once in his life. Let him squirm.

For a hundred yards they stayed silent. Finally Atkinson gave a small cough.

'For whatever it's worth, I had nothing to do with what happened in court yesterday. I didn't even know about it until I heard the gossip after church.'

'Give me one good reason to believe you.'

The man shook his head. 'I can't do that. The only person who can tell you who gave the orders is Hardisty. I believe he left Leeds in a hurry.'

'He did,' Simon said. 'And no one seems to know where he's gone. Strange, isn't it?'

'I've told you the truth. The council will have its reckoning with him when he returns.'

As much as he wanted the man to be a liar, Simon believed him. There was no varnish on his words. He'd left himself open.

'Who else has the power to give orders to a magistrate?'

'Have you heard of Mr Fairfax?'

'Not until yesterday. You're the second person to mention him.'

'Then perhaps you should attend to the advice.' He peered more closely at Simon. 'I know who you are now. You're Westow, the thief-taker.'

'I am.'

Atkinson cocked his head. 'Two years ago, you found something that had been stolen from Mrs Collins.'

'Yes.' It was a hazy memory. A simple job, he recalled, everything done in half a day.

'She was impressed by your work. Said you were honest.'

Simon nodded. 'I try to be.'

'Then perhaps you really will keep my secrets, Mr Westow.' He gave a dark smile. 'But as you say, you hold the cards.'

'Fairfax,' Simon said. 'What do you know about him?'

'He has the ear of everyone important.'

'Why would he help someone like White?'

'You'd need to ask him.'

'I will. Does he come into Leeds much?'

'Rarely,' Atkinson replied. 'When he wants to talk to someone, he summons them.' He paused for a moment. 'People go to him, not the other way round. I believe his wife is a little more social, but I've never met her.'

'If I wanted to see him, what would be the best way?'

'Ingenuity.' He straightened his back. 'With that, I'll trust to your honesty and wish you good day and good luck, Mr Westow.'

Simon watched him go, standing until Atkinson turned between a pair of gateposts and disappeared.

Fairfax.

He needed to find out about the man.

Jane huddled in the long coat as she drifted around the streets, waiting. For once, she hoped that someone would see her. But this was a day when she couldn't make herself visible. No one followed her, no one even seemed to notice she was there.

She talked to people she knew. Old women, children scavenging in the courts, two of the pickpockets who worked Briggate and dreamed of finding a fortune in a purse. But no one had seen Julius White.

But he was here. Somewhere in Leeds. She could feel him in her blood.

*   *   *

Mudie was in the newspaper office, jacket off and shirt sleeves rolled up as he cleaned the printing press.

'Found a buyer for it yet, George?'

The man turned, a broad smile on his face. 'I've done even better. I have two printing jobs lined up.' He wiped his hands on a dirty rag, but he'd never shift the ink from his fingers. 'You wanted information.'

'I still do,' Simon told him.

'I haven't come up with much for your money, I'm afraid. About the only name was Fairfax.'

'Other people have been saying that to me, too. What do you know about him?'

'Well.' He drew the word out slowly as he walked through to the front of the office and sat at his desk. 'He tends to stay out of sight, I can tell you that much. His grandfather made the family money. They were never poor, but he married a woman with proper wealth.' He smiled ruefully. 'Some men have all the luck.'

Simon laughed. 'You love your wife and you know it.'

Mudie sighed. 'Fairfax's father made some good investments. God only knows what they're worth. It's safe to say they'll never need to worry about their next meal.'

'I want to know what he's like, George.'

'I've never met him. I've only seen him a few times, I haven't written about him. But I don't think he's a well man. A while ago he lost weight; he was as thin as a wraith. He might still be. And I've heard he has a temper on him.' The man shrugged. 'That's all I know, Simon.'

'How old is he?'

Mudie thought. 'Thirty-five. Something like that. He inherited about ten years ago, when his father died.'

'Does he have any children?'

'Not with his wife,' the man answered guardedly.

'But?'

'There have been rumours about a mistress.' He frowned. 'I don't have any idea if they're true. You know how people love to gossip.'

'Does she have a name?'

'Mrs Chambers. She's a widow, quite young. Two boys, I'm

not sure how old they are. Probably still quite young. She's only
in her twenties. Very pretty.'

'Where does she live?'

'She took a house in Potternewton a couple of years ago. I
don't know where she lived before that. Someone said Horsforth,
I think.'

Potternewton was close to Chapel Allerton, no more than a few
minutes from Fairfax. It might be a way to get to the man.

Simon rubbed his knuckles along his jaw. 'How does he have
so many people in his pocket?'

'Money.' A simple answer, and plain as day. 'You know how
it works. Money means power, and he likes to exercise it. I think
he enjoys seeing everyone running around, doing his bidding. Like
a boy playing with lead soldiers.'

Could it be as simple as that, something so stupid? A man taking
his pleasure from seeing everyone scuttle and scurry to his whims?
But he didn't even know if Fairfax was involved. It might be
nothing at all. But if he was, then White must know something
about the man, something that could destroy him.

It was the only thing he could imagine.

TWENTY-ONE

'We'll meet back here,' Simon said. They'd walked out
along the road from Leeds as coaches sped past and
carts rumbled slowly by. A pair of cottages stood
close together, their windows looking along the long hill into town.

'I might not see her,' Jane said. 'It'll probably be the cook or
the maid.'

'That's not important. Talk to them, see what you can find out
about her.'

She nodded. Three miles out here through the countryside, it
was safer with company. If people looked, they saw him, not her.
She was just a girl, nothing. And she'd had no feeling of anyone
trailing behind them.

While she went to Mrs Chambers's house, Simon would walk

a little further, into Chapel Allerton, to discover what he might about Fairfax and have a chance to see his property.

She'd been sitting in the kitchen when he came home, honing her knife with a whetstone. She did it every day, keeping the edge keen and brilliant, ready to cut through anything with the lightest touch. As Simon explained what he wanted her to do, she wiped the blade on her dress and slid it away into the sheath in her pocket.

It was a ritual. Her ritual. It made her feel safe.

She touched the hilt now, as she walked down the road on her own. The third house along on the left, Simon had told her. They were dotted on the hillside, a fair distance from each other. Private.

Jane stood at the end of the drive. The place was modest, smaller than she'd expected, the stone still clean, shining in the sunlight, a big window on either side of the door, three of them on the floor above. She pulled the shawl up over her hair and started to walk over the gravel.

The back door. It would always be the back door for someone like her.

Simon watched her go, a small figure blending into the distance, then he walked the last half mile up the road and into the village. It was a quiet place. A church with its graveyard, a pair of inns. A few big houses and more that were smaller, poorer.

Over on Chapeltown Moor he could see the small quarry and the brickworks. They once held the hangings out here, someone had told him. Big crowds would come from all around Leeds to see a guilty man have his neck stretched. Stalls would be set up, selling food, all manner of things, and horse races to finish the day. It seemed impossible to imagine now.

The smith was working in his forge, hammering out a horseshoe as a groom waited, holding his animal by the reins.

'Where's a good place to find something to eat?' Simon asked.

The smith never lost his rhythm.

'There's the Regent and the Nag's Head. You'll have passed the Bowling Green Inn down the hill.'

He lifted the shoe with a pair of tongs, inspected the glowing metal, and tossed it into a bucket of water. Steam rose in a sudden hiss. The man wiped the sweat off his face with a cloth.

'Not too many stop here.' He nodded towards the road. 'Most just go by.'

'I was hoping to see someone,' Simon told him.

'Who's that, then?' His voice turned wary.

'Mr Fairfax.'

The groom snorted. 'You'll not get near him. No one does.'

'No one?'

'He's not partial to people,' the smith said. 'We don't hardly see him and we live here.'

'Which house is his?'

The blacksmith pushed out his chest and folded a pair of thick arms. 'Why?'

'I'm curious, that's all.'

'Quarter of a mile along the road,' the groom told him. 'You can't miss it. Big place.' The smith turned and glared, but the man didn't notice. 'Gates are always closed. Like I said, they don't take too kindly to visitors.'

'I see.' Simon tipped his that. 'Then thank you, gentlemen.'

'I wouldn't be making a nuisance of yourself,' the blacksmith warned. 'Mr Fairfax might not like company, but he's one of us. You understand what I mean.'

'Perfectly.' With a nod, he was gone.

The Regent was a poor place, two cramped rooms and a bar. A pair of men played cards in a corner, their mugs empty. Another talked to a weary barman, who seemed glad to move away and serve a new customer.

'Beer,' Simon said. 'Do you have something to eat?'

'Nothing fresh,' the man replied. 'We get a few in for their dinner and the wife cooks for that. No call later in the day.' He pursed his lips. 'Bread and cheese, I suppose, if you're hungry enough.'

'I'll take it.'

There wasn't much more to learn about Fairfax in this place, and the owner was reluctant to talk. The man had never been a customer, didn't order his wine or ale here. A few of Fairfax's servants sometimes drank in the public houses of an evening. Most went down to the Bowling Green.

Simon finished the beer and food and ambled along the road. Fairfax's house was easy to spot, exactly as the groom had promised. A high fence of metal spikes faced the road, the tall gates

firmly closed. A long expanse of lawn led to the building. No sign
of anyone working. From somewhere behind the building he heard
a shot. Then another, and the faint sound of men laughing.

Getting in could be a deadly test. Doing it legally, impossible.
But he needed to find a way. White could be there now, staring
out at him with a satisfied smile.

Jane knocked on the door and stepped back, staring down at the
flagstones in the yard. She heard movement inside, and a curious
tapping sound. Then a key turned in the lock and she looked up.

A man. One good leg, the other gone at the knee, a carved
wooden stump in its place. He was tall, his hair dark and thick.
A wide scar on his chin, a leather patch covering his right
eye. And a warm, kindly smile on his face.

'What do we have here, then?'

Jane was used to a cook or a housekeeper answering the door.
They were the ones who ruled the servants. She could talk to a
woman. A man standing in front of her, especially one who looked
like this, was unnerving.

'I'm looking for work, sir.'

'Are you, now?' He had a deep, tender voice. 'And what's your
name, love?'

'Jane, sir.'

'What work can you do, Jane?'

'Anything, sir. Scrub, clean.'

'Done it before, have you?' he asked doubtfully.

'I have, sir.'

'Where?'

'At the workhouse.'

It was the lie she'd built with Simon. No one would employ a
girl who had no experience. This explanation sounded possible.

'You don't look as if you've been there in a while.'

'No, sir.' She kept her voice meek. 'I didn't like it there. They
beat us.'

'When did you eat, girl?'

'Supper yesterday, sir.'

'I'll tell you what: I can't offer you any work, but I can give
you some food.' He held the door wide. 'Come in and warm
yourself.'

She stepped into the house, wary. The man might have a wooden leg, but he was big, he had broad shoulders and strong arms. Jane kept her hand in her pocket, fingers round the hilt of her knife, ready.

'Where's the cook, sir?'

He laughed. 'You're looking at him. Cook, the mistress's coachman and bodyguard. There's me and a maid who's also the nanny. We're a strange little house here, Jane.'

The kitchen was spotless. The pans were hung up, shining in the light through the window. The man limped over to a cupboard and brought out a board with some bread and cheese and a jar of pickle.

'Here,' he said. 'No job here for you, I'm afraid, but you can help yourself to that. Take the rest with you, if you like. It's never good to have an empty belly.'

'Thank you.' Jane cocked her head. 'Have you been hungry yourself?'

'Once or twice.' He gave a wistful smile. 'More, after I got back to England. There aren't many willing to employ a man with one leg and one eye.'

'What happened to you, sir?' She nibbled at the bread and broke off a piece of the cheese. 'Was it the French war?'

'No, it was nothing like that. A crocodile did it. Do you know what they are?'

Jane shook her head.

'They're nasty beasts. Don't look like one of God's creatures at all. They've got skin like armour and they can grow to twenty feet long. Mostly they wait in the water to gobble up what they can, but if they come up on land they can move faster than a man. And they weigh more than I can lift. One of them decided he'd like the taste of me.' He shrugged. 'He settled for my leg.'

She'd heard tales of beasts like that, but only from the story-tellers at the market. She'd never believed they really existed.

'Where did it happen?' Jane asked.

'Australia,' he told her. And suddenly she was very alert, paying attention to every word.

'Were you a convict?'

The man laughed again. 'No, thank God. A little better than that. I was a soldier. Only a private, I never wanted rank. After I left the army, I decided to make a life out there and try my hand at farming. Then I met the croc. Bayside isn't any kind of country for a man with one leg.'

She looked at his face. No sign of anger or resentment. It had happened, and that was it.

'You said there's a mistress here, sir?'

'That's right.' His voice softened. 'Mrs Chambers. She's a widow woman, very young. She took a chance on me, and I'd do anything for her. That's why I'll let in someone who comes to the door. It's always good to give a little charity. Someone gave it to me.' His eyes moved around the kitchen. 'I had some good luck for once.'

'How many children does she have?' Jane had finished the cheese. The bread was almost gone, the jar of pickle empty. Soon she'd have to leave. For now, she'd keep asking questions.

'Two. A pair of lads, three and four. Playful as the devil, but well-behaved. Mrs Chambers sees to that herself.'

'What happened to her husband?' She placed the final crumbs in her mouth.

'A seizure, she said. It happened before I came to work for her. She was still carrying Joshua, the youngest. Mrs Chambers took me on when he was still in the cradle, after she moved here.'

'And you have a home now.'

'Yes,' he agreed with a smile. 'A good one, too.' He slid the empty board away from her. 'I hope you can find one, too, Jane. You look like a girl who needs a welcoming place.'

As she sat by the roadside, waiting for Simon, she wondered if she should have mentioned White to the servant. They might have known each other on the other side of the world. No, she decided; silence was safer. The name would have given too much away.

'We're no further along.' Simon kicked at a stone, watching it spin down the road.

'No,' Jane said. 'What can we do?'

'I don't know,' he replied after a moment, his jaw set. 'I don't bloody know.'

'White might not even be in Fairfax's house.'

'Then where is he?' Frustration prickled at him, cut his temper short. 'Tell me that. We can't find him, and he hasn't come after us.'

'Maybe he's not in town any more.'

Simon shook his head. 'He's still here. He's not going to leave Leeds until he's satisfied. He didn't come all this way just to kill Lizzie Henry. He wants all of us.'

White was toying with them. Like a cat biding its time with a mouse before it pounced. The man wanted them so terrified that they'd jump at their own shadows. To live with fear.

'Then we'll wait,' Jane said. 'Let him show himself.'

Simon kicked out at another stone. He was always the hunter. That was his job. It was what he knew. This sat too heavy in his belly. It ate at him. He didn't like to wait. Patience had never been one of his gifts.

'We'll stop at Lady Lodge on the way back,' he said. 'Madeley might have an idea how we can bring White into the open.'

But the door was locked. No servants in the house, the shutters all closed. It looked as though the man had gone away.

Simon could feel his temper rising. Every way they turned today, there'd been a wall in front of them.

'You know that's exactly what he wants,' Rosie said. 'He'll wait until you're so frustrated that you do something stupid. As soon as that happens, he'll be there.'

'I'm going to be careful.'

'Simon.' She placed her hands on her hips and stared at him. 'Look at yourself. You've snapped at me three times since you came home. You're ready to explode.'

'I just want this over. I want the boys back here.' He let out a breath. 'I want everything the way it was.'

Rosie put her arms on his shoulders. 'It will be,' she said softly. 'It will be. Come on, let's go to bed.'

In the middle of the night, Jane rose and stood in the darkness by the window. She thought she'd heard something, a scratch at the door. But Swinegate was empty, no lights showing anywhere.

Quietly, she put on her dress and coat and tucked the shawl around her head. In stockinged feet, she slipped downstairs and out of the door, stopping to lace up her boots. And she vanished into the blackness.

The night didn't scare her. She could use the darkness, hide in it. This was the time when the people she knew would be out. Gathered round their fires, caught in the space between sleep and waking.

No one behind her. Not a soul to be seen.

The river was almost silent, just the faint lapping of water by the wharves. At the entrance to the old blacking factory Jane stood for a moment, letting her eyes adjust to the gloom.

The children slept in the corner, holding each other close for warmth. The adults sat quiet by a small blaze, too lost for sleep. She moved from one to the other, whispering her questions, watching the reflections of flames in their dead eyes.

But none of them had seen Julius White.

It was the same out by Drony Laith at the camp in the woods, and in the cellar off one of the old Briggate courts. She was just leaving, hands pushed deep in her pocket, fingers running along the knife hilt, when she heard someone hiss.

Jane stopped.

'I've seen him.'

It was a boy's voice, thin and high. He was in the shadows, only his face visible. One eye was swollen shut. His lower lip was cut, blood dried on his chin.

'What happened to you?'

'I tried to steal an apple from a cart at the market. He caught me.'

You needed to be quick to survive. Sometimes you weren't fast enough. She'd owned her share of bruises and welts. A scar on her back from a whip.

'You said you'd seen the man I'm looking for.'

'Yes.' He was shivering. Jane moved closer. The lad wore a thin shirt, old trousers holed at the knee, his feet bare.

'When was it?'

'Yesterday.'

'What did he look like?'

'His skin was dark. His face and hands. He was talking to someone and he sounded strange.'

'Strange?' she asked.

He had to think, to try and find the words. 'I don't know,' the boy said finally. 'A bit like he was from here, but it was different.'

'Who was he talking to? Where did you see them?'

'It was in the churchyard, that one on the other side of the Head Row.' He looked down at the ground. 'I ran there after I'd been beaten.'

To hide. So nobody would see him cry. So no one would see his weakness.

'I couldn't hear what they were saying, just the voices. His was different. That's why I remembered it. And how he looked. I've never seen anyone like that.'

It was White. She knew it in her bones.

'What about the other man?'

The boy just shook his head.

'Where did they go?'

'I don't know. I stopped looking.'

Jane took two pennies from her pocket and put them in his hand. His flesh was cold as a corpse. His teeth were chattering.

'Wait,' she told him, then took off the coat and handed it to him. 'Wear that. It'll keep you warm.'

Jane drifted through the darkness, from place to place, camp to camp. But no one remembered him. One sighting was enough. Out in the open, striding around, unafraid. She believed the boy.

A band of pale light glowed on the horizon as she made her way home. The early chill brought goose pimples to her arms. She liked the coat, but she could get another. Anyway, soon enough it would be summer and she wouldn't need one. It was just another possession to weigh her down.

At the bottom of Briggate she stopped suddenly and drew in her breath. There was something. She couldn't see it, couldn't hear it. But she could feel it. Carefully, she moved to the wall, pulling the shawl over her head, and peered around the corner.

Nobody. No movement to catch from the corner of her eye. But there was *something*. She was certain of it.

Jane retraced her steps towards home, picking her way slowly and silently through the ginnels. At the final corner, she stopped again. Crouching down low, she waited, listening until it was there. So faint that she might have imagined it. Someone breathing. Then the soft scrape of a foot shifting on the dirt. It was still too dark to be certain of anything.

Right there. Outside the gate. Someone. Standing, waiting. Jane had the knife in her hand, clutching it so tight that her fingers ached.

The figure was just a blurred, faint shape.

She needed to be patient. Another five minutes and there'd be enough light to make out the figure.

Her gaze never moved. Her body was ready. But she still missed the moment, the shift in the light when black became grey.

The outline began to take form.

A woman? At first she wasn't sure. But a woman could kill as readily as a man. And die just as quickly.

Jane waited, completely still. Ready.

The minutes moved and the brightness grew enough to make out the woman's face. Jane stood slowly and began to walk. She made each step loud. The woman turned. She was wearing a rich silk gown. Her eyes were lost. Helpless. Terrified.

'Hannah Milner,' Jane said softly. 'What are you doing here?'

TWENTY-TWO

In the kitchen, Rosie fussed around the girl. Poured a tot of French brandy that brought the colour back to her face. Built up the fire to give some warmth to the room.

Simon waited. There was food on the table, but no one had eaten. They waited for Hannah's tale. But every time she opened her mouth to speak, she began to cry. He tried a question, but Rosie shook her head sharply. She needed time.

And he needed to know. Something bad had happened. Finally he stood and walked away, pausing at the door and beckoning to Jane.

'Milner's house?' she asked as they hurried along Swinegate. His heels rang on the cobbles. A few men on their way to work paused to stare at them.

'Yes.'

The front door was locked. But the back was only pulled to, the wood splintered around the lock where it had been forced.

Simon pushed the door open with his fingertips, listening for any sounds inside.

The kitchen was empty. All the pots were clean and polished, hanging on their racks. Dishes were stored away. The mess lay on the other side of the door. Blood on the floor of the parlour and the dining room. Still pools of it, mounds of flies feasting. The whole house smelt of iron. Enough blood to fill a bucket. It looked like more than any human could contain.

But no corpse. Simon gestured, and Jane crept slowly up the stairs. Light from the window flickered on the knife in her fist.

He moved from room to room downstairs. The library. A sewing room. Blood in every one of them. No sign of Milner or his wife. No trace of any servant.

He turned quickly at the squeak of a stair tread. But it was only Jane, shaking her head.

'Empty,' she said. 'But there's blood on all the beds and the rugs.'

'And everywhere down here,' Simon said. He chewed on his bottom lip. 'But not a body.'

They searched again, from cellar to attic: nothing.

'I don't know,' he said finally. 'The place looks like a massacre happened here. It doesn't make sense. Maybe Hannah will be ready to talk now. She was just standing by the back gate?'

'She looked as if she'd been there for hours. There was dew in her hair. When I spoke her name, all she could do was look at me.'

'She must have come here and seen all this.'

'Where are they?'

'We'd better hope she can tell us.'

'When I was out, someone told me he'd seen White.'

He stopped suddenly and turned to her. 'What? Why didn't you say something?'

'When did I have the chance?' Jane stared at him. 'Anyway, it happened the day before yesterday. Up at the old church. He was talking to someone.'

White was brazen, open. But still they couldn't find him. Simon clenched his fist tight then opened it again and looked around.

'Where are Milner and his wife?' he asked. 'And whose blood is that?'

*　　*　　*

In the kitchen, Rosie was scouring the table.

'Where is she?' Simon asked.

'I gave her some laudanum and put her in the boys' bed. She needed to rest.'

Damn. He had to *know*.

'Did she say anything at all?'

'Yes.' Rosie pursed her lips. 'What's in the house, Simon? All she could tell me was blood.'

He rubbed his face. 'That's all there is. Gallons of it. Everywhere except the kitchen. But no one dead.' His voice was tired. Weary as death.

All he could do was pace. Wait for her to wake. No boys here to play and laugh and distract him. Jane had vanished, off somewhere without a word. Rosie was in the kitchen, cooking, checking their accounts. Each time he wandered in, she waved him away.

Questions spilled from his brain.

Three hours passed. Four. Finally, he heard a stirring overhead.

Rosie was ahead of him. She crouched by the bed, speaking softly, pushing the girl's hair away from her forehead.

'You're safe. You're with us. Simon Westow and his wife. Do you remember him? He found you when you were taken.'

Hannah Milner nodded dumbly, her gaze moving round the room.

'Where am I?' Her voice was thick from the drug, the words slurred.

'In our house.' Rosie took a glass from the table. 'Nothing can hurt you here. Sit up and drink this.'

Like an obedient child, she did as she was told.

'How . . .' she began.

'Simon has things he wants to ask you.' Rosie's voice was calm and gentle. 'Do you think you can answer him?'

Another nod. 'I'll try.'

The family was staying in York. John Milner had joined his wife and daughter there, the servants with them.

Hannah's friends had wanted to attend a ball in Leeds. It was one of the events of the Yorkshire season, held every spring at the

Mixed Cloth Hall. She'd been reluctant, she felt too scared to come back to Leeds. Not yet. But her friends didn't know what had happened to her. That secret had held. They persisted, sending letters and notes day after day, urging her to come, until they wore her down and convinced her. There would be five of them together. Servants with them and chaperones in attendance at the hall. Everything would be completely safe.

Her father had said no. At least the man had some sense, Simon thought. But her mother had argued. No word of the kidnap had slipped out. And the ball was a good place to meet an eligible young man. After two days of nagging, Milner had given in.

She'd had five dances and drunk three glasses of wine. The evening was filled with laughter and the pleasure of charming company. Too much of it. Hannah had forgotten all her fears. She had a fan at the house that would set off her gown perfectly. It was no more than five minutes' walk each way. She was young, nothing could hurt her. She could slip away and be back before anyone realized she'd gone.

She found the back door open. Yet still she'd gone inside, lit a lamp. And then she'd seen the blood, smelled it everywhere . . . the next thing she remembered was Jane finding her.

'I knew you lived on Swinegate, but I couldn't remember which house.' The tears came again. 'I thought if I waited somewhere . . .'

'You're safe now.' Simon turned to Rosie. 'We need to get a message to the Milners.'

'I'll take care of it.'

He heard the quick scratch of pen on paper as he entered the kitchen. Rosie's writing wasn't copperplate, but it was legible; that was all they needed.

'Is she sleeping again?'

'Yes.'

'Milner's probably already on his way to Leeds,' she said without raising her head. 'By now he'll know she's missing.'

'Very likely,' Simon agreed. 'At least this will put his mind at rest.' He paused for a moment. 'Her mother's, too.'

*   *   *

The hammering on the door came an hour later. Simon looked at his wife and took out his knife.

Turn the key, lift the latch. He stood back, ready, as his hand turned the knob. Milner's servant stood, dusty and dirty from the road.

'Miss Mi—'

'She's inside. Sleeping. Not hurt.'

The man let out his breath. His body sagged. 'Thank God for that.'

'Have you been to your master's house yet?'

'Yes.' A word as heavy as stone.

'She saw it.'

The servant nodded. 'We'll take her back to York.'

'I'll escort you up to Hannah.' He hadn't heard Rosie come through from the kitchen.

'Is Mr Milner in the coach?' Simon asked.

'He is.'

The man looked haggard, deflated. So much older than the last time they'd met.

'She's safe,' Simon said. 'Not harmed. And no one's dead that I know.'

No reply. Just silent, staring eyes. And then: 'Why?'

'I've no idea.'

He'd wondered about it all through the morning. There was no reason to it. White. He didn't even need to think about that. But Milner's part in all this was long over. He'd never had more than a small role. It was just terror. Fear.

He heard the stirring in the house, and the sound of hesitant footsteps on the stair. A thought came to him.

'Do you know a man called Fairfax?' Simon asked.

Milner turned his head. 'Not particularly well. He was a friend of my brother's. Why? Are you saying he's behind all this?'

'Can you write me a letter of introduction?'

The man's gaze shifted and Simon turned. The servant was helping Hannah walk. She leaned against him, barely awake, a coat of Rosie's draped over her body.

'Is it important?' Milner asked.

'It might be.'

'Does it have something to do with all this?' He opened the door and helped the girl inside, settling her tenderly on the seat.

'Yes.'

'I'll see that you'll have it tomorrow.' A short command and the coach pulled away.

Jane walked. She saw Milner and the servant in the coach as it rushed into town. A moment and it was past her.

She moved along Vicar Lane, down to Quarry Hill. Along Mabgate and back. The sound of people. The raw noise of machines. But no one behind her. The invisible girl.

The whistles sounded for dinner, and a flood of chattering mill girls poured out of the doors. She lost herself among them, not even noticing the talk, happy to be part of a crowd for a few minutes.

The Head Row, Woodhouse Lane. A circle round, then she disappeared into Green Dragon Yard.

White was here. He was in Leeds. But he wasn't taking her bait.

Through one court, into the other, and she stood by Catherine Shields's door again.

'So soon, child?' The woman gave her soft smile. 'And look at you. Is something wrong?'

Jane felt safe here; nothing bad could happen to her in this place. Catherine stroked her hair, placed a scoop of powder in a glass, poured in some liquid and passed it to her.

'Drink this.'

It seemed to sparkle in her mouth, as if the woman had somehow captured the heart of spring. A tentative sip at first, then she downed it in three long swallows.

'Better?'

'Yes.' She looked down at the dregs. 'Thank you.'

The old woman patted a space beside her on the settle.

'Now, why don't you come and tell me what's wrong? And don't say it's nothing. I can see it on your face.'

In the daylight the house looked worse. Flies were everywhere, black, shifting hills of them, gorging on the blood. They buzzed and flew, more landing on him as he brushed them away. On his clothes, in his hair, on his skin.

Upstairs was worst. They gathered on the sheets, a crawling, seething mass. More of them than ever he'd seen in his life. This was their banquet.

Simon was glad to leave and try to pull the door closed. To get away from the constant hum. The noise of Leeds – the distant rumble of carts on the road, the hammering of the factories – sounded like music, and the smoke was sweeter than the hard stink of blood.

No need to worry about thieves. One glance inside and they'd run like the devil was after their souls.

No sign that any bodies had been dragged through the house. He'd been right. This was terror. Revenge for losing the ransom money, more likely. His gift to the Milners; they were supposed to discover it when they returned from York.

Jane didn't tell it all. She never told everything. The more you said, the more power you gave away, even to a kind, open woman like Catherine Shields. Some things would always be hidden, unspoken. It was safer to keep pieces locked inside.

'He almost killed you before, child,' she said when Jane finished speaking. 'Why do you want to give him the chance again?'

'This time I'm ready for him.'

'You were then, too. When you were in the house. That's what you said.' Catherine's voice was quiet, not judging, not condemning.

'Then I wasn't prepared enough, was I?' Jane answered.

'You don't have to prove anything, child.'

She did. She had to prove everything. Not to the world. To herself.

'Jane,' Catherine said as the girl stood to leave. Jane felt thin, bony fingers take hold of her hand and press it a little. 'Look after yourself, and may God protect you. I have something I want you to take.'

A ring, a tiny band. Gold. It fitted perfectly on her middle finger.

'My husband gave it to me. No, it's not my wedding ring,' she added with a smile. 'It was for an anniversary. He said it would always look after me. It'll do the same for you.'

For a moment, she didn't know what to say, what to do. She stared at it, the metal shining on flesh. Awkwardly, she hugged Catherine. The woman felt so frail, her skin so thin as if a breeze could gather her up and carry her off into the sky.

'Thank you.'

At the door she didn't dare to stop or look back. Not until she was in Green Dragon Yard. Then she held up her hand and saw the ring there. It felt strange; *she* felt strange. That anyone would trust her with something like this. To carry a memory.

Yet, as she came out on to the Head Row, among the wagons and the people, the sun breaking through the smoke, she felt stronger. Determined.

TWENTY-THREE

Leeds was a town of shadows. The courts and yards that hid from the light. The manufactories that rose and grew and blocked out the sun.

Simon was chasing a shadow. White came and went, and no one seemed to see him.

White didn't forget. He stored up his wounds, he picked at them. They festered inside. The blood in Milner's house proved that. But that was a distraction, a horror. The man's plans were deeper and darker. More deaths, a full settling of accounts.

Rosie or White. Jane or White.

Him or White.

He had to catch the shadow before it caught him.

The day was empty. He trailed home with nothing. Without the boys, the house felt too quiet. He wanted them back. Simon wanted his life to be complete again. He needed this to be over.

He stood by the kitchen table, trying to read the *Mercury*. The advertisements offering rewards for goods that were missing. Five shillings for the return of a bracelet. Ten for anyone who brought back a piece of silver plate. His business. His livelihood. But his mind drifted away every time he stared at the words.

The knock roused him. He opened the door with the knife in his hand. Milner's servant once again, his face drawn, in his hand a folded piece of paper, sealed with wax.

'The master wanted me to deliver this. You asked for an introduction to Mr Fairfax.'

Simon nodded. 'Thank you. How is Miss Milner?'

'Safe,' the man replied after a moment. 'Her mother is still dosing her with laudanum. It helps.'

'The house?'

'I'll see it's cleaned from top to bottom before the family comes back from York. Was it Mr White?'

'Yes,' Simon answered.

The servant stared him in the eye. 'Then I hope you'll kill him for what he's done to Miss Hannah. He's destroyed her.'

'I'll make sure that he hangs,' Simon said. 'I can promise you that.'

The same road, the same walk. Through Chapel Allerton and on to the gates of the house. This time he pushed one open and continued down the drive.

Milner's letter of introduction helped him past the front door, into a place far grander than any he'd ever seen. It made Emma Hart's small mansion look like a pauper's hovel. Wealth of a kind he could never imagine. Large rooms with expensive decoration, the soft hush that only money could buy.

He could hear the guns outside, on the far side of a hill. A flurry of them, then silence. As he waited, Simon began to have doubts about coming here. What kind of power could White have over someone like Fairfax? Men like this were untouchable; they created the justice they wanted with a quiet word. They could buy and sell souls without effort. Back in town, White could be someone. In a house like this one, he'd be nobody. A nuisance.

Half an hour later, Fairfax appeared in the drawing room, still wearing his shooting clothes. A leather jerkin over a white shirt. Black smears of gunpowder on his cheek and the stench of cordite clinging to his body. A large dog followed, lying down as soon as he made a small gesture. As obedient as everything in this house, Simon thought.

He was a handsome man, with thick dark hair and frank blue eyes, a bemused stare on his face.

'You wanted to see me.' He had the lazy drawl of the wealthy.

Simon needed to be direct. A few brief moments were all he'd have with a man like this. An indulgence.

'I'm looking for a man called Julius White. A magistrate illegally released him from custody on Sunday morning. Someone suggested he might be staying here.'

Fairfax listened as Simon talked, an elbow resting on the mantelpiece.

'Whoever said that is wrong,' he answered. 'I have no idea who Julius White is. Did anyone say *why* I should know him?'

Simon took a breath. 'Because you're a powerful man who can make things happen. You can have the guilty freed.'

Fairfax raised an eyebrow. He selected a cheroot from a box and lit it with a taper.

'People seem to believe a great deal of me. Why is that, do you think?'

'You're rich. And from what I can gather, nobody knows you. A little mystery goes a long way.'

The man smiled. 'Perhaps that's it. But whatever power people imagine I have, it doesn't extend to the law. I wouldn't want it to.' His gaze changed. 'What's your interest in this White, anyway?'

'I'm a thief-taker. He's stolen and he's murdered. He's free again, and he wants to kill me and my family.'

'That's quite a list of accusations, Mr—'

'Westow.'

'Do you have proof?'

'I do.'

'Is there anything to suggest my involvement?'

'No. I'm here because three people mentioned your name, that's all.'

'Flattered as I am that people think of me as someone exalted, I can assure you that all this has nothing to do with me. As I told you, the first time I heard the man's name was when you just mentioned it. I've given you what time I have. I wish you good day.'

He walked out. The audience was over. A few seconds later, a servant appeared to escort Simon to the door, out of the rarefied world and back to the road.

He believed Fairfax. White's name really meant nothing at all to him. But not every road had a destination. He'd go back to Leeds and try again. Keep trying until he discovered the answer.

*   *   *

Jane turned the ring on her finger. The gold felt warm to her touch. Soothing.

She spotted someone walking along the street. The boy, bare-headed, lost in the coat she'd given to him. His eyes were wide, frantic as he dodged between people, avoiding the cuffs they tried to give him as he pushed past them. He came to a stop by her.

'He's there. In the churchyard again. With that man.' The words rushed out. The boy turned, starting back up the street, then looked back. 'Are you coming?'

The ring rubbed against the knife hilt in her pocket.

St John's churchyard was empty. Only the gravestones kept watch.

'Where were they?' Jane asked.

'Over there.' He pointed to the porch.

'You stay here,' she told him and saw his mouth turn down. 'It's safer.' She hesitated, and said, 'If anything happens to me, go and tell Simon Westow on Swinegate.'

The boy nodded, his face solemn.

Jane walked around the church. She heard the noise from the small school in the corner of the yard and saw the almshouses in the distance. She halted at every corner, listening, waiting, ready.

White wasn't there. She stepped into the porch, then turned the handle on the heavy door and entered the church. Her footsteps rang off the high ceiling. Dark, carved wood. Stained glass. The glowing smell of wax.

Nobody inside. Nothing except the creak of time and the mustiness of age. She came back out, into the light. The boy pointed towards something in the distance.

'That's him. The one he met.'

A figure on his own, almost a hundred yards away. Pale trousers, a dark coat, hat, a slow, thoughtful stroll.

'Are you sure?'

'Yes.'

She glanced at the boy. He looked back, defiantly, daring her to call him a liar. Jane gave him a penny and began to walk after the man.

Out along Woodhouse Lane, where the houses were grand, standing at a distance from each other. He turned, passing Queens

Square, its buildings surrounding a trim, fenced lawn. Then another
turn, on to Long Balk Lane.

He'd never looked back. No one was behind her, she knew that.
Jane hurried, reaching the corner just as he unlocked a door and
vanished inside. She stood, counting the houses. Then she left again.

The boy had vanished from the churchyard. She sat in the porch
and thought. Simon would be able to discover the man's name.
But White couldn't be far. Not all the way out in Chapel Allerton.
He was much closer to Leeds. Without noticing, she turned the
ring on her finger again.

'I'm coming with you,' Rosie said. 'The boys are off and safe.
There's no need for me to stay at home.'

Simon stared at her and pursed his lips. Then he nodded.

'Make sure you're armed.'

A single, swift movement and she had a dagger in her hand.

'See?' she said with a dark smile.

He turned to Jane. 'Now let's find out who lives there.'

She led the way. Up through town, out along Woodhouse Lane
and Queens Square once more, then stopping at the corner of Long
Balk Lane.

'Five houses along.'

'You're absolutely sure it was that one?'

'Yes.'

Where Arthur Standish lived. The man whose son had been
turned away for Hannah Milner's hand by her father. The first
place he'd gone searching for Hannah. Simon felt as if events had
turned in a circle.

Standish, Madeley . . . had they worked together to destroy
John Milner? How did Standish know Julius White?

'Simon?' Rosie said, and he turned.

'What?'

'You know who lives there, don't you?'

He nodded. A faint memory stirred in his mind: Standish's sister
was married to Hardisty the magistrate.

'You might as well go home,' he said. 'I may be a while.'

At the back of the house, he knocked and waited for the word to
enter. Martha the housekeeper looked him up and down.

'Things must be bad if you're here touting for business again.'

'I need to see Mr Standish.'

'Do you, now?' She placed her hands on her hips. 'And what if he doesn't want to see you?'

'He will,' Simon told her. 'Tell him it's about Julius White.'

She stared a little while longer, then waddled away.

The kitchen smelt of roasting meat. Fat dripped and sizzled on the coals. A pan of vegetables simmered on the stove and a pudding rested on the table, enough to feed eight or more.

His stomach rumbled; he'd had nothing to eat since breakfast. Simon poured a mug of ale and drank it down. At least he could wet his whistle.

'Upstairs. In the library.' The voice surprised him. He hadn't heard Martha return. 'You remember the way?'

Arthur Standish sat surrounded by his books. Two walls filled with shelves that rose from floor to ceiling. More on his desk and on the lectern. The windows looked out on a garden starting to bloom.

The man had a florid face, ruddy from years of drink, a map of red veins just under the skin. A full glass beside him on the table. His belly was too big for his waistcoat, pressing and threatening the buttons.

'You told Martha you wanted to talk about Julius White, Mr Westow.'

'That's right. The man you met in the churchyard earlier today.'

Standish raised thick, grey eyebrows.

'Did I? I must have forgotten that appointment.'

'How is your sister these days, Mr Standish?'

The question caught him off guard. Standish fumbled for a reply.

'Anne? Do you know her? She's—'

'She's married to Magistrate Hardisty, isn't she? Such a pity he had to leave Leeds so suddenly on Sunday morning. Right after a special court hearing, too.'

The man's red face turned darker, purple rising on his cheeks.

'I don't know what you're trying to say, Westow—'

'Yes, you do. You know exactly what I'm saying.'

The silence grew around them.

'Why would I meet someone like White?' Standish asked finally. His voice was cracked and dry.

'You tell me that,' Simon said.

The man was beginning to waver. His gaze slipped from object to object. A vase, a volume open on a chair, the inkwell on the desk, never resting on anything.

Simon could wait. The truth might take a little while yet, but it would come.

Jane walked back beside Rosie. They didn't speak. She could feel the woman's disappointment; she wanted to be part of it, to do *something*. They passed through the crowds on Albion Street, more and more people around them as they neared Boar Lane. Carts swerved around each other. Draymen rolled a barrel of beer down to a cellar. A woman cried out, trying to sell last autumn's lucky heather.

'Your ring,' Rosie said. 'It's new.'

Jane pushed her hand into her pocket to hide it.

'Yes.'

'From a young man?' Rosie's voice teased a little; her eyes twinkled.

'No. A woman. An old woman.'

'It's safe to trust us, Jane. We won't hurt you.'

But the people who promised that were the ones who caused pain. She could rely on herself. Only herself. Catherine Shields would die. Mrs Rigton would die. They understood her without asking. They accepted her as she was. But a few more years and they'd both be in the ground.

It was always safer never to let go, never to let anyone have any hold over you.

No strange faces waiting on Swinegate. She saw Rosie looking round the empty house, hearing its silence. Missing her children.

Jane closed the door quietly as she left.

People walked through the churchyard at St John's. Some hurried, desperately trying to catch up with life. Others moved in twos and threes. She saw an old man stoop awkwardly and brush the dirt from a gravestone with his handkerchief. He stayed a minute, hands clasped and head bowed, then walked slowly away, wrapped tight in his memories. A cat found a patch of sunlight and curled up to sleep.

She sat for an hour, off in the corner, under an old oak. Sooner

or later White would be here again. Jane could wait. She was so
still, nobody would notice her. The shawl over her head. The
invisible girl.

Standish wavered but he didn't break.

'I told you, Westow. I don't know White. I've never met him.'
He gripped the arms of his chair and stared.

'I don't believe you,' Simon said.

'You can either leave now, or I'll send Martha to bring the
constable.'

He'd come so close. The man had been on the edge. But the
admission had never arrived. Perhaps Standish had looked ahead
and seen himself in the dock while a judge handed down the
verdict. Maybe he'd felt the noose tightening around his neck.

'I'd enjoy this place if I were you,' Simon told him. 'You might
be exchanging it for a cell very soon.'

TWENTY-FOUR

The world changed as the daylight faded.

The cat had long since padded away. The footsteps
vanished from the churchyard. The only sounds were urgent,
whispered voices. People moved unseen in the darkness. A shriek
of laughter from a whore and her john; they were finished and
gone almost as soon as they arrived.

Jane sat by a tree. Her belly was empty, but she'd known too
many days like that for it to bother her. Her eyes grew used to the
night. She could make out the shapes as they passed softly.

A soft, waning moon, enough to cast a faint glow. Thousands
of stars, faint pinpricks in the blackness.

White would return. She knew it. She would wait.

Jane must have slept. She woke to feel the dew on her dress,
cool against her skin. The grey light before dawn. She stretched
out her legs and arched her back. All around there was silence, as
if Leeds was holding its breath as it waited for day to begin.

She touched the knife in her pocket, then turned the ring on her finger, as if that might summon the man she wanted to see. He'd be here today. She knew it inside.

A clear night; a sunny morning. Soon a haze of factory smoke would leave the sky as hazy as gossamer.

She waited. Not long now.

'It doesn't mean anything,' Rosie said. 'There are plenty of times she doesn't come home.'

Simon breathed and tried to calm his mind.

'I know. But White's after us. He could have her again. She could be lying dead somewhere.'

'Simon.' She took hold of his hand. 'Do you honestly think either of us could ever stop her going where she likes?'

'No,' he admitted.

'Then there's no point in worrying. If anything's happened, people will let us know. Jane has her own mind. She goes her own way. Whatever she's doing, you won't find her until she's ready.'

'But if she's dead—'

'We'd better hope she's not.' Her voice rose over his, her voice hard. She wasn't going to let herself think that, he could tell. 'Jane can take good care of herself. You know, in some ways she's older than either you or me.'

She was right. Neither of them knew what Jane's life had been like. She'd never told them. She'd hardly said anything about herself. She locked everyone out, she used silence as her defence against the world.

He valued her. Jane was the best he'd ever known. She had a keen gift for the work they did. Sometimes she did seem older than them, that was true. But at other times she was so young. She didn't understand people. She pushed them too far away ever to see what lay in their heads and their hearts.

'I'm going out to look.'

'Find White,' Rosie told him. 'That's what she's doing.'

People came. People went. No one glanced in her direction. The cat arrived, purred, turned three times and settled close to her.

Soon, she thought. Very soon.

The first to arrive was the man from Long Balk Lane. The same coat and trousers as the day before. He stood on a patch of grass, removed his hat and wiped his face with a handkerchief.

He had the look of a man who'd been kept awake by nightmares. Anxious, pacing, taking the watch from his pocket and checking it. A few breaths and he'd pull it out again.

Five minutes passed, ten. And then White appeared, walking as if he didn't have a thing to worry him, the lord of the world. The pair talked in whispers.

The man from Long Balk Lane kept gesturing, arms moving. Fear, she decided. He was scared. White listened, nodded, spoke a little.

People passed by, lost in their own lives, everyone hurrying today. They kept talking. Finally, White reached out and placed his hand on the other's shoulders, squeezing hard, not letting go. Then a nod and he was gone, striding away.

Jane rose. The cat stirred and settled again. No one saw her leave.

Simon could walk around Leeds all day and never spot Jane. Find White, Rosie had said. Easy words but impossible to do. He went to the people who might hear: the upright and the criminal. Nobody knew. Still no one had seen him since the appearance in court.

He was here, though. He was definitely here.

At the top of Briggate, Simon turned and gazed back down the street. A throng of faces. Carts parked, men unloading their goods as others edged by. A coach tried to make time with the crack of a whip.

How many people could he see? Hundreds? A thousand? More? And how many filling all the other streets, the manufactories and mills, the houses?

How much sorrow did they all carry? What memories did they push away, never welcoming their return?

He'd learned to live with his past, to make it his own. To turn it into anger.

He kept looking. What chance was there of picking out one face among so many?

His job was a game of seek and find.

But this . . . this game was deadly. It was one where he had no control.

* * *

White plunged into the crowd on Briggate. Jane stayed close enough to follow and watch as he slid between people. They passed the Moot Hall, where the butchers' shops all clustered together with their stink of meat.

At Wood Street, he turned. She paused. There were too many ways out; he could go straight through to Vicar Lane or slide into a network of yards. But somewhere like this offered her the chance to end everything.

She moved carefully, listening for the ring of his footsteps on stone and keeping a safe distance. There were fewer people back here; all the noise from the road grew muffled by the buildings that rose up around her.

Her hand was tight on the knife as she moved. Jane heard him turn into one of the courts, walking without a care on his mind.

Jane knew exactly how dangerous he was. The way he could appear out of nowhere. And if White had a blade to her throat back here, she knew she would die.

At the corner, she stopped, drawing in her breath before she looked. There he was, pausing, then kneeling to tie his bootlace.

Jane ran. He turned his head as he heard her. Too late. Her knife sliced through his coat and his shirt, biting deep into the flesh on his back. She pulled it out, seeing the blood start to boil and stain. A second blow and he was lying on the ground, huddled down in the piss and the night soil, fingers scrabbling for a weapon.

Jane raised the knife and brought it down. Again and again. On his arms, on his body, anywhere she could reach. With her left hand she turned White's head, holding it, forcing him to look. She wanted him to see who'd done this to him, to know. To understand. The invisible girl made flesh. He was still breathing, a thin, whistling wheeze through his teeth. His eyes were filled with hate. Jane stood and smiled down at him. She had her arm raised for the final slash across his throat when she heard voices. Men, just around the corner. Too close.

A last look and she was gone.

Jane burst into the house and through to the kitchen. She was weightless. She felt as if she could laugh. As if she could dance.

Rosie turned, a metal pan in her hands. Her eyes widened. 'What's happened to you? There's blood—'

'He's dead. White's dead. I killed him.'

'He's dead?' She let the pan fall on the table. 'How? Where?'

'In the court just off Wood Street.' She pulled out her knife. The blade was still red and dripping.

'Listen,' Rosie told her. 'You need to take that dress off. Now. All that blood on it. I'll give you one of mine. And take a bath. It's all over your hands and your face.'

Jane nodded. She couldn't understand. Rosie should be happy. They were free. White was gone from their lives. Why was she like this? So frantic, so worried.

'I'll bring you something to wear and I'll burn this. Did anyone see you?'

'No. Why—'

'Good.' Rosie bit her lip. 'If we don't mention it outside the house, no one will ever know. We'll be safe.' She pinned Jane by the wrists. 'No one can know you killed him. We can't let you hang for murder. Do you understand?'

Jane nodded again. She looked into Rosie's face. 'But he's dead.'

'And I'm glad.' She squeezed the girl's flesh lightly. 'You did well. I just want to make sure that you don't join him.'

An hour later, hair still wet and dripping, Jane sat in the kitchen, wearing a clean brown dress that was too big for her, a leather belt cinched tight around her waist. The knife lay in its sheath. She'd cleaned the knife, oiled and sharpened it even before she took her bath.

The exhilaration had faded. Now she felt nothing at all. She could remember everything, each blow, relive it in her mind. But it didn't mean a thing. It might have been someone else who struck White. It was already the past, something she was slowly leaving behind her.

Simon had heard the rumours on Briggate. A man knifed. He'd dashed into the court, pushing through the press of people eager to see. All that remained were a few dark, wet stains soaking into the flagstones.

Nobody knew the truth, just the gossip that swirled. It was White. It wasn't. He was dead. He was alive and walked away, barely

wounded. Badly wounded. Almost a corpse. One man claimed to
have seen him. Two questions and Simon made him for a liar.

No body. No facts.

He looked from his wife to Jane and saw something in their
eyes.

'You know,' he said.

'Tell him,' Rosie told Jane.

She did. Each moment of it. But this was the last time she'd
talk about it. The final time to think about it before she locked
the thoughts away.

Silence filled the room as her voice faded.

'Was he dead when you left?' Simon asked finally.

Jane shook her head. 'No. But he was close. He must have been.
I wanted him to see me. I wanted him to know who'd done it.'

'He vanished. You didn't kill him.'

'Simon . . .' Rosie began, but he held up his hand.

'How badly did you hurt him?'

'Enough,' Jane answered. 'I stabbed him seven times. He
couldn't stand up. His throat . . . it sounded like a death rattle.'
She stared. 'He can't have survived.'

But men did. They lived through that and much worse. Simon
breathed slowly. There was nothing he could say.

His face softened. 'How about you? How are you?'

'I'm fine.' Her face showed nothing. Every trace of expression
had disappeared.

'We'd better go and discover the truth.' He smiled at her. 'White's
badly wounded, at least. We know that much.' Jane said nothing.
'Don't ever tell anyone what you did.'

'I warned her,' Rosie said. 'When we thought he was dead.'

'Alive or a corpse, keep silent,' Simon warned. 'And let's all
hope he's supping with the devil by now.'

She should have finished the job. All it would have taken was one
more cut. But she'd heard the men approaching . . . another second
and she could have made certain. Given White his last farewell to
the world.

And now . . .

From place to place and no one knew the truth. All she heard
was a tangle of words. Jane stayed out long after darkness had

fallen. She needed the certainty, one way or the other. In the old blacking factory the voices spoke in whispers, but it was all vapour. At Mrs Rigton's, men talked about it. She listened. Nothing.

Finally, up in the attic on Swinegate, she took out her knife and pulled back the sleeve of her dress. Cutting the flesh where it had begun to heal. To make herself bleed, to make herself burn. Make herself pay.

Simon found no certainty. A few who swore they'd seen it happen. But he knew it was boasting. White's body hadn't been found. That was what mattered.

He wanted the man dead. But he wanted to be there when it happened, to see the end, to watch as his soul left his body at the end of a noose. After that, hell could keep Julius White for eternity.

He walked down Briggate in the darkness. All the way to the bridge. It was so old that the stone on the parapets was beginning to crumble. Simon picked off a few fragments and dropped them into the water.

Seven blows, Jane had said. She'd hurt him badly. He believed her. Yet somehow, he'd managed to vanish once again, as if he was made of smoke.

A wounded animal was the most dangerous. That was what people said.

He locked the door behind himself. A lamp was burning in the kitchen. Rosie sat with her head in her hands, staring at the table. She looked up hopefully as he came in. But all he could do was shake his head.

'I need it to be over, Simon. I want my children back here. Where they belong.'

'I know.' He stroked her hair. 'So do I.'

The place felt empty without them. They made life worthwhile. He missed the noise and the chaos they brought.

'Soon,' he promised. 'Soon.'

TWENTY-FIVE

Simon slipped out while Rosie slept. Into the faint light just before dawn. Already people were hurrying towards the factories. He heard the rhythm of clogs on the cobbles, the swish of a dress as a woman walked by.

He followed the path by the river, all the way downstream from Gott's mill at Bean Ing to Fearn's Island, eyes searching the water for White's body. All he could see were streaks of red and black on the surface from the dyeworks, the bobbing corpses of cats and dogs. A tree limb caught in an eddy near the far bank. And everywhere, the stench of waste.

No matter; it was worth looking.

He saw Barnaby Wade through the window of the coffee house. He had his head down, reading a newspaper, only glancing up as Simon slid on to the seat across the table.

'People have been talking about someone we know.'

'Talk and talk and talk,' Simon said. 'About the only thing I haven't heard yet is the truth.'

Wade lowered the newspaper and sipped from a china cup. 'I don't know more than anyone else.'

'He's very badly hurt.'

'Is he?' Wade cocked his head. 'You're sure?'

Simon nodded. 'I'm positive.'

'And you want to see if he lasted through the night?'

'I want to *know*. He's not in the river.'

Wade nodded. 'I can ask. But if there was something definite, you can wager it would be all over Leeds by now. If I were you, I'd stay armed.'

'I am.' He smiled. 'Always.'

'I did hear one curious thing.'

'What's that?'

'A man claimed he heard someone running near the place where White was attacked. He said it could have been a girl.'

Simon shrugged. 'You know what White looks like. He's big. Do you think a girl could get the better of him?'

'I'd say that depends on the girl, wouldn't you?' He closed the newspaper and pushed it away, gathering up his hat. 'Business calls. I'll tell you if I hear anything. And look after yourself, Simon.'

Standing by the attic window, Jane watched him leave. She made out the silhouettes of roofs and chimneys, smoke and slates against the sky.

She'd wrapped a piece of cloth around her arm. The pain remained, fading slowly. She wanted to keep it, to hold it, to cherish it, to be reminded. One more cut . . .

Rosie's dress rubbed and chafed against her skin. She gathered the shawl around her shoulders, laced her boots and followed Simon out into the beginning of the day.

Today she'd finish things. Today she wouldn't fail.

A few stalls were set up for the early workers, selling coffee, pea soup, bread and butter. There was no need to call out their wares; people knew where they were. Only a few stragglers remained, too late for the start of their shifts. One or two more whose lives were on the streets. A man on the tramp, asking hopefully about jobs in the town.

Jane moved by without being seen.

She returned to the court off Wood Street. It was empty now. In the half-light she could see White on the ground, bloody and helpless. Fury on his face as he waited for the last blow.

How could he have vanished?

The day was coming alive as she emerged on to Briggate. The Newcastle coach sped out of the Talbot yard in a flurry of noise, a crooked smile on the driver's face. Down by the White Cloth Hall, the door to Mrs Rigton's beershop was unlocked.

A pair of early drinkers had claimed a corner. They sat, sullen, quiet.

'You've got a new dress,' Mrs Rigton said, raising an eyebrow.

Jane shook her head. 'It's someone else's old dress.'

'Doesn't matter. It looks like new. They could have sold it and made some money.'

'I should be glad it was free, then.' She paused. 'Have you heard anything more about White?'

'Just the rumours that he was attacked.'

'He was,' Jane said. 'And he was close to dead.'

Mrs Rigton chewed her lip and stared. 'Then you know more than I do. No mention of anyone finding a body.' She saw the cloth around Jane's arm. 'What have you been up to, girl?'

'I cut myself. An accident.' It was as much as she was going to tell anyone. It was her business and hers alone. 'I need to find White.'

'If there's any hint, I'll tell you. Just watch out.'

'I will.'

How had he disappeared? Simon worried at the question. But really, it didn't matter. White was nowhere to be found. That was the important fact.

People had plenty to say about it, but the words were like sand, trickling through his fingers.

What would he do if he found the man? Finish the job that Jane had begun? Could he kill in cold blood? He knew himself well enough: no. What, though? Drag the man to the magistrate and swear out a warrant?

White could counter with his own warrant against Jane. Even without witnesses, she'd be arrested and stand trial. Could she survive in a gaol?

All those questions could wait. First he had to find the man.

By evening the frustration had built inside him and his temper was short. He clenched and unclenched his hands, itching for a fight. It was time to go home before he let it all spill out.

He strode down Briggate, caught in his thoughts. Close to the turning on to Swinegate he glanced up and saw a figure against the wall. Jane.

'Someone's watching the house,' she whispered.

'Where?'

'In the shadows.'

'Who is it? White?'

She shook her head. 'Too tall. The wrong shape.'

'We'll take this one and find out who sent him,' Simon said. 'Give me two minutes to slip through the courts to the other end then start to walk.'

He hurried through the darkness. Simon knew every step here. Inside him, the fire was roaring. He was ready for this. He needed it.

At the corner, Simon waited for a moment, letting his breath steady. He took one knife from his belt, another from his boot. He waited until he heard Jane's footsteps. Then he began to run.

The man was in the middle of the street, waiting for Jane to come close. He was leering at her, licking his lips. She knew she looked like a girl who'd be easy to kill, so small and thin and helpless. Then he heard movement behind and whipped his head around, mouth falling open in surprise.

Simon was hungry for violence. It glittered in his eyes. Fists and boots. Jane stood, ready to strike. But this was his fight. As the man's knife clattered away on the cobbles, she gathered it up, alert.

It was over almost as soon as it began. One final kick to the man's side and she watched as Simon took a pace back, breathing hard.

'Who sent you?'

The man rolled on to his side and retched. The answer came out as a croak: 'Hawley.'

Simon looked at her. Jane nodded. She knew that name.

'Why?' He squatted and took hold of the man's shirt, dragging his head off the ground.

'I don't know. He promised me a guinea if I killed the girl.'

'You won't be going back to get your money from Mr Hawley.' He spoke in a quiet, even voice. 'You won't be going anywhere near him. The only thing you'll be doing is leaving Leeds.'

'But—'

'You'd better remember – I know what you look like now.' Jane kept silent as Simon stared into the man's face. 'If either of us ever sees you again, we'll kill you. Do you understand that?'

The man nodded. Simon let him go. He tried to rise, steadying himself against the wall. He kept one hand pressed against his ribs.

'Go. We know your face now. And we won't forget.'

Jane waited as he hobbled along, until he turned the corner, out of sight.

'Hawley's the farmer that White stayed with,' she said. 'You were going to talk to him.'

'We'll visit first thing in the morning. White might still be out there.'

They left just before dawn, the light just enough to guide them up the cart track towards the farms.

'Which one is it?' Simon asked.

'Over there.' Jane pointed.

On the hilltop, with a view down over Leeds and along the valley. It would be easy to spot anyone coming. A heavy gust of wind rocked them.

'Let's cut across,' he said. 'That way they'll only see us if they look.'

It was a sharp climb, holding on to tufts of scrubby grass and stunted bushes to steady them and stop them from falling. Poor land for farming, Simon thought. Closer to the top there was pasture, a dip in the land and a worn path that ran to the farm.

It was a bleak, lonely house. Battered and worn, with a plain stone front, a barn and stable behind.

'You take the other buildings,' Simon said. She slipped away, her brown dress soon blending in with the ground.

The paint had worn off the front door, the wood turned pale grey with age and weather. He knocked and waited until a hard-faced man answered. Thick hands, a face that had been battered by years of sun and rain. The man wore a padded jerkin over an old shirt, a spotted kerchief tied at his neck, heavy breeches and gaiters covering his legs. His hair hung thick and wild, starting to turn grey at the temples.

'Yes?' A curt voice.

'Mr Hawley?'

'Aye. Who are you?'

Simon pulled out his knife. 'I'm Simon Westow. You offered a guinea to have my assistant killed. We're going to have a talk.'

The milkmaid was guiding the cattle towards a field, a switch moving in her hand to keep them from straying. She turned as Jane approached, curious.

'Road don't go through here,' she called. 'You want to go back. Hundred yards or so.' She used the stick to indicate.

'I want to talk to you, if you're Emily.'

That was the name Josh had said. She wondered if he was standing at his stable door, watching all this.

'I am.' Her voice was suspicious. She kept working with the cows, ushering the last of them through to the grass. One or two of the beasts turned to look. The young woman pushed the gate closed and looped a rope over the post to secure it. 'Who are you?'

'I'm Jane. I knew Josh a long time ago.'

A quick nod. 'He's talked about you. He gave you a coat last time you were out.'

'That's right.'

'What do you want with me?'

'You work for Mr Hawley. Why did he send someone to kill me last night?'

'I've got nowt to say to you.' He started to push the door closed, but Simon kept his weight against it. He placed the tip of his blade against the farmer's belly.

'No, Mr Hawley, you've got plenty to say. We'll go inside and talk about it.'

The rooms were plain and spare, smelling of the fields. Flagstone floors, hearths empty. A big, battered table in the kitchen, the only room with any warmth.

Hawley stood, hands resting on the back of a wooden chair. 'What do you want to know?'

'Everything,' Simon told him. 'But let's start with why, shall we? And you needn't worry; the man you sent won't be coming to collect his fee. Jane's outside. I made her wait there. She'd be quite happy to slit your throat, though. She reckons you deserve it. You'd better convince me that you don't.'

Panic on his face, Hawley half-turned. 'He sent me a message. Told me what to do.'

'Who did? White?'

The farmer nodded.

The man was still alive. That was beyond doubt now.

'Let me see it,' Simon told him. Maybe the writing would tell him something. Weak, shaky?

'I burned it. He said I should.'

'And why are you doing favours for him? I know he stayed here for a few days.'

Hawley stared down at the table and said nothing.

'Why?' Simon asked again. He tapped the knife lightly against the wood. 'Why?'

'None of your business.'

'If it involves White, it's my business.'

He stood over the man, waiting. A log dropped in the fire and sparks rushed up in a hiss.

'Years back, he did something for me. Before he were sent away.' He looked up, defiant.

'What?' He let the knife blade hit the wood a few times. An aid to the man's memory.

'I owed some money. From a card game. I'd had a few drinks in one of the inns and started playing.' He looked up, eyes angry. 'They cheated me.'

'What does this have to do with Julius White?'

'I knew him a little. I'd met him here and there. I told him and he said he'd take care of it. Next thing I knew, I had a note saying the debt was cancelled.'

'How much did that cost you?'

'Not much.' He paused. 'Not then, anyway.'

'What happened to the card players?'

'I don't know,' Hawley replied. 'I never saw them again.'

And what you didn't know, you could ignore. For a while, at least. Too many people owed White favours. Since his return, he'd been calling them all in.

'He stayed here for a few days, didn't he? A little while ago.'

'Aye.'

'Where is he?'

'I don't know.' And suddenly Simon's knife was at his throat, pressing tenderly against the sagging flesh. Hawley's eyes were wide, arms flailing.

'I asked you a question.'

'I don't know. I told you. I don't.'

'Then how were you supposed to let him know if your man had succeeded?'

'He said he'd hear about it.'

Simon pulled the blade away. The explanation made sense. The farmer felt at his neck for blood.

'Who brought you the message?'

'Just a lad. Didn't know his way around out here from the look of him.'

'What if you needed to send word to White about something?'

Hawley shook his head. 'That's not his way. He orders, and people obey.'

'Not you,' Simon told him. 'Not any more. Whatever you owed him, that debt has all been paid. And right now, you'd do well to believe you're lucky that your heart's still beating.' He paused to let the man reflect for a moment. 'It's easy enough to commit a murder up here. Keep that thought at the front of your mind.'

'But he wouldn't do something like that,' Emily said.

'He did.' Jane stood, arms by her sides. The wind whipped at her hair. 'You had a man staying here.'

'Josh asked me about that. I never really saw him.'

'He's the one who wanted me dead.'

'Why? Why would someone do that?'

'Because I tried to kill him. He's a murderer, a kidnapper.'

The girl didn't understand. How could she? Her life up here was straightforward. Milk the cows, tend to them. Each day ordered by the seasons. Jane couldn't explain her world to someone like that. They were close to the same age, but there was a gulf as wide as the world between them.

'I haven't seen him since the day he left,' Emily said. 'He hasn't been back.'

Jane nodded and began to walk away. After three paces, she turned. 'Be kind to Josh. He has a good heart.'

'I like him,' Emily answered with a soft smile. 'I wouldn't hurt him.'

TWENTY-SIX

The wind was shaking the young leaves on the branches, making them dance and fly. A sudden gust caught a crow and pushed it across the sky.

Enough to clear the smoke from Leeds, Simon thought. For a

while. A few drops of rain fell and he raised his head, letting them splash on his skin.

They found shelter in the entrance to a court off New Causeway, watching the drops bounce off the road outside.

'Hawley won't help White again,' Simon said.

'What did you tell him?'

'That you'd cut his throat.'

Jane nodded, staring out at the street. She wore the shawl pulled over her head and he couldn't see her face. But how often did she let anything show? Anger? Fear? They stayed hidden inside. Even her eyes gave nothing away, always watching, assessing.

The shower passed and he stepped out, breathing deep. Clean air and a clear sky over the town. It wouldn't last long. But he couldn't enjoy it. They had too much to do. They needed to finish this.

She sensed him long before she could see him. On Kirkgate, just up from the church. Jane glanced in the shop windows, but there were too many people to pick out a single face. She darted across the road in front of a cart, hearing the driver curse her and flick his whip above her head.

He'd have to follow. She saw him in a reflection, hurrying through a gap in the traffic, one hand holding on to his hat. A big man, muscled and broad, sober in his dark coat and trousers, determination in his eyes.

Stocks. That was his name. She'd noticed him around Leeds before, lurking in the dram shops and the cheap coffee houses. And she knew what he did. Pay him enough and he'd maim or murder.

Jane slid her hand into the pocket of her dress and gripped the knife hilt. He was much taller than her, far heavier. Men like Stocks survived by being good at their work. By being ruthless.

She would be better.

Jane slipped around the corner and up the stone steps to Wellington Court. Stocks knew Leeds well; he'd follow.

Through the cramped passageway and another ginnel that brought her out beside the White Cloth Hall. He was too big to move quickly through here. Stocks would be wary that she'd be waiting for him at the other end.

Let him worry. Jane had another plan.

She paused at the far end of the building, watching as he emerged cautiously with a blade in his fist, looking around.

A flash of her dress and she was gone again. She heard him running, knew he'd seen her. A turn to the right, another to the left, and she was in the space behind Mrs Rigton's beershop.

Empty barrels filled one end, waiting for the drayman. There was enough of a brick wall at the entrance to hide behind. She was small, she was fast. A place like this would favour her. Stocks's bulk would work against him.

Jane heard him come closer. One footstep, a hesitation, another, and a third. She was ready, hardly breathing, reading the shadows near her feet.

He took a pace inside, turning his head. But she was deep in the shade, the invisible girl. Her left arm moved, and her shawl floated in the air towards his face. Stocks lunged. It was instinct.

Jane darted forward, beneath his arms, easing her knife under his ribs. She felt the flesh give and pushed harder. Deeper. All the way, until the hilt jammed against his skin, then she drew it out again.

His eyes were wide. He stared at her. Surprise, shock. His hand reached for the wound, as if he might be able to stop the blood streaming out. Stocks opened his mouth, but no words came as he slumped to his knees.

Jane held the edge of her knife against his throat. 'Where is he?'

Only pale pink foam bubbled from his lips as he tried to speak. Stocks was blinking, fighting to stay in the world. But he knew this was one battle he couldn't win. His life was leaking away.

Then he toppled to the ground. Jane stood, waiting until the last breath shuddered from his body. She wiped her knife on his coat, sheathed it, took a final look and walked into the beershop.

'There's a body behind the building.'

Mary Rigton looked up. 'Who?'

'Stocks,' Jane said. Her voice was flat, no trace of emotion. 'He was coming after me.'

The old woman sighed. 'I wish you'd done it somewhere else.' Jane shrugged and said nothing. She didn't want to bring trouble here. But needs must. Her life or his, and she was going to take

her advantages where she found them. Mrs Rigton would understand that. 'You go. I'll take care of it. There won't be a soul in
Leeds who'll miss him. Who was paying him? Do you know?'

'White.'

'Then you'd best kill him, too. Or there'll be more coming.'

'I'm going to.'

She walked back along the street and washed the blood from
her hands in a horse trough. Mrs Rigton would clean out Stocks's
pockets. The coins would pay the men who dumped his corpse in
the river once darkness fell.

Jane felt nothing. No regret. No guilt. He would have killed her
and gone on with his day. All he wanted was to earn his fee. She
was young, a girl. He'd seen her as a few minutes' work and
money in his pocket.

But she was alive and he was dead.

Near the bottom of Briggate, Big Kate was selling pies from a
tray. She bought one, wandering out along the water. The grass
was still damp from the rain, but she sat and ate. Smoke had closed
over the town again; she could taste it in every bite.

The food was just something to warm her belly and keep her
until supper.

Mrs Rigton was right: she needed to find White, to kill him.
Until that happened, there'd be another man after her, then another.
Too many in Leeds were willing to murder for a few coins.

She stood, brushing the crumbs off her lap. Stocks was put
away in her mind, the door to that room closed. She wouldn't let
herself relive it. She wouldn't feel anything.

'You killed Stocks?' Simon asked in disbelief. God Almighty. The
man was twice her size. How had she managed it, and not a scratch
on her?

'I had to. He was going to kill me.' She sat quietly, tearing a
piece of bread into tiny crumbs.

'Where is he now?' He glanced at his wife. She was standing
by the table, her arms folded.

Jane shrugged. 'Probably in the river.'

'Are you all right?' Rosie asked. 'Did he hurt you?'

'No. I never gave him the chance.' No pride in her voice, Simon
thought. Nothing at all.

Simon was thinking aloud. 'White wants his revenge for what you did to him.'

'I tried to ask where White was, but he couldn't speak.'

Stocks. He knew the man's reputation. A killer, a vicious man who took joy in his work. Brutal, deadly. And she'd beaten him.

'Who else knows?' Rosie asked.

'Mrs Rigton. She won't say a word.' Jane gathered the crumbs between her fingers and put them in her mouth.

He nodded and stayed silent. As soon as someone discovered the body, the news would be all over town. Maybe they'd be lucky and the corpse would float far down the Aire before he was found. Somewhere he wasn't known.

Two had come after Jane now. But White would send more. He'd keep men coming. And sooner or later, one would slip past her guard.

Simon didn't want to kill. But he wondered if he still had the luxury of choice.

He spent the evening haunting the inns. As the clock struck ten he walked into the Old George Hotel on Briggate, through to the office at the back of the building. The stench of boiled cabbage filled the air and stuck in his throat.

The door was closed. He didn't knock, just turned the handle and entered. Cartwright was there, pressed against a whore with her back to the wall and her skirts raised, a look of weariness on her face.

'Time for you to go, miss,' Simon said.

Cartwright turned with a snarl that became a smile as he saw Simon. He pulled away, tucking himself into his trousers and buttoning them.

'Pay her, Zack.'

'I've already—'

'Pay her.'

He took out a couple of coins and tossed them at her feet. She picked them up and left without another look at the men.

All evening, Simon had gnawed at a thought. How was White contacting people? He was badly hurt, that was certain. He couldn't be walking around. But if someone was doing the job for him . . .

'You owe me fourpence,' Cartwright said.

'Take it from the money White sent you.'

Simon stood near the door, waiting. He felt his heart thudding in his chest. Cartwright would break quickly. He always did. This time he'd keep him broken.

'I haven't heard from him.'

'You might as well stop lying, Zack.'

'I'm not, Mr Westow.'

Simon took a pace forward. A movement, and a knife was in his hand. 'You are.'

He could smell it on the man. The lies, the terror. But truth would cleanse him.

Jane sat on her bed and sharpened the knife with a whetstone. Stroke after stroke, for five full minutes, until the edge was keener than it had ever been. Gently, she wiped the dust off the blade and held it up to the lamp light.

She'd be ready.

Simon strode along Kirkgate, moving so quickly that she could barely keep pace with him.

'Zack Cartwright was arranging everything for White,' he said. 'Tempt him with a few shillings and he'd murder his own mother.' He gave a wolfish smile. 'The good thing is he crumbles so easily.'

'Where's White now?'

'Mrs Pascoe's lodging house on the Calls.'

He'd been there often enough in the past. The place was riddled with thieves. He'd lost count of the number of times he'd found them in the rooms, the goods they'd stolen in a pack or bag by their beds. Just waiting for him to arrive and return them to their owners. As long as White paid each day, Mrs Pascoe wouldn't care. She wouldn't ask questions.

Simon had dragged it all from Cartwright. The note he'd received, the demand that he visit. A weak, infirm hand that struggled to make the letters, but definitely from White. He'd gone to see him at the lodging house.

'He looked close to dead, Mr Westow. Honest to God, I swear it. It hurt him to move, I could see that.' Cartwright rubbed his wrist. 'But he still had a grip on him.'

And still something in his purse.

'He told me to send word to Hawley. What he wanted to do. Said he was a friend he could trust. Then when that lass of yours was still around, he told me to hire Stocks.'

'How much did he pay?'

'Two guineas. That's what Stocks charges for a job like that.'

'Then he wasted it.'

'What do you mean? Stocks is dead?' he asked, as if it was impossible.

'No one's ever going to see him again.' He let the words sink in. 'If you help White again, the same thing is going to happen to you.'

Promises. Desperate, begging promises. None of them worth the breath the man had used to make them. But he'd reminded Zack about fear. And he knew where White was now.

There was still a chill in the early air, enough to make him wish he'd worn a cape over his jacket. Jane didn't seem to feel it. He wondered what had happened to the coat she'd worn for a few days; he thought he'd seen a boy in it up near St John's Church.

The door had been painted, but it had peeled in long, curling strips. Mortar was crumbling between the bricks. It was an old house, lost among the new warehouses and the chandlers and the dram shops of the Calls that took money from the barge men. A farthing a night for a bed, tuppence if you wanted it to yourself.

He hammered on the wood for two minutes before Mrs Pascoe turned the key. She was pinch-faced, cheeks sunk where her teeth had been drawn. Hard-eyed, her arms all sinew and bone.

'What do you want?'

'Julius White.'

She snorted. 'Gone, 'ent he?' Her stare was triumphant. 'Go in and tek a look if you don't believe me.'

Simon nodded to Jane. She slipped by Mrs Pascoe.

'When did he leave?'

'He din't. They carried him out. Dead, wan't he? Stiffer than that doorpost. I found him first thing. Had the coroner round and they took his body.'

He wanted to believe it. He hated to believe it. It was too easy. Simon felt cheated. It was wrong. White couldn't die that way, beyond justice. He needed to be there when it happened, to see it all with his own eyes. To *know* beyond doubt.

'How much money did he have on him?'

'Nowt.' Mrs Pascoe stared, defying him to call her a liar. 'Not even anything to pay his bill. They took him off and they'll be burying him for a pauper.'

He heard Jane coming down the stairs. She shook her head.

He saw the gravediggers working at the far end of the churchyard. Already a yard down into the soft ground, shovels moving, a pile of earth beside the hole.

Simon hurried between the headstones, Jane on his heels, to the open ground where the bodies lay without markers or memorials. Too poor to be worth remembering. Gone without names. The men put up their spades as they approached, arms resting on the handles.

'Help you?' one said.

The corpse lay on the grass, hidden inside the twisted winding sheet.

Simon took out a silver sixpence, held it up and tossed it to the man.

'Must be thirsty work. Why don't you go and get yourselves a drink?'

The gravedigger stared, suspicious as he clutched the coin in his fist.

'Why? What do you want here? You can't—'

Jane was already on her knees, knife slicing through the old canvas of the shroud. She tore it away until she could see the face.

'It's not him,' she said.

Simon looked. It was a man. Old, withered, hairless and pale. But it wasn't Julius White.

TWENTY-SEVEN

'Who else have you buried this morning?'

'Just this one.' The man turned his head and spat.

'Any more coming?' Simon asked.

'Not as they've told us.' He snorted. 'Why, isn't it who you were expecting?'

Jane was stalking away. Simon caught up to her.

'Where are you going?'

'Back to see that woman.'

He placed a hand on Jane's arm. 'Leave her to me.'

She stared at him defiantly, then gave a short nod before walking off.

Mrs Pascoe knew, Jane had no doubt. But Simon wouldn't be able to persuade her to give up those secrets. That was one skill he didn't possess. She'd visit later, when the woman didn't expect it.

No one behind her today. She kept checking as she moved swiftly through courts and ginnels, all the ways she knew without thinking. She finished up at St John's Church. No patches of sunlight today, just grey, dull weather.

She spotted the boy immediately, half-hidden behind a tree in the corner. He was still wearing the coat she'd given him. Quietly she approached, settling beside him before he realized anyone was there.

In a panic, he started to rise, one small hand grabbing the food he'd found somewhere. Then he recognized her.

'How did you do that?' he asked.

'You learn,' Jane said.

He took a bite from a small, withered apple and held it out to her. She shook her head.

'Those men you told me about. Have you seen either of them again?'

The boy shook his head. 'People were saying one of them was dead.'

'They're wrong. He's not.'

He had a gaze far older than his years. She knew it. She understood it.

'Did you hurt him?' he asked.

'Not enough,' Jane answered. 'He's still breathing. Do you remember what to do if you see him? The one with the dark skin.'

'I have to go to Simon Westow's house on Swinegate.' He closed his eyes as he recited the words, conjuring them from memory.

'There'll be money in it for you.' She stood. 'Just make sure it's true.'

'I wouldn't lie to you.'

Jane dropped two pennies on the grass before she left. He'd survive.

'Where is he?' Simon asked.

'I told you.' Mrs Pascoe folded her arms over her apron. She stood solid in the doorway. 'He's dead.'

'No, he isn't.'

'Trying to call me a liar now, are you?' She raised her voice, wanting the neighbours to hear. But people passed without lifting their heads.

'Where did he go?'

She began to close the door. He put his hand against it. A big man appeared behind her. A dirty face, unshaved, his hair matted.

'Is he giving you trouble, missus?'

'He is,' she said. The woman had a glint of triumph in her eye.

'You,' the man said slowly. 'You're going to leave now. Or we can fight. It's your choice. And you won't win, I'll tell you that.'

A brawl on the street might bring the watch. The constable would relish the chance to issue him a summons and have him fined in court. He grimaced and turned, hearing the door slam behind him.

Early afternoon. Yesterday's lodgers would all be gone. No more would arrive until dark, weary or drunk or too poor for anything better.

Jane counted the backs of the houses, softly lifting the latch on the gate. A small yard, cluttered with rubbish. She climbed the steps, took out her knife, and banged her fist against the wood.

The woman would never expect danger at the back door.

'What do you—' A hard, angry voice. Stopped in mid-sentence as she saw the blade.

Jane forced her back into the scullery, out of sight. The house was silent. A scrawny cat slept on a rocking chair close to the stove.

'Liars get themselves cut.' She moved the knife in a small circle.

'I told the truth.' But the woman sounded weak and feeble now.

'I opened the shroud,' Jane said.

Mrs Pascoe crossed herself. She stayed silent for a moment, lips pushed together.

'One of the men staying here died. Natural. White said to tell the coroner it was him.'

'How bad is he?'

'Bad enough,' Mrs Pascoe said. 'He needs help to walk. I was giving him laudanum for the pain.'

'Where did he go?'

'He had me send for a carter. They left during the night.'

'Which carter?' Jane moved closer. The woman never took her eyes from the point of the knife. 'Which?'

'Joe. I don't know his surname. He lives on Garden Street.'

It was enough. Her hand was on the doorknob when the woman said, 'I could have you killed for this. Only cost a florin.'

Jane hesitated, thought about replying, then moved on. If Mrs Pascoe needed to salvage her pride with words, let her. The woman's sharp tongue couldn't hurt her.

Rosie had left early for Kirkstall to visit the boys. He'd seen the longing on her face when she suggested it, knew she'd spent too long without them. She needed the chance to hold them and hear their voices. A hunger that had to be fed.

'I won't stay too long, Simon. I'll be back this afternoon, I promise. I just want . . .'

He understood. Still, he'd made her leave the back way, through the yards and ginnels, and to wear her old blue housedress, a shawl held over her head. Richard and Amos would know her, but no one else would.

Jane looked questioningly around the kitchen as she entered. Simon explained. For a moment she looked ready to speak, then shook her head and cut a piece of cheese.

'I went back to see that woman,' she said.

'So did I. Got nothing from her.'

'She told me what happened to White.'

He listened intently as she spoke.

'This Joe will know where he is,' Simon said.

'I went to Garden Street,' Jane said. 'He's not there now.'

'Then we'll have to wait for him to come home.'

Four hours standing. Time crawled by. Simon found a sheltered place, hidden from the breeze, and waited.

How had Jane persuaded Mrs Pascoe to talk? He hadn't asked; she wouldn't have told him, anyway. It was done. They had the information. Be grateful.

He stirred as he heard the slow rumble of cart wheels over the cobbles. It halted outside one of the houses. The man unhitched the horse and led it to a small piece of empty ground. Some grass for it to crop, a bucket of water to drink. It was a scrawny, sorry beast, swaybacked and dull. The carter tethered it to a long rope, patted its neck and walked away.

Before he could reach his door, Simon was there.

'You're Joe?'

'I am.' Alarm filled his eyes. He turned his head, as if he wanted to run. But Jane was close, her knife drawn. 'I don't have anything you can steal.'

'I don't want any of that.' Relief flooded the carter's face. 'What I'm after is information about the man you picked up from the lodging house last night.'

The carter looked relieved. But he kept a hand over the purse hanging from his belt.

'What about him?'

'Where did you take him?'

'That's all?' He gave a short laugh. 'A house on Long Balk Lane.'

Simon knew exactly which house it would be. Standish's home. The circle had closed once again.

'I'll tell you this for nowt,' the man added. 'He dun't look long for this world.'

'He isn't. Not long at all.'

The back door was unlocked. No Martha in the kitchen. No smell of cooking, not any sign that anyone had been in there recently. There was a dangerous silence to the place. Simon kept the knife in his hand. He took a second from his boot and moved quietly. Through to the empty dining room and parlour.

He sensed Jane behind him, tense and ready.

Nothing. Simon jerked his head towards the stairs. He tested each tread, stepping over two that gave a little too easily under his sole. At the top, he placed his mouth against Jane's ear.

'We stay together.' It was barely a whisper.

One bedroom belonged to Standish. The bed was unmade, clothes laid over a chair, the door to the wardrobe open. Another looked like his son's, a few items on a table, everything musty; no one had slept there for weeks.

And then there was one door left.

He reached out for the handle and took a breath.

A fire was burning in the hearth, the air close and stifling. Standish sat in a chair, his head jerking up as Simon entered. The room smelt of disease and the withering of death.

Julius White lay in the bed, propped up on pillows. He was bandaged, bruised, drawn. One eye was swollen, almost closed. He turned his head slowly, trying to hide the pain.

'Finally.' His voice was ruined, little more than a harsh croak. The carter was right: Julius White wasn't long for this life. 'And the girl, too. That's who I wanted.' He nodded at Standish. 'Tell them.'

The man's face was bland. His voice shook as he spoke.

'Mr White is willing to make a bargain with you.'

'Why?' Simon asked. 'He doesn't look in a position to demand anything.'

'You'd be surprised, Westow.' White brought his hands from under the covers, each one holding a pistol. 'They're loaded.' His glance flickered across the room. 'Tell him,' he ordered.

Standish swallowed. 'The life of the girl in exchange for your wife.'

Simon shook his head. 'You don't have my wife.'

Standish glanced at White, saw him nod once more, then continued: 'She left your house this morning wearing a blue dress and a shawl. Someone took her while she was on the way to visit your children in Kirkstall.'

The world stopped turning.

TWENTY-EIGHT

'Does that convince you?' White said. He had to fight for the breath to speak. 'You kill the girl. Here and now. I'll send word and your wife goes free.'

Simon was desperate to think. To clutch on to anything at all. To find a way out. They had her. *They had her.* White was going to kill Rosie. He was going to kill all of them.

Was he quick enough to take White first?

'If you slice my throat, you'll never find out where she is.' The man's laugh was a raw cackle. He started to cough and groped for a glass at the bedside. Standish hurried to help, holding it and letting him sip. Talking seemed a little easier after he swallowed. 'It's your choice. Who's more important to you, Westow? The girl or your wife?'

A choice that gave him no choice at all. The room was hot, but he felt bitterly cold. Jane stood utterly still beside him. Simon tried to breathe; his lungs hurt.

'I don't believe you.'

'Yes, you do,' White told him. 'It's written on your face. You believe every damned word.'

It was true. They knew what she'd been wearing, where she was going.

Rosie knew how to fight. She carried a knife, she could defend herself. But her mind would be full of the twins, easy enough to take her by surprise. He believed. His heart was falling through the air.

He daren't look at Jane.

He couldn't look at her. He knew what his decision had to be. But there had to be something they could do. A way to stop it. A way to make them all safe.

'I don't believe you,' he repeated. The words sounded empty even as he spoke them.

White's mouth curved into a smile. 'Why don't you go and see for yourself?' The sense of power seemed to bring some life to his face. 'I'll give you an hour. No more than that. After all, your little wife should be home by now, shouldn't she? Go to that house of yours and you'll see she isn't there. It'll give you time to make your decision.'

'How do I know you won't kill Jane while I'm gone?'

'Because I want the satisfaction of seeing you do it as I watch. You won't be late and you won't bring anyone back with you.' He let the words dangle. 'Not if you want your wife to live.'

'You're going to kill all of us anyway.'

'Maybe I am. Maybe I'll be satisfied with seeing her dead for the damage she gave me.' He waved his pistol towards Jane. 'I

might have found a little mercy. It's your wager, and you've got
that sliver of hope in your eye. Try holding on to it while you
can.'

Still Simon didn't move. He was frozen, paralysed. But he
couldn't let the man win. Not when he had come so close. There
had to be a way, something he could do.

'The girl won't give me any trouble while we wait,' White said.
'You have to learn to shoot if you try to farm Bayside. A few
kangaroos meant meat on the table. Put your knife on the floor,' he
ordered Jane, and waited until she did it. He turned back to Simon.
'Go. Your time's already started. Not a second more than an hour.'

Jane wouldn't let herself feel. She wouldn't let herself see the men
watching her. And she couldn't think about what Simon would have
to do when he returned. No hope, no fear. Nothing. She left them
all behind, leaning against the wall and remembering afternoons
with Catherine Shields at the house behind Green Dragon Yard.

She closed her eyes. Shut it all out. For the last hour of life
she'd feel free.

A longclock ticked in the corner. Jane refused to hear it. She
breathed slowly. She could wait. She had patience.

White didn't speak. Standish shuffled on his chair. After a few
minutes she barely knew they were in the same room. She'd
vanished inside herself. The invisible girl once again. All they saw
was the shell, still unmoving.

Simon ran. He barged people aside. He didn't care. If he knocked
them over, they could stand up again. A few people called his
name, but he ignored them. He needed to be home. He had to see
for himself.

Panic scalded him. He gulped for breath, as if his heart might
explode in his chest. He ran along Woodhouse Lane, down the
long hill on Albion Street. He dodged between the carts and
the coaches backed up on Boar Lane.

He could abandon Jane and go searching for Rosie. But the
thought evaporated as soon as it came. He couldn't do that to her.
He needed to find a way out of this. His mind raced. Idea after
idea. And none of them would work.

Just the smallest chance. That was all he needed. A fragment.

Nothing's impossible. That was what the man who taught him to
use a knife had said. You just need to think.

He tried, but all he found was terror pressing on his throat.

His wife or Jane. Soon enough White would force him to make
the devil's bargain. And even then he'd probably kill them all.

A fragment. A crumb. That was all he needed.

But where? Where was it? Something, just something.

Simon ducked into Byrd's Court, cut through the passageway
and into the ginnel that led behind the house. His fingers fumbled
with the key, trying to make it fit in the lock, then turn it.

He closed his eyes and opened the door.

'You'd better hope Westow is running,' White said.

Jane heard the sound of his voice, but not the words. Her
fingertips rubbed the cuts she'd made on her arm. The old scars
felt smooth, the new ones still rough. She felt an odd comfort in
them. She'd done each one to make herself feel. To make herself
pay. They made her real.

Each one made her a little freer. Of pain. Of life. Every one
was a memory.

White would never understand it.

In the corner, the longclock kept ticking.

She was there. Rosie was there.

Sitting at the kitchen table, head in her hands, weeping. Next
to her, a knife dripped blood on to the wood.

For a moment, Simon stood, not daring to believe his eyes. It
couldn't be. She was a ghost. A phantom. He was seeing what he
hoped to see. Then she turned, and he knew it was real.

She was here.

He drew her close against his chest, feeling her body shudder,
wanting to have her by him forever. Simon kissed her, closing his
eyes as he tasted his lips and smelled her skin.

'Thank God.'

He pulled back to look at her. There was blood on her hands,
on her dress, a smear of it across her cheek. He felt her skin, her
hair. She was alive.

'Are you . . .' He tried to speak, but his throat swallowed the
words.

Rosie shook her head. 'It's not my blood.' Her voice was a whisper.

He took a breath. She was real. She was alive. She was here, with him.

'We need to go. Both of us.' She looked at him, not understanding. He grabbed Rosie's hand, pulling her to her feet. 'Bring the knife. We have to hurry. I'll tell you on the way.'

'This was pushed under the door when I came home.' She took a folded note from her pocket. Quickly, he broke open the seal.

I finally tracked down the name of the man who had White cover up the murder he'd committed. It was Arthur Standish.

Mudie

And the final piece of the puzzle tumbled into place. That was White's grip on Standish.

Rosie had her arm through his, the shawl hiding her head as they moved through the streets. Walking, not running. Quick enough to draw a glance, but not alarm.

'What is it, Simon? What's happening? Where are we going?'

He tried to push it all into a few short sentences. Her eyes widened in horror as she understood.

'White said that? Me or Jane?'

'Yes.' He didn't want to talk about it. No time. But now he wouldn't have to decide. His wife was with him, at his side. They could beat him. Julius White had lost after all.

She stayed silent for a long time. Just the noise of people all around them. Albion Street. Starting out along Woodhouse Lane.

'I could hear someone behind me,' Rosie began. 'I didn't even think about it at first. I was looking forward to seeing Richard and Amos again. But the footsteps didn't go away.'

'What did you do?' he asked quietly.

'We were out past Drony Laith. You know it's all country there.' He nodded. Fields and copses. 'Hardly any carts went by. The footsteps were still there. I couldn't even make myself look.'

'Yes.' He gave her the assurance of his voice.

'I turned into the woods. Out of sight so he'd think . . . you know. He waited just long enough. I was ready for him. He must have imagined it would be simple.' She gave a bleak smile.

'How badly did you hurt him?'

'He's dead.' There was emptiness in her words. 'I left him there and I ran all the way home.' Rosie shook her head and the tears began again. 'I've never killed anyone before, Simon.'

He held her and wiped her cheeks clean. But they had to go. The minutes were passing too quickly.

'It'll all be over very soon,' he promised.

At the door to Standish's house he put a finger to his lips and whispered, 'Follow me. Stay outside the room until I tell you.'

Jane came alert as the door handle began to turn. It was time. She didn't need this world any more.

Propped on his pillows, White tightened the grip on his pistols. From his seat, Standish looked up, trying to hide the fear on his face.

Simon appeared, knife in his hand. His eyes showed nothing as he stepped into the room.

Jane felt her heart thudding.

'I'm not going to kill anyone,' Simon said.

'But you are,' White told him. 'If you want to dream of seeing your wife again.'

'No.'

White was distracted; Simon had all his attention. Jane began to shuffle forward, unnoticed, inching closer to the knife she'd let fall. This time there would be one cut. This time she'd make certain.

'You'll be in mourning. Is that what you want?'

Another movement, a tiny piece closer. Jane glanced down. Close enough to duck and grab the knife. All she needed was the opportunity.

'She won't have the chance to watch your boys grow. Or maybe you'd rather they asked you what happened to their mama. How you got her killed,' White snorted.

Simon took a pace forward as White raised the pistol.

'Now!' he shouted.

That was all she needed. Jane let herself crumple to the floor, landing on the thick rug. As she fell, her hand was already reaching for the knife.

The shot was deafening.

But she wasn't hurt. Her skin wasn't burning. No pain. Her fingers tightened on the knife as she pushed herself back to her feet and launched herself at the bed.

One pistol lay on top of the covers, smoke still rising from the empty barrel.

And suddenly Rosie was there, out of nowhere, back from death, holding her knife to White's throat, her lips curled in a snarl. Jane placed the flat of her blade along the side of White's neck and stroked it lovingly against his skin, relishing the touch.

A single moment and all his fortunes had fallen.

'You've lost,' Simon said. White still had one loaded pistol in his fist. Simon tried to force his arm down. It was like pushing iron. For someone dying, White had the devil's strength. 'Your man wasn't as good as you thought. Rosie killed him. Give up. It's over.'

He stared into the man's eyes. White was looking straight ahead, at some place beyond the far wall. His jaw was set, lips pushed firmly together. He didn't blink, didn't flinch.

By his side, Simon could feel the warmth of Rosie's breath close to his ear. White's face was his world now. He wanted to see his fear.

It seemed to last an age. The first sheen of sweat appeared on White's forehead as he resisted. The muscles were taut in his neck, veins standing out. Christ Almighty, the man was strong. Simon squeezed White's forearm, pressing down hard, nails digging into the flesh. The skin felt tough as leather, slowly turning white under his fingertips.

He couldn't pry White's fingers away from the trigger. There was only one thing left to do.

Instead he pushed down. He'd force the man to fire. One second. Two.

Then everything exploded.

Simon couldn't hear. The smoke rose and blinded him.

He let go. The gun tumbled to the floor.

Behind him, he felt something falling and turned.

Standish. He'd been cowering on his chair against the wall.

'Sweet God.' His voice, yelling, but it sounded as though the words came from a hundred miles away.

Simon knelt over Standish. He was sprawled on the floor, half his face gone, blood and gore sprayed across the wall and the rug. The jagged remains of his skull showed clean and white. One eye stared emptily at the ceiling. The other was gone.

Simon felt for a pulse on the man's wrist, hoping to God he wouldn't find one.

Jane never moved. The light caught the gold ring Catherine Shields had given her. And finally she saw it: defeat on White's face. His muscles slackened and he lay back on the pillow.

She felt Rosie shift. Simon was shouting. Jane breathed out. She had the ghost of a smile on her face.

'Standish is dead.'

The longclock ticked.

TWENTY-NINE

S imon stood slowly. Moving seemed to take too much effort.

'We need the constable,' he said to Rosie. 'And the coroner.' With a glance at White, she was gone.

He lay still, his eyes closed. His chest rose and fell as he breathed. Impossible to imagine what he was thinking. Jane kept her knife an inch from his face. Simon placed his hand on her arm. A light touch, nothing to disturb her.

'Enough.' He said the word softly. 'It's done.' She moved away to the wall, the blade still ready in her hands.

Simon knelt once again, taking time to examine Standish properly. The ball must have entered just below his left eye. No damage to the man's mouth. It was open wide, caught in a scream that never had a chance to be heard.

He felt no pity; the man had brought it on himself. He'd helped when he could have turned White away. Standish had washed his hands in death and guilt, and now it had visited itself on him. Life was brutal. It took joy in cruelty. But he'd been wealthy for too long. Money had made him forget the tricks life played.

They had something no judge dare deny. Murder was a capital crime. Three witnesses who'd seen it happen. White would hang for this.

Simon stood by the window, staring out but not really seeing.

His thoughts flickered, dark and terrifying. It was over, but wouldn't end until they tightened the noose around White's neck and no reprieve came from the king.

Jane didn't need words. She didn't need to think, only watch. The pistols were spent, empty. Expensive pieces of metal and wood that were useless now.

She saw White's right hand start to move, burrowing slowly under the cover.

He had a weapon there.

'Simon!' She screamed out his name. From the corner of her eye she saw him turn, just as White's hand came out, holding a knife by its long, shining blade.

The man wasn't quick enough. As he drew his arm back, ready to throw it, she was already there, bringing her dagger down.

She was swift. A clean cut. The edge she'd honed every night sliced through skin and bone on White's thumb. A short screech of pain as the blood bloomed. His knife fell to the ground.

Jane was panting, the breath bursting out of her. Why? she wondered. She'd hardly done a thing. One stroke, that was all. One simple stroke.

White's face was contorted. He was biting his lip, trying to keep the pain inside. He pressed his good hand over the wound.

All the colour had left Simon's face. He took a pace, reached out and pulled back the bedclothes. No more weapons. Nothing more than an empty man with his skin turned brown by years of Australian sun. A man who'd believed the world owed him everything. Bandages covered all his wounds, brown and dried where the blood had leaked.

'You've no more cards to play, Julius.'

The longclock kept ticking.

And Jane smiled.

Simon felt as if a year had gone by before he heard feet coming up the stairs. Then Constable Freeman was in the room. He stopped short as he saw Standish's body.

'My God.' He looked around the faces. 'What happened? Westow?'

It was straightforward enough to explain, to watch the disbelief and horror grow on the man's face as he listened.

'Murder.' Simon let the word hang as he finished the tale. 'You know what that means.' He waited as the constable nodded. 'There's a cart down in the yard. Your men can take him to the jail in that. You'd better let a doctor examine him. We don't want him dying before he's in court tomorrow.'

'Yes.' Freeman stepped aside so two of the night watch could enter. The best pair he had, dishevelled and dirty, but still young enough to carry a load. White said nothing. His face was pinched with pain, the creases and scars deep and worn on his cheeks. His eyes moved. To Jane first, then he stared at Simon and spat.

'I'll stay for the coroner,' the constable said. Simon nodded.

'And no Hardisty on the bench tomorrow,' he said quietly. 'Make sure it's an honest judge.'

No need to look back. He'd spent long enough in the room. He'd never forget it. He'd felt its heat, smelled his death. On the landing, he took Rosie's hand and squeezed it. Behind him, he could hear Jane's light tread.

The longclock ticked the minutes away.

Simon gave his evidence to the magistrate the next morning. He heard the eager gasps as he described the choice White had given him: kill Jane or his wife would die. The struggle for the pistol, the shot. Standish's body.

In the dock, White was silent. His hands gripped tight against the rail to keep himself upright. His head was bowed as he listened, staring at the floor, not letting anyone see his face.

The room was full. Simon looked around as he spoke. Mudie, noting everything down in his quick hand. Barnaby Wade, listening thoughtfully. Hawley and Madeley, their faces pale and worried in case Simon should name them. And Milner, with a grim smile of satisfaction on his lips.

White's lawyer rose to ask his questions, but his heart wasn't in them; he knew the cause was already lost.

And it was; the magistrate committed the prisoner to the Assizes in York. He'd stand trial there on the tenth of May.

The afternoon before, Simon had borrowed Enoch's cart and driven down to Kirkstall to bring the boys home. Suddenly the house was full of noise again.

Jane stayed in her attic, away from it all as they celebrated.

* * *

The courthouse in York lay close to the old ruin of Clifford's Tower, standing on top of its hill. A faded reminder of royal pasts, glory and death. Pomp and glory. The procession of judges in robes and wigs marched from their lodgings to the Assizes to begin their season.

A trial full of formality and grand phrases.

Simon waited to give his evidence again. More statements, more questions, but he knew there was never any doubt about the verdict. Dismissed, he withdrew to his seat and waited.

As the jury retired, the crowd were already making bets on how long they'd be gone. Ten minutes and they returned. Two of them were laughing and joking. The others kept sober faces.

The word was passed to the judge in a whisper. A short nod. Slowly, he drew on a pair of black gloves and placed the dark cloth over his wig. The room was silent, expectant.

'Julius White, the law is that thou shalt return to the place whence thou camest and thence to a place of execution where thou shalt hang by the neck 'til the body be dead. Dead. Dead. And the Lord have mercy upon thy soul. Amen.'

The court officers took hold of White's arms. For the first time, he raised his head and stared at Simon. His gaze burned. His voice rang out like a preacher.

'Don't believe you're safe. Not you, not your wife, those brats of yours or the girl who works for you. Don't you ever believe you're safe.'

They dragged him away.

THIRTY

A grey morning, dull and windless. Not warm, not cold. Jane kept her hand in the pocket of her dress. She felt the press of people around her as she stood next to Simon and his family. A city she didn't know. Too many strange faces.

She stood, eyes fixed on the gallows.

She'd travelled up on the coach with Rosie and the twins; the first time she'd ever been a passenger. It disturbed her to be so high off the ground, to fly along so quickly, with the constant drumming of hooves and the squeak of the wheels. She stared out of the window, watching it all pass: the fields and the farms, the villages that were here and gone in a blink.

And finally, York. The towers of a big church someone called the Minster looming in the distance. Ancient walls around the city and stone entrances to guard it. An overwhelming pressure of history every way she turned her eyes.

A hanging always drew a crowd. She saw old soldiers with missing limbs and the faded tatters of Waterloo uniforms. Children, legs bowed with disease, skittered and ran and laughed. The pickpockets moved slowly, hands sly as they dipped into pockets and purses. Prostitutes with torn, fluttering fans covering rotten mouths looked for custom. Good folk and bad.

The first people must have arrived early, she thought, to claim their place close to the scaffold. They were eager to see every detail of White's face as the trapdoor opened and he plunged.

But all she needed was to see the end of Julius White. That would be satisfaction enough.

She could see the heavy wooden beams and the rope with its noose. The executioner was testing the knots to be certain they'd hold.

A stir of noise. She heard Simon tell the boys, 'They're bringing him now.'

Two men helped him up the stairs as the cheers rose, and they showed him off, forcing him to march around the platform. White was dressed in good clothes, hair trimmed and combed, a fresh shave to his face.

His right hand was bound where Jane had taken his thumb. He seemed to wince with pain at every step. The executioner whispered something to him, offering a blindfold, and White shook his head. He was standing without aid now, legs already beginning to sag.

Then the noose was in place around his neck.

She watched as the parson moved forward. In an instant, people were quiet. Even here, fifty yards back, she could hear every word of the hanging psalm.

'"*Have mercy upon me, O God, according to thy loving kindness: according unto the multitude of thy tender mercies blot out my transgressions.*

Wash me thoroughly from mine iniquity, and cleanse me from my sin.

For I acknowledge my transgressions: and my sin is ever before me.

Against thee, thee only, have I sinned, and done this evil in thy sight: that thou mightest be justified when thou speakest, and be clear when thou judgest. Behold, I was shapen in iniquity; and in sin did my mother conceive me.

Behold, thou desirest truth in the inward parts: and in the hidden part thou shalt make me to know wisdom.

Purge me with hyssop, and I shall be clean: wash me, and I shall be whiter than snow.

Make me to hear joy and gladness; that the bones which thou hast broken may rejoice.

Hide thy face from my sins, and blot out all mine iniquities."'

Jane kept her gaze on White. She felt Simon and Rosie lift the boys to watch.

'That's the man who wanted to kill your mother and father,' he told them. 'You'll see what happens to him.'

Like a conjurer in the market, the executioner let the anticipation grow. A final moment, the last chance for a pardon. But no mercy came.

Then, in one movement, he slipped the bolt and White made the drop.

Noise rained down on her. People shouting, people cheering. Some clapped their hands. A wave of sound that rose and slowly faded.

It had happened. It was done. Some began to turn away. Time to get on with their lives. Others tried to press closer, clamouring to buy a piece of the rope for good luck. She stayed still, letting them all wash around her. She'd stand in this place until she was certain White's breath was gone, that he hadn't managed to cheat death again.

It took five minutes before the word passed, flying from mouth to mouth. Julius White was dead. Then Simon placed a hand on her shoulder. Time to leave.

He woke and stretched. Next to him, Rosie slept on, her hair a thick, dark tangle on the pillow. He slipped out of bed, dressed, then gazed at the boys curled under their blankets before he crept downstairs.

Julius White. Soon enough his name would slide away into memory. A year from now, people would barely remember who he was. Simon knew he should be glad. But he felt nothing at all. No satisfaction, no pride.

The note lay on the kitchen table. He'd found it pushed under the door when they returned from York. From Martin Holden, the Radical who was campaigning for children to work fewer hours: *Please meet me at eight in the morning outside the Moot Hall. It is important. Dress well.*

When his business was done; that was what Simon had promised. Now it was finished. They'd returned to Leeds on the last coach, crammed in with five other people, the land dark around them. Then a walk home from the Bull and Mouth, Amos fast asleep in his arms, Rosie carrying Richard.

Home.

He'd held Rosie close in bed. No need for words, just love and the warmth of her body. They'd won.

In the distance the clock was striking eight as he reached the Moot Hall. Along the street, boys were selling broadsides, calling out White's execution as the story to draw in their buyers.

Holden looked anxious, peering into the moving crowds, shuffling from foot to foot.

'Simon!' Relief flooded his face. 'There you are. I hoped you'd be able to come after . . .' The words seemed to fall away from him.

'What is it? What's so urgent?'

'The commissioners came back to Leeds yesterday. They've been in Manchester and Bolton. They want more testimony. They asked to talk to you again.'

'Me? Why?' He'd imagined they'd forgotten his words as soon as he left the room.

'They said it was very powerful. It had an effect on them, Simon. *You* had an effect on them.' His eyes shone with excitement. 'I really think we might be getting somewhere. They've been talking about a report to Parliament. Something might really happen, if you're willing to help.'

Simon nodded. He'd relived it all in his mind so often. Opening up the scars once more wouldn't make any difference. Maybe Holden was right. It might help if hundreds more like him, up and down the country, gave their evidence. It might stop the same things happening to more children. In his heart, he doubted anything would happen. Promises were cheap and too easily broken. But he'd try; maybe he owed Holden that much.

'All right.'

The same room, polished and clean. The same three men sitting behind their table. The same clerk hidden in the corner. As if time had curled around on itself.

He felt as if he'd been here in another life. That it had happened to someone else and he'd stood by and observed it all. So long ago it was seen through a veil.

'Thank you for coming, Mr Westow. We have a few more questions we'd like to ask.'

None of this could touch him any more. The pain of the past had gone. All that remained was the anger. But that was fine. It stayed. It burned. The flames kept you alert. They kept you alive.

'I believe that you became a bobbin-hugger when you were ten years old. Can you describe that?'

Words to men with grave faces who'd forget everything he said as soon as he left the room.

Anger. That was pure. That was real.

'I was big, so they chose me for the job. I had to carry baskets full of bobbins on my back up to the weaving room. They weighed about forty pounds and they were kept in place with a leather strap around my forehead . . .'

Jane sat in the darkness of the attic, rubbing her knife over the whetstone, honing the edge. She'd spent the day wandering through Leeds, one more invisible girl in the throng. Into the yard off Wood Street. White's blood had gone from the flagstones. Washed away, covered with dirt. Down towards Lady Lodge, the place where he'd bested her, held her by the hair with his blade to her throat. She stared and imagined it all crumbling to dust before her eyes.

Down in the old blacking factory by the river, the small fire was dead ashes. Nobody there, just a few old sacks tossed into the corner. With night, the people would return. To sleep, to be safe.

Late in the afternoon she'd gone to the copse beyond Drony Laith, making sure no one saw her. She dug up a tin box covered in oilcloth and opened it. From her pocket, Jane took the money Simon had given her. Half the amount Lizzie Henry had paid for White's death, and her share of the fee for finding Hannah Milner. She added it to the money already hidden.

Two hundred and fifty pounds. That was what she had now. Enough to live like a lady if she wanted. To vanish somewhere and have a comfortable existence. Money made you weightless. You could go anywhere. Be whoever you wanted to be. So simple, just a step and a heartbeat.

No. She had no reason. Not yet.

Jane never would ask Simon about the choice White had given him. She didn't want to hear a lie and she didn't dare to hear the truth. And she didn't want to see his eyes as he spoke. Silence was better than words. It was safer.

Silence could keep the world from shattering.

A bowl of hot stew for supper as Rosie and Simon fussed around the boys. Jane asked about their time in Kirkstall and heard their halting replies. But she wasn't really there. She was alone, behind her walls and doors. Locked away.

Now the house was silent. She moved to the window, standing and gazing down at the street as she twisted the gold ring on her finger.

No one watching. Not a soul to be seen.

CPSIA information can be obtained
at www.ICGtesting.com
Printed in the USA
BVHW031210310119
539101BV00001B/2/P